KILLER CURVES

a Guarding Her Body novel

NAIMA SIMONE

Entangled Publishing, LLC
2614 South Timberline Road
Suite 109
Fort Collins, CO 80525
Visit our website at www.entangledpublishing.com.

Ignite is an imprint of Entangled Publishing, LLC.

Edited by Tracy Montoya
Cover design by Louisa Maggio
Cover art from iStock

Manufactured in the United States of America

First Edition December 2015

ignite

To Gary. 143.

Chapter One

"*Maybe if you weren't such a fat bitch and got laid more, you wouldn't be so uptight.*"

The vicious words played in Sloane Barrett's head on a relentless, taunting loop.

Fat bitch…laid more…uptight… Fatbitch…laidmore… uptight… Fatbitchlaidmoreuptight…

She tightened her grip on her clutch purse while heat coursed up her neck and poured over her face, combatting the cool air of the August evening. *Like I care what a smug, spoiled brat like Drake Morriston thinks of me, or calls me.* She shouldn't. He was an eighteen-year-old toddler with more money than sense or morals. He was destined to end up as one of the FBI's Most Wanted on the lam in some European country with his indulgent parents footing the bill. So no, she shouldn't care if some future dissolute criminal called her fat or a bitch…

But damn it, the little rat bastard had hurt her feelings.

Like a ghostly specter refusing to be exorcised, the humiliation from Drake's voice rushed over her again before she could stem the tide. The entitlement. The condescension. The insults. She would love to say the message had been abnormal, but, unfortunately, she couldn't. As a teacher at the prestigious and very elite Kennedy-Lewis Preparatory Academy, a prep school that catered to the children of Massachusetts's obscenely wealthy, she was viewed as more of a servant than a degree-holding, professional educator. That she hailed from the same background as most of her students didn't matter a damn. Not when she—*gasp*—worked for a living.

She snorted as she tugged open the glass door to the Boston Harbor Walk restaurant. The disrespectful punk should count his blessings he hadn't been in front of her when she received his nasty voicemail. With her five-feet, ten-inch—over six feet in heels—one hundred fifty-five-pound frame, she could've taken him.

All this because she refused to change his grade from the *D* in her government class that he rightly deserved after she'd caught him cheating on the final. Apparently, Harvard—and his parents—frowned on the low mark marring his transcripts. The principal would probably end up changing the grade anyway. Not that it mattered to Drake or his parents. They wanted her head.

She sighed. Sometimes she couldn't help but wonder just what the hell she was doing with her life. When she'd proudly received her degree in education, babysitting trust-fund teens with pathological tendencies hadn't been in the plans.

Dammit. She so didn't need this harassment on top of the other things going on in her life.

First the eerie hang-ups in the middle of the night. Then the disturbing emails. And earlier this evening, the flat tires. If Mr. Hall, the geometry teacher, hadn't been leaving the school at the same time as she had, she would've had to call a tow truck and been late to Fallon's engagement party. Her Boston society parents had taught her manners, perfect etiquette, and how to plan and host a dinner party, but not the particulars of changing a tire.

God. What a shitty three weeks.

As if to underscore her summation, her cell phone chimed, signaling a new email. Her feet stumbled to a halt as her heart stuttered before free-falling toward her stomach. Nausea coiled in her stomach, tightening like a boa constrictor.

I'm not going to look. Ignore it. The command whispered through her head. Even as she fished the phone from the pocket of her wide skirt and swiped her thumb over the screen. Dread curdled inside her like milk left out on the counter too long. Because a part of her knew what awaited her in her inbox.

Stop being so melodramatic. It could be an email from her principal about the upcoming school year. It could be Facebook spam from a Montana rancher telling her in broken English how they were spiritual soulmates. It could be—

Yourenext@yahoo.com. No subject line. Just like the others.

Bile raced up within her, scalding the back of her throat before she convulsively swallowed the acid back down. The phone shook in her trembling hand. She knew what awaited her even as her thumb hovered over the ominous email address. Terror and disgust congealed in her belly. But she opened the mail. She had to. Otherwise it would just sit there like a bomb waiting to explode.

No words greeted her.

But the picture quickly filling up the screen of her phone didn't need a menacing message. In this case the picture wasn't just worth a thousand words, but a damn book.

Death. Pain. Horror.

The tortured expression and glassy stare in the unnaturally pale face of the woman. The broken body lying on the dark, grimy ground of a shadowed alley, the large green dumpster, the woman's only companion. The necklace of bruises around her neck.

A different woman in each email. But the same gruesome image of death.

The same warning in the email address: *you're next.*

She powered down her cell with a jerky, abrupt motion and shoved it back into her pocket.

Not tonight. Whoever this, this sicko was who had been sending her these messages would not shake her. They wouldn't *win.*

Hand still trembling, she pulled open the restaurant door and stepped inside. She briefly closed her eyes as the cool, air-conditioned air drifted over her face, clammy skin, still-boiling temper, and wounded pride. The low murmur of voices greeted her in the nearly empty lobby of the bar and bistro, the delicious scents of Italian spices and grilling seafood teasing her nostrils. She forced her lips into what she hoped passed as a polite smile as a hostess approached her.

Hell, who was she kidding? Neither Drake Morriston, the emails, nor tires could claim full blame for her foul mood.

Walking into an engagement party and toasting the happy couple when Phillip Rison, her ex-fiancé, graced the pages of Boston's social columns with a new girlfriend on his arm—well, yeah. That definitely accounted for the other half of her self-pity funk.

Thomas Edison, inventor of the light bulb, was afraid of the dark.

The useless bit of trivia popped into her head, and she inhaled a calming breath. Hey, some people used martinis or chocolate to soothe their nerves; she memorized obscure facts.

Tom-ay-to, tom-ah-to.

And the trivia kept more inches off her size-fourteen hips

and ass than the chocolate did.

"Sloane," an excited voice called out her name as soon as she entered the beautifully decorated main room of the restaurant. "Get your gorgeous ass over here! I'm so glad you could make it tonight."

Fallon Wayland, the bride-to-be, sailed across the room, throwing her arms around Sloane, and squeezing her in a tight hug. Grinning, Sloane returned her old college friend's exuberant greeting and embrace with equal enthusiasm.

"You look beautiful," Sloane said once Fallon released her. And it was nothing short of the truth. Fallon, with her wild curls, golden skin, and startling gray eyes, had always been a striking woman. But with love settling over her like an honest-to-God glow exclusive to mind-shattering orgasms and pregnancy, Fallon was even more beautiful.

Sloane had never experienced either.

"Aw, go on." Fallon waved a hand. With a wicked twinkle lighting her gaze, she leaned forward and stage-whispered, "It's all the fantastic sex."

"Oh Jesus."

Fallon cackled and, looping her arm through Sloane's, led her toward a table with a big, silver fountain. Reaching past the flutes of golden champagne, Fallon grabbed a Sam Adams Rebel Rider. Sloane grinned. Fallon definitely knew her.

"Here." Fallon pressed the bottle into Sloane's hand. "Drink up. I was a little worried you wouldn't be able to make it. You're preparing for the new school year, right?"

"Yes. I was at the school today getting some things ready for the parent-student open house tomorrow evening." An image of the email as well as her tires flashed in her head. The ugly slashes had been too long and clean for a nail or a blowout. An unsettling twist clenched her stomach. A knife — a very sharp blade — could've caused the slices, though...

Shoving the disquieting thought aside, she pasted a

smile on her face, determined to concentrate on her friend's happiness. "Where's your future husband?"

She'd met Shane Roarke a couple of times. Though the security specialist had a reserve about him that could be faintly intimidating, the aloofness melted like chocolate left out in the sun whenever he so much as glanced at Fallon. If witnessing the obvious adoration between the pair caused a there-and-gone pang of envy to reverberate in her chest, well…hey. It didn't lessen Sloane's happiness for them.

"He had to tie something up at the office, but he's on his way." Several more people entered the room, and Fallon laid a hand on Sloane's forearm. "Excuse me for a moment. Enjoy the booze, and the hors d'oeuvres are being circled around, okay?"

With a squeeze to Sloane's arm, Fallon glided across the room to greet her guests, leaving Sloane feeling oddly bereft and alone. Sighing, she twisted the cap off the beer and tried to ignore the voice echoing in her head that sounded too much like her mother. *Guzzling from a bottle is so common, Sloane. A man wants a lady, not a drinking buddy.*

She snorted. According to her proper, socialite mother, just one more thing to add to the list of why Sloane wasn't proper marriage material. Chalk it down right next to can't wear knit dresses without Spanx, has too many opinions, and boring in bed. Well, the last complaint was courtesy of her ex-fiancé.

Maintaining the polite, impersonal smile her mother had drilled into her from birth, she strolled over to the large French doors along the far wall. Beyond the doors and the restaurant's terrace, the dark waters of Boston Harbor rippled gently in the deepening evening. Farther out, lights on a cruise ship flickered and glowed, and she could just imagine the laughter and chatter flowing as freely as the wine. Like here. A time of celebration and happiness. And it all intensified her sense of isolation and loneliness.

Like a perfect storm everything—the troubling events of the last three weeks, Phillip's new relationship just two months after their disastrous break-up, Fallon's engagement—seemed to converge at once, reminding her she was like that cruise ship on the harbor. Bright and gay on the outside, but at its core alone and circling pointlessly with no purposeful destination.

Well, damn. Apparently she needed to stop DVRing *The Young and the Restless* because she was becoming way too melodramatic.

Shaking her head, she tossed the cap into a nearby trashcan. The bottle was halfway to her lips before she felt it.

A stare.

Not like the expectant or bored gazes of her students. Or the avaricious, gleeful scrutiny of her peers as they watched her for any sign of blood at Phillip's defection.

No, this was…intense. Unsettling. Hot.

Turning from the serene view, she scanned the room.

And collided with eyes the color of a cloudless, beautiful summer sky.

Flawless. Absolutely flawless. Like Michelangelo's David-meets-the-last-guy-who-played-Superman flawless. Dark, thick eyebrows emphasized the brilliance of his blue gaze. Elegant but sharp angles prevented his masculine beauty from edging into pretty, while a wide, sinfully curved mouth obliterated any notion of sweetness. Black loose waves and curls brushed his cheekbones, ears, and the collar of his black suit jacket. A black jacket clung perfectly to his wide shoulders and muscled arms like a shameless slut. With that hard body, he must work in construction or some other profession that required strength and muscles capable of shaming Vin Diesel into picking up his dumbbells and going home.

She dragged her greedy inspection back up his tall frame

in time to catch that electric stare skim down her face and throat and loiter on her breasts. Unconsciously she sucked in her gut, praying that sometime between this morning's glance in the mirror and now a miracle had occurred and God had granted her abs tight enough to bounce a quarter off of.

After another visual caress that left her flesh tingling and heavy beneath her dress, he returned his attention upward. The heat in his eyes blasted her like a furnace dialed up to incinerate. She blinked. Surely, that flash of desire had been a figment of her overactive and undersexed imagination. A man who exuded sex and sin like a high-priced cologne wouldn't give *her* a second glance much less a long, lingering one.

A pregnant goldfish is called a twit.

The obscure trivia whispered through her mind, and she grasped on to the calming mechanism like a lifeline. She lifted her bottle and gulped from it, averting her gaze. His wasn't the first gorgeous face she'd ever seen—hell, she'd been raised in a world where beauty was a commodity. But none of those men had almost…smoldered with raw sexuality. A sexuality that seemed to be barely leashed by golden skin and steely control. Against her brain's sharp commands, she shot him a furtive glance. None of those aforementioned men looked like they could break a woman apart piece-by-piece with pleasure then calmly put her back together. Only to do it again…

A tall, whipcord-lean man with shoulder-length, dark brown hair approached the stranger, claiming his attention. She exhaled, as if granted a reprieve.

And like any intelligent person presented with an unexpected escape route, she ran.

Pushing down the handle on the French door, she emerged onto the covered terrace. The gentle breeze off the waterfront caressed and cooled her flushed skin. Around her, the wait staff bustled, lighting hurricane lamps suspended from wooden beams as well as on the tables to dispel the deepening shadows of the evening. Pale-colored flowers, the flicker of white fairy lights, and bolts of white, ethereal cloth added to the ambiance of romance. Fallon's doing, Sloane surmised, striding to the railing. As a talented event planner, Fallon had an elegant but luxuriant point of view that was rapidly growing in demand. If things had worked out differently, Sloane would've hired Fallon for her engagement party and wedding with Phillip.

If things had worked out differently…

"Differently" meaning if Phillip hadn't cheated and then blamed his infidelity on her "irrational refusal to lose thirty pounds." After all, how could he be expected to fuck or wed a lazy cow who would be a direct reflection of him?

She gasped at the quick and sharp stab of pain and humiliation, pressing a fist to her chest. Even months later, her ex's remembered derision and contempt still contained the power to wound…

"Hello."

Holy hell. That voice. The fingers of the hand not grasping the beer bottle like a lifeline curled around the patio railing. Her lashes fluttered and lowered. One word, and yet the deep rumble of it stroked over her skin, evoking images of shadowed bedrooms, rumpled sheets, and sweaty bodies. Good God, that voice needed to be bottled and sold in sex shops worldwide. Who needed porn with that purring dark velvet in your ear?

Shit. *Purring dark velvet*? What. The. Hell?

She turned around, and *whoa.*

The railing pressed into her back as she instinctively leaned away from the overwhelming, intense male towering over her, just inches short of invading her personal space.

Not that he probably gives a damn about little things like appropriate, polite distance. The thought popped into her head, and though she couldn't possibly know that about him, she didn't doubt the veracity of the statement, either. She had a feeling the "inches" were for her benefit, not his.

She inhaled a shaky breath—then immediately wished she hadn't. But too late. She couldn't scrub the woodsy, earthy fragrance of his cologne from her nostrils. *Damn*. Before this moment she wouldn't have believed a man's scent could be foreplay.

He said hello, the part of her brain still functioning hissed. *Get it together, dammit!*

Right, right. Oh Jesus Christ. Wasn't talking to oneself a precursor to Prozac and rubber-walled rooms?

Again, she forced her social smile to her lips. "Hi."

That inner voice sighed at her inane stupidity.

A corner of his mouth lifted in a half smile, and a dent in his cheek made a brief appearance. *Dimples*. Really? Because beautiful eyes, a gorgeous face, and hard body weren't enough? Butterflies took to flight in her belly. Damn butterflies. Raptors. Freaking pterodactyls.

"Ciaran." He held out his hand, and for several long seconds she studied his big, wide palm. Something instinctive, primeval, yelled a warning not to touch him. That if she did, there would be no turning back, no do-overs. But in spite of her earlier thoughts of comparing herself to lonely, aimlessly circulating cruise ships, she wasn't a fanciful woman but a realist. A pragmatist, a rationalist, she reminded herself as she pressed her hand to his...

And an idiot.

His big palm nearly engulfed hers. Electric. Stunning. She swallowed a gasp as a jolt speared her chest and traveled at lightning speed to the faintly pulsing flesh between her thighs. A handshake. He'd set her sex swelling and quivering with a simple handshake.

She shouldn't have touched him.

"Nice to meet you, Ciaran." *Kee-ran*. She silently repeated his name, rolled it on her tongue like a delicious, decadent treat. It suited him. Unique. Strong. Sexy. "Sloane Barrett."

"Sloane," he repeated. "It's my pleasure."

She'd never been a fan of her name. Her parents had christened their youngest daughter Chelsea—perky, pretty, bright, fun. Perfect for her sister. As the first-born child, Sloane had received her mother's maiden family name—Sloane. Stately. Stodgy. Gender generic. Boring. Hell, if she'd been a boy, she still would've been Sloane. Her parents had deliberated, considered, and finally selected the ideal match for their second child. They hadn't done the same for Sloane. Probably from the moment they'd discovered her mother was pregnant, the decision had been made, regardless of whether the name would fit. Regardless of whether the weight of it was too heavy for a child. All that had mattered was Mallory Johanna Sloane Barrett's legacy.

So, no, she'd never been a fan of her name.

Until now.

Until the moment a midnight-and-sin voice stroked that one, resented syllable and transformed it into something—*someone*—sexy and mysterious instead of dull, stuffy... flawed.

God, he was dangerous.

"You're staring," she whispered. Like she wasn't doing some major ogling right back at him. Jesus Christ, lust had eradicated all but a few brain cells.

Amusement flickered in his bright gaze. "I am," he agreed. "I like looking at you, duchess." His voice lowered as if imparting a secret. A secret that should only be voiced in the darkest part of the night when sighs and whimpers are the only form of communication.

Heat scorched her throat and face even as she latched on to the one part of his admission, choosing to ignore the rest for her sanity—and panties'—sake. "Duchess?"

He lifted a shoulder in a half-shrug again. "You look like one. Beautiful, wealthy, composed…untouchable."

His description unnerved her. She was none of those things. Her parents were wealthy, but she lived off her teacher's salary. And her mother had never been able to drill a proper lady's composure into Sloane; she'd always been too shy, too sensitive. Now she could pretend with the best of them…but the mask only lasted a little while. Sooner or later the emotions inside her landed on her sleeve for all to see like a Hell's Angel patch. And beautiful? Well, her father called her so. As had Phillip at one time. But he'd changed his tune soon enough.

The reminder of her ex swilled in her gut like sour alcohol. "Yes, well, looks can be deceiving." She tugged her hand but his fingers tightened, refusing to release her.

"Which one," he challenged.

"Which one, what?" Frowning, she tried to pull free again. But once more, his hold tightened. She narrowed her eyes on him, and his hooded gaze dropped to their clasped hands before lifting back to her face. And he *still* didn't let her go.

"Which one is deceiving?" he clarified. "I have eyes, so I know you're beautiful. Composed, too. You walked in here tonight like you owned it and chose a beer when every other woman in this place has a glass of champagne. Which was hot as hell." His scrutiny briefly dipped to her mouth as if he envisioned her drinking from the bottle at that moment. "From the cut of your hair and the red soles of those shoes, you can afford material things. So that leaves untouchable." He cocked his head to the side. "Are you untouchable, duchess?"

"First, my name isn't duchess. And second, my touchability or lack thereof is usually reserved for people I've known for twenty minutes, not two," she bit out. And the Louboutins had been a gift from her mother, who firmly believed the designer shoes should be a staple in every woman's closet.

Buy the expensive shoes on a teacher's salary? Not hardly.

His smile widened, those damn dimples flashing another appearance.

Hell. So much for putting him in his place. Apparently sarcasm was wasted on him.

She jerked on her hand again, and this time he released her. But it wasn't lost on her that her freedom was a direct result of his choice, not her strength. The knowledge shouldn't have turned the screw of lust inside her, but damn if it didn't.

"Wedding or engagement?"

"What?"

He grasped her hand again and brushed his thumb back and forth over the pale strip of skin on her ring finger. The tell-tale sign of a recently removed ring.

Just that quick, the reminder of her ex and their spectacular failure of a relationship doused the desire simmering within her in a frigid wave of humiliation. Pain and something darker—uglier—convulsed inside her chest. With Herculean effort, she schooled her features into a smooth mask and extracted her hand from his grip.

"Engagement," she said, interjecting a whole bunch of *let it go* into the flat monotone.

He tipped his bottle and sipped from it. The silence stretched between them as he lowered the beer, his brooding gaze fixed on her face.

"Does he need maiming or killing?"

She frowned, her aloof facade slipping into surprise and then confusion. *Uh… What the hell?* "I-I'm sorry," she stammered. "Does *who* need maiming or killing?"

"The man who made you feel…" He paused, his full, sensual lips firming into a grim line.

"Feel like what?" she pressed, although part of her didn't want to hear his answer.

Another beat of silence passed before he murmured,

"Small. Like you didn't matter to him."

Ouch. That hurt. Did she wear her hurt and shame over Phillip's betrayal so vividly that even a stranger noticed? Forcing a laugh that sounded serrated and bitter even to her ears, she waved off his observation. "Small," she repeated with a wry smile. "Well, no one's ever called me that before."

"Ah." He nodded, eyes narrowing with a piercing intensity that had her fighting the need to turn away and hide from that too-perceptive stare. "Killing, then."

She blinked, momentarily stunned into silence. Unbidden pleasure at his unsolicited—and unconditional—defense crept through her like a stealthy invader. It was silly; at twenty-six, she was too old and cynical for a white knight on a liveried steed. Yet the sinuous slide of warmth in her veins belied that belief. No one had ever championed her like this hot, blue-eyed stranger. Even if instead of a sword and shield, he wielded a proposal to off the man who'd hurt her—a proposition she was only half convinced he said in jest…

She shook her head, chuckling under her breath. "You just don't give a damn about proper decorum or manners, do you?" She shook her head, bemused. "Because I am quite certain offering to carry out a contract killing violates at least two of Emily Post's etiquette rules."

He laughed, and the low, sexy rumble stroked over her skin. Lowering her lashes, she sipped from her beer. But the cool alcohol did nothing to quench the thirst that went so much deeper, burned so much hotter than something capable of being doused with a cold beverage. Suddenly nervous, she slid her tongue over her bottom lip.

A dark, growling sound—a sound caught somewhere between a groan and a purr—emanated from him. She sucked in a breath and her gaze jerked up to meet his.

Oh God.

Such focus. It was intoxicating. Stimulating. Arousing. The

hot intensity of his eyes branded her. Whew, boy. Her fingers tightened on the beer bottle as if the touch could ground her to reason, to logic, and not allow her to get swept away and lost in feeling. God, he made her *want*. Made her crave things she'd only read about or watched on late-night cable shows. Made her consider doing things…

She'd never been that sleep-with-a-man-you-just-met kind of woman. It smacked of low self-esteem and no respect. And in this day and age, a girl might go home with Mr. Nice and Normal, but wake up shackled to the bed by Mr. I-Have-A-Nice-Hot-Bath-of-Hydrochloric-Acid-to-Dissolve-Your-Body-Parts. So yes, entertaining a one-night stand with a guy she barely knew smacked of stupidity. But that had been before tonight. Before a man with eyes the color of a flawless gem, the face of a pagan fertility god, and the body of a Celtic warrior had asked her if she was untouchable. And then offered to kill someone for making her feel "small."

She shuddered.

"Cold?" Ciaran murmured.

Cold? God, no. Any hotter, and she would make the Human Torch look like a little kid playing with matches.

A dragonfly has a lifespan of twenty-four hours.

"That really sucks for it," he said.

She frowned. "I'm sorry?"

A corner of his mouth quirked. "For the dragonfly."

She'd said that out loud? *Well, shit.* She swallowed a groan. He must think she was the village idiot's long-lost twin.

"Sloane."

He shifted closer, and the glow from the hurricane lamps highlighted the angles and shadows of his face. Her belly clenched, and traitorous warmth unfurled, winding its way south. Apparently her body chose not to remember the last time she'd fallen for a handsome man. She'd been so enamored with Phillip's pretty looks, she'd failed to recognize the ugliness hidden beneath the mask. She hadn't heeded the signs of control and mental and verbal abuse until she'd been ensnared in their insidious, sticky webs. Logic argued that not all good-looking men were narcissistic assholes. Still, feeding on her issues about being the chubby, shy, more-tarnished-than-gold Barrett, Phillip had hammered home the doubts and insecurities of why a handsome man would find her attractive. And Ciaran...well, he exceeded mere "handsome." Describing him with such a bland and anemic description was like calling the Sistine Chapel a pretty church.

"We should return to the party," she murmured, not waiting for his agreement. She eased past him and headed toward the patio entrance. Yes, strategic retreat presented itself as the wisest course of action. She needed to return to the safety of the party with people she didn't know, where she could wrap herself in the protective and cold distance of polite conversation. Escape before she did something to embarrass herself—like beg him to touch her and end her four-month celibacy streak.

"Sloane."

Keep it moving! Her mind blared the order, but as if of their own volition, her feet jerked to a halt.

"If you keep running from me, I'm going to start taking it personally."

Running? That was ridiculous. Absurd.

And she would've told him so...if she wasn't already making a beeline for the restaurant.

Chapter Two

Okay, so her vagina was really, *really* pissed off with her.

Sloane snorted, striding up the sidewalk to her Bay Village brownstone. Not that she could blame her lady bits. Even two hours after the weird and stimulating conversation with the mysterious and sexy Ciaran, she still tingled like a lightning rod drawing electricity to her body, transmitting currents to her breasts, belly, and sex. It was a wonder she didn't light up like a freakin' glow stick at a Lady Gaga concert.

She sighed. And yet, here she was, walking up to her home — alone.

Because she was a coward. After scurrying off the shadowed restaurant patio, she'd spent the rest of her time at the engagement party avoiding the temptation and...hurt Ciaran represented. Like a child burned by a flame, she only needed to look at the thing responsible for once hurting her to shy away. Not that Ciaran had inflicted the pain, but he represented the source. A handsome, charismatic man. The wonder of attraction. And ultimately, the disappointment of knowing she wasn't enough.

Been there, done that, had the matching T-shirt and refrigerator magnet to prove it.

Her cell rang, and the muffled notes of LL Cool J's "Mama Said Knock You Out" reverberated from her purse. Groaning, she removed the phone and, for a second, considered not answering it. *Like that would stop her.* Gritting her teeth, Sloane swiped her thumb over the Accept Call bar. "Hello, Mother."

"Sloane, I have been trying to reach you all day and evening," her mother, Mallory Johanna Sloane Barrett, complained without preamble.

Sloane swallowed another sigh. "School starts in another week. And besides preparing for it and the open house Monday night, I've been pretty busy."

"You also have next week to pack for. I won't take no for an answer, Sloane. Nor will I accept any excuses. It's your father's and my anniversary, and you will be here."

Sloane paused at the low, wrought-iron gate bordering her building. *God*, she pinched the bridge of her nose, her lips moving in a soundless prayer for patience. Oblivious to Sloane's plea for divine assistance, her mother continued to drone on in Sloane's ear. Usually, all her mother required was an occasional "uh-huh" or "yes, Mother" to ensure Sloane was listening, but today she wanted actual conversation. Or rather, acquiescence.

"Mother, I'm just arriving home from Fallon's engagement party," Sloane said, interrupting her mother mid-admonishment. "I haven't even walked into the house yet. Can I call you back?"

"Fallon's engagement party." Mallory *tsked*. "This is precisely what I'm talking about, Sloane. Even Fallon has found a husband. And here you are, school hasn't even started yet, for goodness sake, and you're already wrapped up in work. How do you expect to have any kind of social life or relationship when that's all you ever do? A paycheck cannot keep you company or marry you or give you children. No man wants to play second fiddle to a job." Most people usually reserved the sneer her mother applied to "job" for dog poop on the sidewalk or Justin Bieber. Only Mallory would consider honest employment to be on the level of shit and spoiled, mop-bucket-peeing pop stars.

"Yes, Mother, I know."

This line of conversation was so old, cobwebs dangled from it. If her mother would allow her to *breathe*, then maybe Sloane could wedge into the exchange that she already planned on driving down to the Hamptons next Thursday. Yes, for her parents' anniversary party, but also to get out of Boston for at least a few days.

She shifted her attention to the front door of her brownstone, and a slight shiver skated over her skin. She hated it—hated the unease that tripped through her when her home should only bring comfort and relief. But her haven had become tainted by ominous phone calls that ended in hang-ups and emails containing disturbing images like the one she'd received earlier that evening. Calls and emails bombarded her daily, fraying her nerves until she dreaded the ring of a phone or the notice of an unread message in her Inbox. A report to the police had resulted in a "There's not much we can do" that infuriated her even as she understood the response. Their resources were limited, and with nothing to go on but a bogus email address and untraceable calls... She shook her head. At least they'd offered to subpoena Yahoo for the owner of the email address.

But God knew how long that would take or even if the records would reveal the identity of the person harassing her. As for the other incidents... Even if she could convince the police her tires hadn't been a coincidence, no one had witnessed the incident. Because the vandalism hadn't been a coincidence. A shiver crawled down her spine. She'd seen tires punctured by a nail or flattened by a slow leak before. Hers, on the other hand, had been slashed.

Yes, she needed to escape her home and the total helplessness she'd been experiencing these last few weeks, if just for a little while.

"Guests are arriving Thursday afternoon, so you need to be here by then to help greet them with the family." Mallory's world-weary sigh interrupted Sloane's morose thoughts. "And with all that's going on with your sister, now more than ever we have to appear like a strong, united front."

"What? Wait. What's going on with Chelsea?" Sloane and her younger sister didn't speak often, but Chelsea was busy with her life as wife to a very successful attorney, mother to two gorgeous children, and a social titan. The two of them had almost nothing in common except genetics—and Sloane had questioned that at times.

Another heavy sigh. "She and Greg have separated. Chelsea's tossing around divorce."

Shock ricocheted through her. Divorce? What? How? God, Chelsea—

"So if *work* crops up between now and then," her mother continued, "it needs to take a back seat to your obligations. I can only handle so much this weekend."

"I'm not going to argue with you on an empty stomach." And as if on cue, her belly grumbled. She'd been so nervous and acutely aware of Ciaran's presence at the party, she'd only nibbled on the massive amount of food the restaurant had provided. "I need stamina to go another round about my impending spinsterhood."

"Sarcasm is not necessary, Sloane." Mallory sniffed. Jesus take the wheel, no one did a guilt trip like her mother. "But speaking of eating..." A long pause had Sloane squeezing her eyes shut. *Oh. Hell.* "Did you receive the name of the dietician

I emailed you?"

Sloane groaned, the slight pounding in her temples edging toward full-blown headache. This topic was nothing new either, yet the sour swill in her stomach and tight squeeze in her chest never eased. Her mother honestly meant no harm with her "helpful tips." Neither of her parents were—or had been—openly demonstrative. Not with each other or their children. Reserved was a good description. "Decorum above all" should be the family motto. Still, in her own way, her mother saw recommendations for nutritionists, trainers, and surgeons as concern and her own brand of affection. Mallory couldn't see that each piece of advice poked at the tender place in her soul that never felt good enough.

"Don't pout, Sloane," her mother chided. "I only sent you that information because he came highly recommended from several of the women I lunch with."

"Great," Sloane drawled. "So the topic of conversation at the country club has been my weight. Wonderful." The same women she would most likely have to spend the weekend with, socializing. Oh goody.

"Oh stop. Dr. Colbert could help you manage your lifestyle, give you better nutrition tips, and assist you in being more active. What is the harm in that, Sloane? You have such a pretty face."

The *"If only your body matched"* remained silent but blared so loudly, her elderly neighbor could've caught it without her hearing aid. The vise on her chest squeezed harder.

Clinophobia is the fear of beds.

She inhaled, and after a moment, slowly exhaled, the grip on her rib cage easing a fraction.

Part of her understood the criticism didn't originate from a place of malice—her mother honestly did worry about Sloane's happiness and future. But the other half... God, the other half longed to ask her mother if she could just lay off and accept her for who and what she was. Mallory's concept of a fulfilling, purposeful life differed from Sloane's. Did she sometimes wish she possessed the slender, hipless builds her mother and sister had been blessed with? Yes. Did she sometimes envy them their marriages and children? Of course. Especially in the last two months since her engagement ended, and the house seemed to echo with deafening silence. And loneliness. Even if her sister had separated from her husband, she'd experienced the fulfillment of companionship, family, and security. Of love.

An image of sky-blue eyes in a face of strong, sexy angles flashed across her mind followed by a hot spiral of heat coiled low in her belly. If she hadn't run from the patio and avoided Ciaran for the rest of the evening, she might have ended up under him in her bed, writhing in orgasm. She'd called him dangerous, and the label fit. With one conversation, he'd had her questioning herself. Had her contemplating taking another risk. Had her—just for an instant—considering the risk would be worth the one night of sin his piercing gaze had promised. Yes, he was dangerous. Even more so than she'd originally supposed.

Phillip had enchanted her with his attractive features, flawless charm, and pretty compliments. But Ciaran's blunt honesty and unapologetic sexual magnetism had captivated and aroused her in ways her ex hadn't in the two years they'd been together. At the end of her relationship with Phillip, she'd been a timid, bullied shell of who she used to be. Phillip had battered her pride; she suspected Ciaran would destroy it, not even leaving scraps.

A wry smile twisted her mouth. Not that it mattered. Ciaran hadn't approached her, either. Which solidified her assumption that she'd either been a lark, an amusing distraction to pass some time, or wasn't worth the chase to him. At this moment, he'd probably forgotten all about the size-fourteen school teacher whose panties he'd melted with an offer to maim or kill and had picked up a Victoria's Secret model wannabe who didn't need to wear Spanx beneath her dress. Why that thought should sting so badly was beyond her.

God, I'm so pathetic. She continued up the sidewalk, eager to get inside, down some aspirin, and veg out in front of the television and whatever Housewives were cat-fighting tonight.

"Sloane, there's another reason I called." Well, damn. She'd almost forgotten her mother was still on the line. Sighing, she tuned back in to the conversation, but Mallory's uncharacteristic hesitation echoed in her ear, and disquiet pulsed inside Sloane like a flashing caution signal. "I should have let you know earlier, but..." Her mother cleared her throat. "Phillip is coming to the party."

She screeched to a halt at the bottom of the stoop steps as if a road block had sprung up before her. A road block that warned *Caution: Betrayal Ahead.* Shock encased her, but the bright flames of anger quickly dissolved the icy disbelief.

"What?" She stared at her front door, her voice low, trembling. "Please tell me you didn't just say my ex-fiancé will be spending the weekend with my family. With *me.*"

"When we invited him, you two were still together. We couldn't just rescind his invitation. He's still a business associate of your father's, and John loves him like a son. That didn't change just because your relationship did."

Tears, sudden and hot, burned her eyes and clogged her throat. Pain radiated from her chest. Not because in a matter of days she would be facing the man who'd eviscerated her pride and esteem before he'd walked out the door. God knows she wasn't looking forward to that, but once—*just once*—she wished her parents would take her side. Okay, Phillip was *like* a son. But she *was* their daughter. Besides, would they

be so eager to include him if they knew how he'd treated—
*mis*treated—her? Too bad shame had kept her lips sealed...
still did.

She squeezed her eyes close, refusing to allow one tear
to drop.

"Sloane—"

"Thanks for letting me know, Mother. I really have to go,
so I'll call you later."

She didn't wait for Mallory's reply, instead she ended the
call and stared blindly down at the phone's screen for several
long seconds. As if any moment, her mother's telephone
number and name would pop up. As if she would call back to
promise to retract her invitation to her asshole ex.

As if.

Sloane tucked the cell into her purse and climbed the
brownstone's stairs, her tread heavier than only minutes
earlier. If the celebration wasn't in honor of her parents'
thirtieth anniversary, she would say to hell with it and skip
the party. But she couldn't. She loved her parents; they didn't
see eye-to-eye on her appearance, her career choice, or her
personal life, but she wouldn't deliberately hurt them. And
not showing up next week would fall squarely in that category.

Possessing a conscience truly sucked sometimes.

Slipping her keys free of her pants pocket, she grabbed
the door knob.

God, she smothered a groan. *What if he brings his new
girlfriend—*

The front door creaked open.

Stunned, Sloane stilled, the hand clutching her house keys
frozen midair. Her heart *thudded* in her ears like a bass drum.
Ice slid through her veins, replacing blood with a burgeoning,
oily fear.

She'd closed and locked the front door before leaving for
school that morning. She was certain of it. With the emails

and phone calls, she didn't take chances. So why...

Her breath burst from her lungs in rapid, loud puffs that seemed to boom in the eerie, suffocating silence. She pushed the door and it swung wide, the *creak* like nails scraping down a chalkboard. The light spilling in from the street lamps did little to dispel the shadows in the foyer and hallway. Swallowing, she stepped over the threshold.

And gasped.

Horror filled her.

The pretty, delicate table she'd found at a Charles Street antique shop lay overturned on the floor, pieces of the Tiffany lamp that had sat upon it scattered across the hardwood. The gilded, oval mirror that had hung on the wall now occupied a corner, bits of glass clinging to the frame like silver tears. Her purse and bag drooped down her arm, and they dropped to the floor with a dull thud. She barely noticed as she moved farther into the foyer. Something cracked under her foot. A glance down revealed one of the Thomas Kinkade Victorian lighthouse figurines she collected. Shards of the porcelain as it'd been broken—destroyed.

A harsh sob escaped her. She lifted her hand, encircling her neck as if she could manually contain the whimper. Grief welled inside her like a geyser. Her home, her things. Who would do—

A floorboard *groaned*.

She knew that sound. When she'd bought the brownstone, the squeaky step at the top of the staircase had been delightful, part of the old building's charm. Now...

She slowly lifted her gaze, her pounding heart lodged in her throat.

He stood on the second floor landing, one foot planted on the creaky step.

As if God had pressed pause on the video of life, they stood there, staring at one another. The dark eyes that peered at her from the red-rimmed slits of a black ski mask seemed to glitter in the dusk-deepened shadows. A gloved hand gripped the newel post cap. It was the sight of that black glove that shattered her paralysis.

She backpedaled, and the movement triggered the intruder like a bullet expelled from a gun. He charged down the stairs. With a strangled cry, she whirled. The open front door loomed just several feet in front of her, but it might as well as have been miles. She dashed for the entrance, but her heel slipped on the shattered pieces of the figurine. With another low scream, she slipped, her shoulder slamming into the wall, her hip clipping the small mail table. Pain radiated through her, snatching her breath.

Move! Move now!

Horror clawed at her chest, but she obeyed the shriek in her mind. She shoved off the wall. Darted for the door. For freedom. For safety.

Her fingernails scraped the edge of the jam, relief and an almost hysterical joy surged inside her chest. *Please, God. Thank you, God...*

Pain exploded at the side of her head, her scream muffled by a gloved hand. She blinked rapidly, trying to clear the burst of black and gold stars that crowded her vision. A whimper escaped her as a cruel grip jerked on her hair, arching her neck until tendons whined in complaint.

"Where do you think you're going?" The raspy question contained a note of malicious glee that caused nausea to churn and roil in her gut before racing for her throat. He wrenched harder on her ponytail, his fingers biting into her skin. Even through the knit mask, she swore she could feel the heat of his breath against her cheek. Feel the hum of a nasty chuckle. "You and me, we got—*bitch!*"

Terror transformed her into a wild thing. She couldn't hear the rest of his sentence—was terrified to hear it. She bit the fingers covering her mouth, clamping down hard. The thin material of the gloves didn't provide him protection against her desperate attack.

"Goddammit!" he howled. "Get off me."

But she only clenched harder. And drove the heel of her shoe down the inside of his ankle and into his instep.

With a vicious curse, he yanked his arm away and shoved her.

Toward the entrance.

Stumbling, she quickly steadied herself and lunged, barreling out of the house and onto the stoop. And didn't stop. She bolted down the steps and onto the sidewalk, running for her life as if the masked intruder chased her, intent on dragging her back into her home to finish whatever he'd broken into the house to do.

Chapter Three

"**O**oh. You look like hell."

Ciaran Ross grunted as he stepped into the lobby of GDG Security Solutions. Functioning on three hours of sleep, the grumble of sound was all he could manage prior to coffee. Speaking of…

He flipped the tab on the insulated cup in his hand. The strong, fragrant aroma of dark roast teased his nose, and like Pavlov's dogs, he felt his stomach tighten in anticipation of the first hit of the brew hitting his tongue. When he'd been a DEA agent, he'd come across more than his fair share of drug addicts. His reaction to the coffee with two creams and three sugars wasn't very far off from that of a junkie feenin' for their next high. He tipped the cup and sipped. Oh yeah. He might be edging into crackhead behavior, but fuck it. He so needed this.

Only after a couple of more gulps did he meet the amused gaze of the petite woman with raven black hair and violet eyes manning the receptionist's desk.

"Uh, rough night?" Willow Clark arched an eyebrow with

a pointed glance at his coffee cup.

Ciaran visually swept the open, empty space of the lobby before answering. The warm browns, deep reds, and blues of the area put a person more in the mind of a friendly doctor's office rather than a personal security firm that contracted ex-soldiers and cops who weren't afraid to kick ass and take names. But the décor as well as the careful restoration of the Back Bay brownstone that housed the offices of GDG Security Solutions had been deliberate. From the garden-level meeting rooms to the parlor floor offices, he and his partners had tried to keep in mind that their clients wanted to feel secure in the knowledge that former military and law enforcement guarded them, not have the hell scared out of them.

Returning his attention to Willow, he stated, "Reinhold."

"Aah." Willow nodded with an exaggerated grimace. "'Nuff said."

Yeah, the name of one of their most recent—and difficult—clients was indeed enough explanation. Instead of heading home after Shane and Fallon's engagement party, he'd received a call from the security detail assigned to Carlton Reinhold's home. The business executive had hired GDG to protect him from the threats of a disgruntled employee... disgruntled because the exec had been boning the employee's wife. Just stupid as hell.

Ciaran's number-one rule: Don't shit where you eat. As Reinhold had discovered, becoming involved with employees or clients only ended one way—threats to his dick and a brick with "Burn in hell" painted on it catapulting through the living-room window.

Or worse.

God knew it could be so much worse.

Ruthlessly squashing that particular line of thought, Ciaran strode to the front desk and picked up the small stack of envelopes in his inbox tray. Most of the mail was addressed to the GDG marketing department. As one of the four owners of the private security firm, he'd drawn the short straw and ended up in charge of promotion, advertisement, and media. Which, considering his partners, made sense. Shane and Khalil ranked networking—hell, *smiling*—just above a *Hallmark Channel* marathon. And Maddox...well, since no one could ever predict what the hell would come out of Maddox's mouth, they'd found it safer to keep him behind the scenes.

He, Shane Roarke, Maddox Wright, and Khalil Jordan founded the firm three years ago, employing and contracting personnel to provide security and protection for high and low-risk clients. When he'd left the Drug Enforcement Administration four years ago after serving in their Operations Division, he'd floundered like a fish scooped out of its bowl and abandoned to flop around and struggle to survive in a suddenly new and alien environment. Leaving the agency had left him adrift—until GDG. His friends and the company blessed him with purpose. Granted him direction.

Offered him absolution.

"Exactly. Where's Lauren?" While Willow was one of their most valued employees, the Artful Dodger, as they called her around the office, was more known for her talents with discreet retrieval of sensitive documentation and items rather than answering the phones.

"Her son's daycare called, and she had to go pick him up. Apparently he and the Cream of Wheat he ate for breakfast didn't agree." She grinned and the piercing at the corner of her bottom lip lifted. "So you have me manning the helm for the rest of the day. Lucky you."

"Lucky. Now there's a word," he drawled. "Not the first one that came to my mind, but..."

She laughed. "Now who's the sweet talker?"

"Uh, excuse me," a voice rang out.

Both he and Willow glanced toward the lobby entrance. But while she rose and circled the desk to greet their newcomer, Ciaran remained rooted to the spot. Lust tended to do that to a man. Grab him by the balls. Stop him dead in his tracks.

Sloane Barrett.

God*damn*.

The impact of her slammed into his chest with the force of a sledgehammer. Just as it had the night before. Then, he'd noticed her as soon as she'd entered the dining rom. How could he have missed that long, dark hair that looked like it'd been styled in one of those high-end salons that served mimosas and canapés along with its shampoos and cuts? Thick, luxurious, rich—and perfect for a man to twist his fist in. Perfect for tugging. The waves framed a face that could have graced the cameo his grandma had worn every Sunday morning to mass. Cool and composed, with graceful brows arching over beautiful almond-shaped eyes. Elegant bone structure, high cheek bones, and the faint, sexy-as-hell indentation in her chin lent her features an air that could have been haughty except for the wide, almost carnal mouth that was stunning in its sensuaity.

The ends of her hair brushed her breasts that had his mouth watering for a taste. Not the flat or barely-there flesh that seemed so fashionable in magazines and catwalks around the world. Anyone looking at her would know she was a woman, not some prepubescent girl. A narrow waist, a sensual flare of hips, and legs the perfect length for wrapping around a man's hips...and holding tight for a rough ride.

All that beauty, and then she'd picked up a Sam Adams. In a bottle.

Last night, his response to her had been too visceral, too deep...too hungry. Sex was a physical release, a stress reliever.

Not the craving that had gnawed at him just at the sight of her. That should've been his first warning to keep his distance from her. The second should've been that she was obviously a friend of Fallon's. A wealthy, Beacon Hill friend. In other words, the women he stayed away from. Women like Sloane Barrett weren't the hit-it-and-quit-it kind. She would expect cuddling, whispered praise, and reassurance in the morning after. Hell, she would expect a fucking morning after. And with him, there was no such animal; he hadn't slept beside a lover in four years. Not since...

His fingers tightened around his coffee cup, and he detonated the tracks on that train of thought before it could pull any further out of the station.

Yet, the knowledge and back-the-fuck-off warnings blaring in his head hadn't stopped him from following her out on the patio. And even when she'd walked away from him, avoiding him from the rest of the evening, he'd been consumed with a mixture of relief and *hell no*. When she'd left the restaurant, part of him had wanted to turn around and return at least a little of the interest the blonde flirting with him exhibited. And the other half...that half burned to charge after her, guide her into the back of a cab, and carry her to his bed where she belonged.

Where she belonged. Shit, even the thought—the unfamiliar *possessiveness* behind the thought—had caused a fist of panic to tighten around his throat.

Like it did now in the lobby of his firm.

And damn, the sight of her. His cock jumped, pressing against his zipper like a fucking voyeur vying for a peek.

At some point between soothing a client over a brick arriving unannounced through his front window and arriving at work this morning, he'd convinced himself Sloane Barrett couldn't be as gorgeous as his sleep-deprived brain had convinced him. Yeah, well his memories hadn't lied. If anything, they'd fucking low-balled the truth.

Eyes still the vivid green of a rain forest. Face as smooth and lovely as a painting. Mouth as lush and ripe as the juiciest piece of fruit. A body—shit, a body so wicked, it should've been the eighth deadly sin. Even the simple lines of the strapless, floor-length dress couldn't hide the sexy-as-hell curves. Strapless. Hell. He deviated between envying and hating the material that supported the generous weight of those beautiful breasts.

The low lighting of the restaurant patio hadn't allowed him to catch the smaller, less obvious details. Such as the faint mark at the lower end of her eyebrow. Surprise and delight sparked within him. Apparently, at some point, the duchess had been pierced. He also noticed the light smattering of freckles across her nose and cheekbones, the specks a slightly darker shade of gold than her skin…

Sloane blinked up at him and swept the tip of her tongue over her parted lips. He smothered a pained groan. Just like the night before, the nervous gesture had him imagining the same moist swipe over his cock instead of her bottom lip. "What are you doing here?" she asked, voice barely above a whisper.

"I believe that's my question, since I work here, duchess," he drawled.

A flare of satisfaction and need sparked in his chest at the firming of her mouth and the anger that flickered in her eyes at the "duchess." She hadn't appreciated the nickname while on the patio. But with all that rich, dark brown hair drawn away from her face to stream in a luxurious, sleek fall down her tautly held shoulders and straight back, she earned the title. Regal. Gorgeous. Distant. But, goddamn, his fingers itched to discover if she was touchable.

She frowned. "You didn't mention…" Shaking her head, she waved a hand. "Never mind, I supposed it doesn't matter."

Turning to Willow, she smiled, but now it was his turn to frown and edge closer. Something about that smile was off… "I have an appointment to see Fallon Wayland and Shane Roarke, please. My name is Sloane Barrett."

"Uh, yeah," Willow said, her curious and way-too-perceptive gaze darting back and forth between him and Sloane. "I'll give 'em both a heads-up."

"Yeah, you do that." He narrowed his gaze on the slow grin spreading over Willow's lips as she circled the desk and picked up the phone. "What's wrong, Sloane? Did something happen?"

Unease wormed under his skin. Since she'd just seen Fallon at the party hours earlier, he doubted this visit to the office was social.

"No. Yes," she stammered, pinching her nose and briefly squeezing her eyes closed. When she looked at him again, her lovely features had shaped into an aloof, reserved mask. But she'd been seconds too late. He'd detected the traces of fear before she concealed it. *What the hell happened?* "I'm fine."

"Ms. Barrett, they're waiting for you in Shane's office." Willow rounded the desk. "Just follow me—"

"I'll show her, Willow," he interrupted, eliminating the space between them and placing a hand on her lower back.

She stiffened. "Thank you, but—"

"No problem. I was headed there myself." Giving her no choice, he gently but firmly pushed her forward in the direction of Shane's office.

"This really isn't necessary—"

"Trust me, duchess, it's necessary." He opened the door to Shane's office just as she jerked to a stop and glared fire and brimstone at him.

"Can I please finish a sentence without you interrupting?" she snapped.

"Umm…hi?" Fallon greeted.

Heat flooded Sloane's face, staining it an adorable shade of Embarrassed as Hell. He grinned as she turned to face a fascinated Fallon, who watched Ciaran and Sloane with a gleam most people reserved for chocolate and football.

Shooting him another irritated scowl, Sloane recovered with an admirable quickness and entered the office. She crossed the spacious but Spartan room and hugged Fallon. Shane, Ciaran's business partner and best friend as well as Fallon's fiancé, rose from behind his desk. He glanced at Sloane, then cocked an eyebrow. Ciaran shrugged a shoulder in silent reply.

"I'm so glad you came in," Fallon said, kissing Sloane on the cheek. "I couldn't sleep last night, I was so worried about you. I still wish you would've come over and slept at our place."

Worried about you? Slept at our place? All traces of humor evaporated like fog burned away by the mid-morning sun.

"What's going on?" he demanded of everyone. He didn't care who answered, as long as someone did. And five seconds ago.

"That's what we're here to find out," Shane murmured, rounding the desk and leaning against the edge, arms crossed. Again, he arched a dark brow. "Why don't you join us?" he invited, voice dry.

"I, uh, take it you two know each other?" Fallon asked, her gaze shifting from Sloane to Ciaran.

"No," Sloane stated firmly.

"Yes," Ciaran contradicted at the same time.

"Well, that certainly clears that up," Shane drawled.

"Later," Ciaran growled, stalking to the nearest wall and propping a shoulder against it. He returned Sloane's stare with one of his own. Fuck that. She could aim as many frosty glowers and frowns his way as she wanted, he wasn't going anywhere. "What's going on?"

"Someone broke into Sloane's house yesterday evening. He grabbed her, but she escaped before he could hurt her," Fallon explained softly, clasping Sloane's hand as the other woman sank into one of the visitor chairs flanking the front of the desk.

A cold fist smashed into his chest, seized his heart, and squeezed. He straightened and fought the instinctive urge to charge across the room and draw Sloane into his arms, shielding her from not just the horrifying violation that must still be tormenting her, but also from any more threats and danger. The need to touch her, soothe away the fear, and murmur his promise that no harm would come to her was a living thing inside him. But he smothered it, forcing himself to remain at his post against the wall. Not only would she reject any overture from him, but he didn't comfort clients. He didn't soothe. And he damn sure didn't issue promises.

"Start at the beginning, Sloane," Shane instructed gently. "Leave nothing out."

Sloane sighed, and her shoulders slumped the tiniest bit, weariness settling on her like a heavy blanket. "Three weeks ago, I started receiving late-night phone calls with no one speaking on the other end. And"—she paused, and he caught the slight shudder that rippled over her body—"unsettling emails."

"What do you mean by 'unsettling?'" he asked before Shane or Fallon could.

She didn't glance at him, but the fatigue disappeared, her body going rigid. "They're images of women," she explained, voice flat. "Dead women."

Fallon sucked in an audible gust of breath while Ciaran swore, harsh and hot. Shane's mouth straightened into a grim line.

"How do you know they're dead?" Fallon asked, her face

pale.

"The eyes. They're glassy. Empty," Sloane whispered. Then, shaking her head, she cleared her throat. "There are also bruises around their necks as if they were strangled."

"The emails. You don't recognize the sender's address?" Shane questioned.

Again, she shook her head. "The address is yourenext at yahoo-dot-com."

"And the emails and phone calls? They started three weeks ago? Just out of the blue?" Ciaran stalked across the office, halting at the edge of the desk.

She nodded. "Yes. And yesterday afternoon when I left school, two of my tires were flat. I think"—she hesitated—"I think they were slashed."

"Slashed tires?" Fallon frowned. "Sloane, you didn't say anything last night."

Sloane lifted a shoulder in a half shrug. "It was your evening. I didn't want to spoil it. And besides, it's my *belief* they were, I don't have proof, yet. I asked my mechanic to check, so I'll know today when I pick my car up."

"How often do you receive these calls and emails?" Ciaran gently steered the topic back to the immediate threats.

"That first week, it was only a few times. But the following two, I received them every day. I turned off the ringer on my cell at night so I could get some sleep, and I blocked the email address, but somehow, they keep coming through."

"And last night?" Shane prodded.

Sloane closed her eyes, but her lids immediately popped open, almost as if she couldn't bear the momentary darkness.

"I arrived home and noticed that my door was open..."

As Sloane relayed the events of the night before, anger and fear rolled through him. And that old motherfucker helplessness washed up right behind them. For several long moments, he slowly, silently inhaled through his nose, exhaled through parted lips. He blinked back the walls of black that darkened his peripheral vision, threatening to blind him completely.

Sam had been killed the same way. The safe house broken into. Dragged to another location. Gunned down in front of him.

Ciaran pressed a hand to the middle of his chest. Right over the circular scar that had once been a bullet hole. For a second, the searing blaze infiltrated his flesh, radiated from behind his rib cage...

"Ciaran." Shane's deep rumble penetrated the dark fog wrapping around him and halted his spiral into the blood-soaked past. Back then, Shane had seen him at his worst, had yanked him back from the abyss... And he recognized the signs of Ciaran teetering on the edge of it now.

"Yeah," Ciaran rasped. He thrust his hands in the front pockets of his pants, hiding the fists his fingers had curled into. "Do you know how he got into your house? Do you have an alarm system?"

Sloane studied him, those emerald eyes incisive and questioning. Apparently she hadn't missed his momentary furlough into hell. He struggled with the urge to return to his post against the wall and hide from her stare that seemed to cut too deep.

"The police haven't verified it, but I assumed through the front door, since it was unlocked. I always lock the door and set the alarm. I've been even more conscious than usual with the emails and calls," she explained. "I've been trying to figure out how he disarmed the system..." she trailed off, frowning.

"Is the code your birthday?" The slight widening of her eyes affirmed his guess. He nodded. "Most people use either their own or their kids' birthdays as codes. Which tells us whoever did this must know you in some way. At least enough to have knowledge of your birthday or have access to the info," Shane added. "Sloane, do you have any thoughts to who might be behind this?"

"As a matter of fact, I do," she said with a grim smile. "Drake Morriston."

"Who?" Fallon demanded. "You've never mentioned that name to me before."

"He's a senior in my government class. Well, was." She went on to tell them about Drake, his rage at the failing grade she'd given him and the voicemail he'd left on her phone. "He's the only person I can think of who has anything against me."

Ciaran snorted. "True, he sounds like a spoiled douche, but that's thin. And a B&E and attempted assault is a steep upgrade from a tantrum and voicemail."

"I can't think of anyone else who would hate me enough to destroy my home and come after me," Sloane admitted softly.

Truth be told, he couldn't either. From the short amount of time they'd spent together, she'd struck him as strong but vulnerable. Reserved but sensitive. And sweet. So fucking sweet.

Jesus H. Christ, *focus.*

"Does your school have security cameras installed on their campus?" Ciaran's mind already turned, setting on the methods he and his colleagues could use to identify the asshole stalking Sloane.

"Inside, yes. But I'm not sure about whether they cover the parking lots." A rueful, humorless smile twisted her lips. "Either way, good luck with convincing the principal to let you have access. The administration is very…careful of their privacy and reputation."

Meaning they wouldn't want even the smallest hint of negativity attached to their prestigious name. Not even if it meant protecting a teacher who might be in danger. Fuckers.

"Don't worry about that. We'll manage."

GDG wasn't the police. Sometimes, permission was a nicety instead of a necessity. Especially when you had a world-class hacker on your payroll. After outsourcing the technical side of their business for several years, they'd finally hired Jake Reid, ex-CIA and a computer genius-slash-mad-scientist.

"I'll get Jake to track the IP address on those emails. Find out what computer they originated from. Even if we can't get a name, we might be able to come up with a location," Ciaran said.

Shane pushed himself off the desk and rounded the piece of furniture to drop into his office chair. "And I'll get Maddox to install a tracker on your home and cell phones, see if we can trace the calls the next time they come in." Shane dipped his chin in Sloane's direction. "If that's okay with you, Sloane."

"Of course, thank you," Sloane murmured, that cool mask firmly back in place. He would've believed this conversation didn't affect her if not for her twisting her fingers on her lap. The sight of the nervous gesture sent an unsolicited and unwanted tenderness stretching in his gut. He shut it down so hard and quick, a phantom muscle twinged in his chest.

Ciaran turned to face Shane and away from the temptation to...*feel* that Sloane represented. He hadn't allowed anything stronger than lust, anger, and grief to fill him in three years. And unless he intended to crack right down the middle and have all his fucked-up shit spill out, he didn't see a reason to start feeling now.

"What about putting someone on her?" Ciaran proposed.

"Just what I was thinking." Fallon shot a look at Shane, her fear for Sloane so obvious, Stevie Wonder wouldn't need braille to read it. The severe lines of Shane's face softened as he gazed back at the woman he loved, and Ciaran had to look away. He was happy for the two of them, he truly was. But the intimacy in their silent communication jabbed at an emotion he wasn't too proud of—an emotion that he detested experiencing at all: jealousy. He didn't want love or even companionship. The females he fucked understood what he offered them—one night. He never failed to make his limitations abundantly clear. Anything more than several hours of pleasure led to hopes of a relationship, and he didn't do relationships.

Commitment, love, selflessness—those were his biggest deficits.

And unlike some knuckleheads, he didn't need to ride the merry-go-round of insanity over and over again before jumping off. Shane was his best friend, and Ciaran considered Fallon his little sister, but he couldn't help but call them reckless and crazy for risking their sanity and their lives, if one of them were hurt...or died.

Because loving meant losing.

"I don't think that's necessary," Sloane interjected, drawing Ciaran's attention back to her like a dinner bell lured a horde of ravenous men. "I'm staying in a hotel now and am leaving town next week."

"Leaving town?" he barked. *Calm the hell down*, a soft voice whispered against his mind. Why should he care? *I don't*, he assured himself. Still... "Where are you going?"

"To the Hamptons for my parents' anniversary. I'll be there Thursday through Monday."

Refusing to analyze the absurd strength of the relief that coursed through him at the knowledge she was leaving town and would temporarily be out of harm's way, he nodded. "Okay, but I still believe we need to sit someone on you until then."

"Just because you leave Boston doesn't mean whoever is doing this will wait patiently for your return. I still say you should have someone watching your back on your trip, too,"

Fallon insisted. Her expression cleared, brightening as she turned fully toward Sloane. "You mentioned this party to me. Isn't your mother expecting you to bring a plus one? So take a guard and pretend he's your date. No one would suspect the truth, and you'll be protected."

Before Sloane could control her reaction, horror flashed across her features. The accompanying flinch was small, but he noticed it. Filed it away to question and examine later. Why did the thought of bringing a "boyfriend" to meet her family disturb her so much?

"Absolutely not," she said flatly. "Not only would I hate having to lie to everyone, but my parents wouldn't buy it. And, like I said, it's not necessary. I will be surrounded by people the entire time. I'll be safe."

"Sloane—"

"Let it go, Fallon," she murmured, gentling the command with a squeeze of her friend's shoulder. "I get you're worried, and I appreciate it and love you for it. But I'm going to be okay." She rose from her chair. "I have to go. I have to pick up my car, and I have an open house for new students on Monday to prepare for. You'll let me know what you find, Shane?"

"Of course," he said, also standing. "We'll get started right away."

"I'll walk you out," Fallon offered.

"I'll do it," Ciaran interceded, already moving forward.

"Not necessary," Sloane gritted out between clenched teeth.

"It's not a problem," he returned, opening the office door.

"It is for me," she snapped, then tried to soften the sharp tone with a polite smile. Too bad it came off as more of a snarl. "I mean, surely you have more important things to do."

"Not really."

They stared at one another, a Mexican standoff without

guns. Well, she was armed. If looks could kill…

The corner of his mouth quirked. The duchess fascinated him. But the passionate woman beneath the elegant veneer… she made his dick harden until it resembled a damn steel pipe.

Made him wonder what that passion looked like when a mouth teased and licked her pussy, sucked on her clit. No, not "a mouth." His. He lowered his gaze down the walking wet dream masquerading as a body, settling on the area where her thighs would connect with her torso. The spot where half his fantasies focused. Lust snaked through his veins, an answering tribal beat taking up in his dick. In his perverted mind, when he parted her pretty legs and exposed her pink, swollen flesh, he discovered the sugar and cinnamon flavor was concentrated in her folds. In the thick, wet sweetness that coated her sex.

That comprised only half his imaginings, though.

The other part had him sinking inside her. Being surrounded, squeezed, milked by her. Being held by her.

As he studied the defiance in her glare, he indulged in the ultimate fantasy. Forgetfulness. Peace.

Redemption.

He balked, recoiling from the bright, warm illusion. He clung to the cold, the dark. Not because he relished the pain and loneliness. But because he'd earned it.

"Soooo, I'm going to go out on a limb and guess that you two *do* know each other." Fallon's dry observation snapped him free of his demons.

"I have a call to make," he said, voice hard, abrupt. He had to get out of the office, away from her. Away from the temptation she represented. Yet, before escaping, he turned to Shane. "You'll keep me posted?"

Shane nodded. "I will."

"Good." With a sharp dip of his chin in Sloane's direction, he stalked out, heading for his own office where he could hunker down, regroup.

Still… Too bad he couldn't dodge the suspicion that he was only slapping a Band-Aid on a bleeding wound.

He might've won this round by walking away from Sloane, but the battle was far from over.

Chapter Four

"Good-night." Sloane smiled, following the last pair of parents to the door of her classroom. They stepped out, disappearing into the hall, carting the last of her hope for a new, *different* school year with them.

She sighed, slipping her heels from her feet. Her toes sank into the thick carpet—one of the perks of working at a prestigious school. No tiled floors for the wealthy, elite students of Kennedy-Lewis Preparatory Academy. Only the best amenities, technology, and accommodations. But hey, their parents paid for the privilege of not having their darlings mingle with the dirty masses.

"God." She groaned. *I'm getting on my own nerves.*

"Well, hello, *Ms.* Barrett," a voice drawled.

Damn. From the insolent tone and disrespectful way he stressed the Ms., as if emphasizing her single status, she knew exactly who'd addressed her.

Turning toward her classroom door, she schooled her features into a cool mask and rose. "Hello, Drake."

Her former student could've graced the cover of a fashion

magazine, his handsome face and impeccable clothing a photographer's dream. Too bad they hid a meanness that exceeded simple spoiled entitlement. Drake Morriston was rotten on the inside. He'd taken great delight in tormenting his classmates by ruining reputations, intimidating them with his size and social influence. And though it hadn't been proven, she suspected he'd been behind the horrific social media barrage that had made a former student attempt suicide. If she'd met Drake on a dark street, she would cross the road and run with mace in hand.

"Getting ready for another school year, *Ms*. Barrett? Another year of"—he grinned—"wasting on the vine."

She didn't respond. Engaging him would only encourage him, and that's what he sought. A response to his taunting. Not that it stopped him from poking at the wound. And it was a wound. How he'd discovered her single status, she didn't know, but she also didn't put anything past him.

"You know…" He strolled into the room as if he owned it. Well, that was the library his parents had endowed, not this building. "My parents are urging Mr. Cole to fire you. But I convinced them to let you have this sad, pathetic job. I mean, I'm a legacy, and someone as insignificant as you won't keep me out of Harvard. But if we took this position away from you, what else would you have? You already have so little." He scanned her from head to her bare feet, a sneer tipping the corner of his mouth, his opinion of her appearance clear. "No fiancé, no family, and now you've obviously pissed somebody off enough that your house has been broken into and vandalized?" He *tsked*. "Yeah, it would be cruel of us to take this away."

Rage, hurt, and humiliation crowded into her chest. By sheer will, she remained standing when her knees trembled. By the power of self-preservation she kept her hands hanging loosely at her sides, when they itched to curl into fists and swing at this little punk. By the force of her pride, she held the stinging moisture in check, when she wanted to tear up at his spiteful insults.

Inhaling a deep, quiet breath, she laser-beamed in on the one thing he'd said that sounded incriminating to her. "How did you know about the break-in, Drake?"

His eyes widened in mock innocence. "Word gets around, *Ms*. Barrett. The school grapevine is a fast and reliable thing. While I may have graduated, I still have eyes and ears here."

She nodded. Slowly, without removing her eyes from him, she patted her desk for her cell phone. After a couple of seconds, she picked it up.

Drake snorted. "Calling 911?"

"No," she said, tone calm as she swept a thumb across the screen. "I'm recording this conversation so I will have proof of your harassment." She pressed her video app. "Okay, go ahead. As you were saying?"

The sneer on his mouth deepened, but it was his flat gaze, not unlike a snake, that had her gripping the phone tighter. Finally, he dipped his chin and slid his hands in the pockets of his perfectly creased pants.

"You have a wonderful evening, *Ms*. Barrett. And keep safe." He pivoted and exited the room, leaving the echo of her pounding heart in her ears. Logic insisted she was safe in this school that hadn't emptied out yet. But…there was something unsettling about Drake Morriston.

Exhaling, she dropped into her chair once more. The visit from him had only verified what she'd been experiencing for a while now. For two years, this restlessness had been growing inside her. No. "Restlessness" was the wrong word. Something larger, wider, *hungrier* than mere restlessness spread in her chest like a sink hole. Not that every student at the school was spoiled and entitled—or sadistic like Drake. Actually, the majority of them were exuberant, fun-loving, smart teens and, she enjoyed them. It wasn't their fault she didn't feel… needed.

The joy that had filled her like a hot air balloon after her college graduation, lifting her higher and higher into the sky, into a welcoming, bright future, had seeped away like a slow leak. Her dream had been to watch a child's eyes light up with understanding. To forge a new educational path in a well-worn field instead of aimlessly treading the same road over and over again until she herself wanted to weep with frustration. To leave a positive mark on a child's life.

Walking into the school this afternoon, preparing to meet the parents of incoming and returning students, she'd hoped— *prayed*—she would find that joy again. That excitement and anticipation. But she'd encountered nothing but the mourning. Honed even sharper because of the fragile, futile hope.

Hooking the straps of her shoes over a finger, she strode to her desk and dropped into the chair. She reached for the copies of the syllabi and curriculum she'd handed out earlier. For a long moment, her hands hovered above the stack before shifting direction seemingly of their own volition. As if her fingers were detached from her brain, they changed course and headed toward her messenger bag and removed a folder. A folder she'd been carrying around for weeks.

She placed the white and green file on her desk and warily flipped it open as if it contained a coiled snake—or a beautifully wrapped gift. Though she removed the sheaf of papers, she didn't need to read them. The words were branded into her memory from the countless number of times she'd repeated this very action in the weeks since she'd received the folder.

The information on Boston's newest charter school. The five-year charter had already been awarded, and the school would open the following year. Meanwhile, teachers were being hired, curriculum and teaching methods being planned.

And Sloane wanted to be in on it. Forget that, she *yearned* to be in on it. The freedom, the opportunity to cause change. This school, situated in inner-city Roxbury, veered as far from Kennedy-Lewis Prep as champagne differed from Kool-Aid. The pay would be less, the prestige would be nil, and the environment rougher. She would be stepping out into the unknown, by herself...alone.

God, she wanted in.

But leaving the cloistered, cushy position at Kennedy-Lewis would mean disappointing her parents...again. For most twenty-six-year-olds, this wouldn't be a big deal. But when her life had been one frustration and let down after another, she hated heaping one more to the steaming pile. Her parents' wishes for her to mirror Chelsea's life—beautiful, bubbly, married, two gorgeous children, a perfect hostess. Not shy, single, childless, shackled to her job. And, oh yes, a size fourteen instead of a four. They believed this pampered existence would bring her happiness and fulfilment—even though it obviously hadn't worked out for Chelsea. Her father hadn't understood her choices, but he'd supported her. And had been excited when he'd called her to announce he'd tugged on his connections to procure her the job at Kennedy-Lewis. Her usually reserved father had been *excited* he could do something to encourage and help her in a dream he might not have agreed with but aided. Leaving would be like kicking dirt on his show of support.

Still...Sloane drew in a breath and closed the folder, tracing the slightly raised letters on the front. Still, did she wake up one morning ten years from now, filled with bitterness over how her life had turned out? Did she allow what was her passion to become her burden, her albatross?

Shaking her head, she replaced the file in her bag and returned to the little bit of work left on her desk. Or she would have if her cell hadn't rang out. She grinned, already reaching for the phone and cutting off Tom Jones mid-croon.

"Hi, Uncle Matt," she greeted her godfather and father's oldest and best friend, pleasure a warm glow in her chest and banishing the guilt-filled shadows as well as the residual dregs of uneasiness from Drake's unexpected visit. "Shouldn't you and Aunt Grace be preparing for the Hamptons?"

Matthew Daniels' rusty chuckle echoed in her ear, and her smile grew. Hearing his laughter was like winning a medal since joy from the man she loved like a second father was so rare these days. Four months ago, he'd lost his only son, Matthew Daniels II, to suicide. He'd only been several years older than Sloane, and though they hadn't been very close, he'd always been a kind, quiet man. Like his father.

"I'm just staying out of the way. After thirty-five years of marriage, I've learned it's much easier this way." His soft snort had her laughing. "Just as I've learned when I'm ordered to do something, I do it."

Sloane groaned. "Who? Aunt Grace or my mother?"

"Your mother with your aunt aiding and abetting. Mallory wanted me to call and make sure you're coming this weekend. Although with that jackass Phillip coming as well, I wouldn't blame you if you decided to skip it," he grumbled.

Even as exasperation welled up inside her, love for her godfather tempered the frustration. "It's okay. Dad has a relationship with him, so I understand." *Like hell.* "Uncle Matt, you promised…"

Matthew grunted. "I won't say anything, but I still think you should let John and Mallory know what a jackass he is."

It'd been in a moment of weakness a couple of days after Phillip left that she'd confided in Matthew about the true nature of their relationship. Angered, he'd encouraged her to talk to her parents, but fresh in her head had been Phillip's mocking laughter and taunt that they would blame her for being unable to hold on to a man…again. That she was the fat, ugly daughter they would end up having to pay someone to marry. Though common sense argued her parents loved her, shame, hurt, and embarrassment had kept her mouth shut.

"I will, or at least I'll try. But their anniversary party isn't the time or place." God, she could just imagine the conniption fit her mother would throw if Sloane dared to interject unpleasantness in their special weekend. Between the break-in and Phillip, there was plenty of unpleasantness to go around. "And you can assure Mother that I will be there Thursday on time and ready to play the shiny, happy family."

"I'll make sure to relay your assurance without the sarcasm," Matthew drawled.

Sloane laughed. "I appreciate it."

After several more minutes where she promised to come to dinner the following week, she ended the call and finished up the work on her desk. A half hour later, she shut off the light in her classroom and shut the door behind her. Hiking her messenger bag and purse straps higher on her shoulder, she strode down the silent, abandoned halls. Damn it. She'd lost track of time. Being one of the last people to leave the building had *not* been on her agenda. Since the lights were still on, a janitor and maybe even the principal probably lurked somewhere. The rational logic didn't stop her from speeding up, the echo of her shoes *clacking* on the hardwood floor bouncing back at her like a shout in a wide cave.

She burst through the front entrance like the hounds of hell were nipping at the heels of her knock-off Manolo Blahniks. The cool night air closed around her, and she inhaled, then released the breath on an embarrassed chuckle. Jesus, next thing she would be imagining a machete-wielding, hockey-masked maniac stalking her through the campus. Although she was walking by herself to her car in a nearly deserted parking lot. After all the events of the past few days—weeks—that alone had to nominate her for some kind of Darwin Award.

With a relieved sigh she couldn't quite swallow, she reached her car, hitting the valet key to electronically unlock the doors. A quick glance at the ground revealed she wouldn't have to call the tow truck once again. Her tires were all in working, *inflated* order. Oh goody. She was already in better condition than she'd been on Friday.

Jerking open the passenger door, she dropped her bags, binder, and a couple of text books onto the seat. Calling herself about five kinds of paranoid, she glanced in the back seat, scanning it for anything hulking and darker than the shadows, before shutting the door and hurrying around the tail of the car. The same unease that had trickled down her spine when she'd approached her vandalized home days ago now skated over her skin. She snorted. *Get it together*, she berated herself, gripping the driver's door handle. *You're a grown woman on the grounds of a school, not some air-headed teenager in a horror mov—*

A palm slapped over her mouth. Pain and terror ripped the breath from her throat. On reflex, she tried to inhale through her mouth, clawing at the big hand cutting off her air flow. Ashes. Grease. She gagged on the dirty, oily taste coating the flesh pressed to her lips. For an instant she started sliding toward unconsciousness before primal instinct kicked in. She sucked in a breath through her nose. The black creeping edges started to retreat, and she screamed, or tried to with a hand covering her mouth.

The muffled cry reverberated in her head, the desperate, panicked roar almost blocking out her assailant's "Shut it, bitch."

Ruthless fingers manacled her wrists and jerked her arms behind her back, but her mouth remained covered. Two attackers. *Oh God.* Her stomach bottomed out, then filled to the brim with dread and a hopelessness that almost buckled her knees. For a second, as her hands were bound at the base of her spine, she gave up. Two against one. Jesus, she was gone…

Hell no. Hell. No.

She yelled, jerked, twisted. Fire raced up her arms and pulsed in her shoulders like an open wound. But she didn't stop. She lunged forward, not caring that with her hands bound, that she would likely face-plant. *Get away. Run. Scream.* The mantra ran through her mind on a frantic loop.

"Shit, man," the one covering her mouth from behind snapped. "Knock her the fuck out so we can get her in the car and get the hell out of here."

"Well, hold her, then," the other assailant ordered.

A large pair of black boots filled her vision. And she fought harder. If they hit her, if she blacked out, she was dead. Every *48 Hours: Hard Evidence* episode about kidnapped women she'd ever seen ran through her brain in warp speed. Once the victim was carried to a second, likely more remote location, her chances of survival plummeted. She couldn't die. Couldn't…

She leaned her head forward…and snapped it back. Pain exploded at the back of her skull.

"Fuck!" came an agonized howl from behind her. The hand covering her mouth disappeared, and she gasped in a breath. Nausea churned in her belly and scalded a path up her chest to the back of her throat, but she fought it down. She stumbled forward, her shoulder bumping into the chest of the attacker in front of her.

Cruel fingers dug into her upper arm just as her head was wrenched back by her hair, sending more painful pricks stabbing into her scalp. She cried out, the tendons in her neck screaming, stretched until they burned, as if on the verge of snapping.

"You're gonna pay for that, bitch," a nasally voice sneered

in her ear with another vicious jerk on her head. Obviously her head-butt had damaged his nose. And he was pissed. She squeezed her eyes shut as a hand closed around her throat… squeezed…

"What the—"

The hands gripping her hair and choking her neck disappeared, leaving her staggering. The ground rose up to meet her, and at the last second, she twisted, clenching her teeth against the impact of her shoulder, arm, and hip slamming to the pavement. But as she rolled to sit on her behind, she couldn't contain her groan. Fire throbbed in her muscles and joints. Her heart hammered against her ribcage. Bile razed the lining of her throat.

Move, a voice screamed in her head. *Fuck the pain.* Move.

She obeyed. Whimpering, she staggered to her knees, ignoring the tiny bits of gravel biting into her—*holy shit*. She froze, the throbbing in her body momentarily forgotten.

Ciaran.

Moving like a honed weapon. Quick. Silent. Slashing. Precise. Deadly. Fury darkened his features into a taut, ruthless mask, but he fought with cold efficiency. Though her two attackers—her first look at the hooded men—outnumbered him, and their bulky, wide builds seemed to outweigh him, Ciaran cut through the assailants like a hot knife slicing through butter.

A jab to the throat. A kick that could've been choreographed in a Jackie Chan movie. A flurry of punches that elicited pained grunts and rage-filled curses. He shifted, glided, and struck with a lethal grace and beauty. He was both awesome and frightening.

With a hard, two-palmed shove to one of the thug's chests that had the asshole crashing into the side of her car, Ciaran pivoted and delivered an audible, jaw-cracking punch to the other. He quickly followed up the blow with a knee to the gut and an elbow to the spine. The guy crumbled to the ground and didn't move.

Metal glinted in the light of the parking lot lamps behind him.

"Ciaran," she rasped, the warning like sandpaper over her raw throat.

But she must've been loud enough. Ciaran whirled around, gripped the attacker's wrist, and in a complicated but seamless move, rotated and rolled, ending up behind the other guy with the asshole's hand twisted and the gun on the ground. In seconds, Ciaran released the thug, only to wrap his arm around the other man's neck in a merciless chokehold. Her attacker slapped at Ciaran, grabbed at him, even tried to elbow him. But Ciaran, his mouth flattened in a straight, grim line, his blue eyes glittering, didn't flinch or ease up. Not until the other man slumped, unconscious in the implacable hold. Only then did Ciaran allow him to drop to the ground with a dull, heavy *thud*.

He crouched over the prone figure at his feet and reached into the thigh pocket of his cargo pants, removing a clear zip-tie. "Are you hurt?"

She flinched at the quiet tone which belied the rage burning in his narrowed gaze. With sure, economic movements, he trussed up both men, shackling their wrists and ankles. A fierce satisfaction blazed through her. *Good.* When the assholes woke, they would know how it felt to be trapped and helpless... Good, dammit.

"Sloane?"

She jerked her attention back to Ciaran. "No, I'm okay."

Her shoulders ached and her wrists burned, but he'd most likely just saved her life. Yes, parts of her complained like nagging fishwives, but dammit, she was alive.

Thanks to Ciaran.

Chapter Five

"Thank you."

Ciaran glanced at the passenger seat of his Range Rover where Sloane sat staring out the window. Dirt smudged her skirt, and a tear ruined the hem. Yet, at some point, she'd brushed her hair and tucked her shirt nice and neat in the waistband of her skirt. Though signs of her terrifying ordeal and brush with possible death marred her, the duchess had stepped in. With her straight shoulders and regal bearing that had probably been drilled into her from the cradle, he could easily imagine her riding in a horse-drawn, covered carriage, separated by birth and blood from the teeming masses.

Except she wasn't separate. A couple of the "teeming masses" had assaulted her less than two hours ago. Put their hands over her mouth, around her neck. Had cuffed her. Rage poured through him like a molten wave of lava. He curled his fingers around the steering wheel, squeezing so hard, the ridges underneath bit into his flesh.

Seconds. That's all it'd taken for him to jump out of his vehicle and run across the parking lot to reach Sloane and those two bastards who had appeared out of the shadows to attack her. Those seconds, though, had seemed like years, and the small distance had yawned wider with each step he'd taken. As a DEA agent and a security specialist, he'd faced down criminals. Had neutralized threats. But not since his first drug bust had his heart pounded so hard in his chest, it'd nearly burst through his rib cage like a wild, rabid animal.

Even now the sour, acrid remnants of fear that had flooded his mouth and nose lingered in his throat, his tongue. *Not again, not again*, his mind had chanted. *I can't lose another one again.* For a moment, he'd been back on that dirty, oil-splattered warehouse floor, blood pumping out of his chest, spilling over his hands. For a moment, the *boom* of another gunshot had filled his ears.

For a moment, his eyes had connected with the dark, blank, lifeless stare of the woman he loved.

Ciaran swallowed hard and narrowed his gaze on the white lines and reflectors on the dark street. He'd reached Sloane in time. He'd subdued her attackers. He hadn't failed to keep someone safe…again.

"Ciaran?"

Her soft voice drew him back those last few inches from the crumbling, fragile edge. Inhaling, he consciously eased his grip on the steering wheel and quietly, deliberately exhaled.

"You're welcome." He didn't pretend to misunderstand why she was grateful. "Are you sure you're okay?"

"Yes," she murmured.

From the corner of his eye, he caught a subtle movement. Sloane rubbed her wrists where the zip-ties, not unlike the ones he'd used to cuff her assailants, had bit into her flesh. After he'd snapped the restraints loose, the sight of her reddened and raw skin had almost sent him over to the assholes to slap them awake so he could beat them into unconsciousness all over again. The angry welts and bloody chafing had seemed sacrilegious against her delicate, soft skin. Once more, he tightened his hold on the steering wheel. This time to keep him from reaching across the console and rubbing his thumb over the irritated and bruised area.

"So I take it you weren't there by accident," she said, a wry note creeping into her voice. "You were following me?"

He nodded. "Since Saturday afternoon." In their office earlier that day, she hadn't exactly forbidden them to tail her. She'd claimed a surveillance team hadn't been necessary. Not that her wishes in the matter of her safety would've mattered anyway. Between the emails, late-night phone calls, and the assault and break-in at her home, there was no way in hell Ciaran wasn't putting someone on her. "We've had a small detail assigned to you."

And if he assumed a shift every day, then it was only because Sloane held a special place in Fallon's life.

He smothered a snort. Yeah, he didn't even buy that bullshit.

Still, he retreated from examining why. It didn't matter if the reason behind his compulsive vigilance was because she reminded him of Sam or because she, herself, was the one he couldn't exorcise from his mind and dreams. Both options sucked and scared the shit out of him. One meant he teetered closer to the abyss than he imagined, and the other suggested he was obsessed.

She sighed. "I guess it would be completely useless to point out that I didn't want to be followed, since your disregard of my wishes saved my life." She shook her head and chuckled, but the low burst of laughter didn't contain the slightest hint of humor. "You know, this morning I had myself convinced Friday night had been a random burglary gone wrong." She emitted another of those dry, self-deprecating laughs. "I didn't want it to be anything more. What's the saying? There are none so blind as those who will not see." Then, quieter,

"Normal. All I want is a little bit of normal."

He frowned, almost asking what the cryptic words meant, but at the last moment, he swallowed back the questioned and focused on the events of the night. "We're going to have to talk about what happened tonight." Not rehash the details of the attack; he'd witnessed it, and the cops had already taken her statement. Besides, making her relive those moments when she'd been restrained and abused seemed cruel. And the idea of causing her any further pain tonight—even mental anguish—sickened him.

"Yes." She nodded. "Starting with how I need to get my head out of my ass and face this thing head on."

A corner of his mouth quirked as he hit the turn signal for the Copley Square, Back Bay exit. "Careful, duchess, you just said 'ass,'" he teased.

She snorted. "I do curse, Ciaran."

"With that pretty mouth? Say it isn't so," he drawled. He chuckled at her short huff and rumble of irritation. Actually, imagining those plump, created-for-a-blow-job lips uttering "fuck me" while he rode her into his mattress summed up one of his most lurid fantasies. Just one.

Silence descended in the vehicle until he turned onto Boylston Street and neared the hotel parking entrance. Pressing a button on his earpiece, he stated, "Mark," and in seconds the GDG man he'd had sitting on the hotel, Mark Granger, answered.

"Mark, I'm arriving with Ms. Barrett. Come meet me on the lower level at parking. I need you to stand with her while I park. ETA three minutes."

"Got it. See you in a few."

The line disconnected. Ciaran's diligence might seem like a little too much, but he didn't want Sloane out of his sight even for a second. Not after tonight's events.

"They have valet parking," she said, but he shook his

head.

"I don't trust anyone with my car."

"First the guard meeting me and now this. Are you always so paranoid?"

He glanced at her, an eyebrow arched. "I get paid to be paranoid. Once, I worked an assignment for a four-star hotel like this one that was experiencing a theft issue. Turned out one of the sources was a couple of valets with sticky fingers. Not all of them are dishonest, but that small handful convinced me to secure my own vehicle."

And then there was the hard, cold fact he was just an untrusting bastard. He mentally shrugged. Some people bit their nails and others chain smoked. He didn't trust motherfuckers as far as his newborn nephew could throw them.

"Do you think the police will be able to determine who sent those two after me?"

Ciaran slowed the Range Rover to a stop in front of the ornate glass doors and staircase leading to the hotel's lobby. A liveried valet approached the vehicle, but Ciaran ignored him, instead focusing every ounce of his attention on the battered, trembling but proud woman next to him. Most women would've broken, been a sobbing, inconsolable mess after enduring the attack she'd suffered. But not the duchess. Bruised, but definitely not broken.

That kind of strength was sexy as hell. As alluring as the siren call of her curves. Sloane returned his stare without even an uncertain demure dip of her gaze. He fucking liked that, too.

Damn, he just enjoyed looking at her. But he forced himself to keep his attention from lowering to her mouth. One glance at the erotic shape of her lips, and all he could imagine was how they would feel under his. Or how pretty they would look sliding over his chest…or parting around his cock. His flesh thumped behind his zipper, totally on board with that idea.

The hard throb of arousal forced him to concentrate, to remember why he sat in this truck with her. Why she was there. Not for *him*, but what he—GDG—could offer. Protection. Security. Safety. Nothing else. Not his depraved thoughts or gnawing hunger. If Sloane had a glimpse of the pictures tramping around in his head, she would smack the shit out of him then hightail it out of his car like the damn thing had exploded into flames.

"You want complete honesty from me?"

"Of course," she said. "Always."

A wry smile twisted his lips. "Be careful what you wish for, duchess. But no, I don't think the police will find out who is behind tonight's kidnapping attempt." A beat of silence passed between them. "And make no mistake, Sloane. It was a kidnapping. If they only intended to hurt or even kill you, they could've done it there in the parking lot. Instead, they bound your hands and tried to drag you to their car and a second location."

Her lashes lowered, and an audible breath escaped her parted lips. When she met his gaze again, the green in her eyes had darkened, appearing almost black in the shadowed interior of the vehicle.

"Well, I asked for honesty, didn't I?" she murmured.

Humor even with terror staining her eyes. Yeah, definitely sexy as hell.

"Yes, you did. Those two assholes probably have long criminal records, and a simple snatch-and-grab is nothing to them." He would find out for sure since both geniuses had been carrying wallets in their pockets—pockets Ciaran had picked, stashing the contents in his trunk before the police had shown up. With their identification, Jake would be able to pull up any existing criminal records, violations—hell, the last time they'd shit. The man was that good…and scary. "But if the person who hired them possesses even a couple of brain cells, he made sure a go-between stood between them and him. Which means, they might, *might*, give up the name of who directly contacted them—if they have that—but not the identity of the person who wants to get to you." But he had a feeling the cops would find two men with a sudden case of deaf and dumbness on their hands. *Snitches get stitches* was the code of the street—and the pen. "And where they came from, there are plenty more willing to step up and take their places. So what I'm saying, Sloane, is this attack was the latest, not the last."

"I guessed as much," she whispered, shoving a hand through her hair. "Jesus. Why?"

The valet peered into the window and gently rapped on it.

"We don't know yet, but we'll find out. I promise you that. Sloane"—he leaned forward, ignoring the tap on the glass—"I intended to wait and bring this up, but you do understand that just because you leave Boston later this week doesn't mean this person won't send someone after you again."

"But what are the chances…"

"The fact is there is a chance. One we're"—*I'm*—"not willing to take. I know in the office you objected to the idea, but you need someone to accompany you out of town."

She was already shaking her head before he finished his sentence. "No. That's not an option."

"In the office, Fallon suggested you take a date with you to the Hamptons. I agree. We could send one of our people, and no one at your party would think twice about him being with you at all times," he insisted.

"No," she repeated, her pretty mouth flattened into a grim, *stubborn* line. "This is my parents' anniversary party for God's sake, not a sting operation. Whoever this is has already turned my life on its ass. I'm not giving him any more." Again she shook her head. "I won't be a prisoner. Not again," she murmured.

A prisoner? What the hell did that mean?

"Sloane, I've examined the plan backward and forward, and it's solid." Clenching his jaw, he palmed the back of her seat, resisting the urge to grasp her shoulder, touch her. "I get this is an inconvenience— "

She snorted. "You don't get anything. I refuse to let this, this *psycho* control where I go, who I go with, how I live. He doesn't get to do that."

The vehemence in her voice took him aback. He studied the clenched fists on her lap, the set line of her jaw. Something else was going on here... But he couldn't allow whatever it was to sway him. He'd been here before. And damned if he would allow emotion to trump duty again.

"I'm not asking permission, Sloane," he said softly but injecting a whole lot of "deal with it" into his tone.

He didn't miss her swift, hard inhalation of breath or the stiffening of her body. Yes, he was being a hard-ass, but he couldn't bring himself to care. Not when her life hung in the balance. And he harbored no doubt it did. What had seemed on the surface like a stalking case had transformed into something much more ominous and threatening tonight. There was only one reason a person had another kidnapped. They wanted to spend time with their victim. Torment and torture her before eventually putting her down once her body and spirit were broken. He'd seen it in his line of work.

Once, he'd failed to protect a woman he'd been responsible for—the woman he'd adored. He'd failed to keep her safe. Alive.

He'd proven himself incapable. Unworthy.

But that wouldn't be Sloane.

Not on his watch.

Not again.

"Ciaran, I understand you take your job seriously—"

"Very."

She again tunneled her fingers through her hair. "But what employee will consent to carrying on a charade of posing as my boyfriend for five days? Especially if they have families. It's unfair, and I can't do that," she insisted, shaking her head.

"You're right. I won't ask an employee to do it," he agreed.

"Exactly." She sighed, reaching for the door handle and giving him a small, relieved smile. "Thank you for seeing—"

"But I'm not an employee, am I?"

Chapter Six

"Hell no."

Those had been the words she'd growled before shock had propelled her from Ciaran's SUV minutes earlier. And she hadn't uttered another syllable since. Not even when the door to her hotel suite closed behind her and the watchful, brooding, freaking *infuriating* man at her back. Proper decorum prevented her from shrieking like a banshee in the lobby of a four-star hotel. And since any attempt to speak to him prior to reaching the privacy of her room would result in a brawl, she deemed it best to keep quiet. Him. Pretending to be her boyfriend. At her parents'. Just. Hell. No.

"I'm not asking permission, Sloane."

The words echoed in her head, rebounding against the walls of her skull. Panic, fear, and anger coalesced and congealed into a lump in her chest. Already she could feel the worn ropes of the fragile control she'd just managed to weave back together over her life unraveling. For two years she'd been subject to Phillip—to the thinly veiled, and then not-so-thinly-veiled barbs and criticisms that had ruled her opinions, her movements, her decisions. Her life had become a shadow of his, determined by his needs. In the months they'd been over, she'd begun the process of recapturing herself, of being in control after handing it over to someone else for so long.

And now, Ciaran wanted her to submit everything—her decisions, her opinions, her power—to him. Yes, she got his primary concern was her safety, and she was grateful for the protection. But only those who'd experienced being helpless, fucking powerless could understand the fear of it being ripped away again. The panic at returning to that place where her concerns, her thoughts, her choices didn't matter. The anger at allowing herself to fold under…again.

He, with his confidence and strength, couldn't comprehend why she detested giving away the pieces of herself she'd just managed to hold together after two years of emotional and verbal abuse. Even in his concern, he was forcing his will on her, making her bend to his decisions. She couldn't do it again. She couldn't be imprisoned by someone else's orders again. Not when she'd tasted freedom.

She set her purse and messenger bag on the beautifully upholstered couch with its peach and gold pillows, the deliberate motion belying the storm whirling in her head like a Kansas twister. A glance over her shoulder revealed Ciaran scanning the room, and no doubt the quiet elegance and obvious opulence confirmed his "duchess" impression. Beautiful chairs with sumptuous cushions and gleaming woods. Paintings that looked like they could grace the walls of the Louvre. Everything from the wallpaper to the dark but large fireplace radiated wealth. Usually she eschewed the luxury hotels that catered to the affluent and privileged. Unlike her family and the society she was born into, she wasn't a slave to the trappings of wealth. But leaving her home with the shattered and torn evidence of violation and assault still littering the floor, she'd run to a place she would feel safe—

or at least offered the illusion of safety. And this hotel, with its security and discretion, had been ideal and necessary. She wasn't an idiot incapable of making intelligent decisions about her safety.

She could try to explain this to Ciaran, but part of her detested having him see her as weak. Again. Since she'd met him, she'd been running from him, then running to him for help. No wonder he saw her as pampered, spoiled—a duchess who needed to be contained.

Crossing the room toward the bar, she twisted her fingers in front of her.

Antarctica is the only continent without reptiles or snakes.

Bypassing the wine and cocktail mixes, she slapped down a squat, thick tumbler and poured herself a finger of Scotch. She fortified herself with a large sip, and waited for the smooth but fiery burn to slide over her tongue and down her throat before turning around to face Ciaran.

"*If* I agree to this plan," she began, her fingers tightening around the glass as he arched a dark eyebrow, "you going as my *significant other* is out of the question."

Okay, so on the elevator ride up to her floor, she'd reconsidered taking a guard with her to the Hamptons and her parents' anniversary party weekend. It wasn't an *awful* idea. A: She would be leaving Boston for a few days. B: After the attack tonight, she would feel safer knowing someone was there guarding her.

And C:

She wouldn't be pathetically alone when Phillip arrived with his new, gorgeous girlfriend.

In the hidden, most honest depths of her soul, she could admit that A and B edged out C by the smallest of margins.

Still, showing up with Ciaran...*Ciaran.* The man she simultaneously wanted to strangle and lick like a man-pop? Not likely.

"Forget it," he said, his hard voice brooking no argument. "That point is non-negotiable."

"Nothing is non-negotiable," she countered. "This is my life—literally. So as far as I'm concerned, everything is up for discussion."

"Exactly," he agreed. "This is your life, and protecting lives is my job. And I'm damn good at it."

She emitted a sound caught somewhere between a growl and a moan, and one hundred percent frustration. "Surely as the owner of a business, there is plenty of work keeping you busy. I can only imagine being away from the office for several days at a time will be a huge inconvenience."

"I have three partners who can handle whatever comes up until I get back." He slid his hands in the front pockets of his cargo pants, that infernal eyebrow still arched. "Next."

"My parents, sister, their friends. They'll never believe we"—she waved a hand back and forth between them—"are a couple. They'll never buy it," she reiterated.

A hard-edged coldness descended over his face, flattening his gaze and the sensual curves of his mouth. "I assure you, duchess," he drawled, the lazy tone belying the hardness of his features. "I clean up well."

His words slapped her in the face. Quickly, she rewound the last part of the conversation and hit play. Shit. He'd misunderstood. She hadn't meant to insult him. No, with his stunning male beauty and heir of steely confidence, her family would more than approve of him. What none of them would be able to fathom was why someone who looked like *him* was with *her*. Not the other way around.

"You don't understand." She whirled around, setting the glass on the bar top with a snap. The amber alcohol sloshed against the sides.

"Then, please, by all means. Explain."

Explain. The request sounded so simple, yet it was anything

but. He wanted her to say that not only would her family and their friends find the notion of him being her boyfriend—her lover—laughable, but also reveal that she didn't trust herself. Not with him. And not just because he wanted to strip her of the control she'd fought for and scraped together over the last few months. That entailed only half of her issue with him accompanying her.

This…charade would require acting. As if they were in a relationship. As if they cared for one another. As if they possessed intimate knowledge of each other.

As if she knew what his kiss tasted like. Knew whether he preferred long, lazy licks and a sensual tangling of tongues or a wild, greedy clash of mouths and harsh moans. Knew if he would leisurely allow her to take his cock into her mouth, slowly engulfing him, or if he would grip her hair in his large fists and hold her head steady for a demanding, rough face-fuck.

If he growled low and deep when he came or if he roared his pleasure.

A lover would know all these things.

The problem was, she hungered to discover the answers to all those questions.

Since the night of Fallon's engagement party, she hadn't been able to exorcise Ciaran from her mind. Electric blue eyes. A stunning face of elegant and hard angles. A body worthy of commemoration in chiseled marble. The heat she'd imagined had darkened his gaze when he'd stared at her on that shadowed patio.

A shiver coursed through her, pebbling her skin. That heat made him the most dangerous to her. Because she would long to warm herself in that heat. Bask in it. Lose herself in it.

With a stranger—a stranger who didn't cause lust to tighten her belly or her sex to clench with empty need—she could endure the casual touches, kisses, and displays of affection required of couples. With a stranger she wouldn't lose sight of the reason why she required his presence. With a stranger she wouldn't permit her heart and need to convince her make-believe was reality.

So, no, Ciaran couldn't accompany her.

"You're not like the usual type of man I date," she hedged. Because Ciaran, with his smoldering, *tangible* sexuality, was like no man she'd encountered, much less dated.

"Turn around, Sloane." From the way her nipples perked up and her panties dampened, he might as well as said "fuck me" in that dark, velvet-soft murmur. "Look at me when you lie."

Now *that* brought her around.

"I'm not lying," she gritted out. Omitting the whole truth? Yes. But lying? No. Ciaran was *nothing* like the men she'd previously been involved with. None of them possessed a face capable of stopping traffic...or were capable of stirring an unprecedented hunger inside her with just a glance.

"Then, tell me, duchess, what's your *usual type*?" He didn't wait for her to reply, but advanced, erasing the safe distance between them. "Polite? Boring? Harmless? Great manners....even in the bedroom?" He stalked even closer. "Well, you might have me there. I'd never mistreat a woman, but I'm damn sure no gentleman. Especially when she's under or over me. I'll be courteous and place my hand along her back in public, but in private, I'll push that same hand to the back of her neck, lowering her to the bed as I fuck her from behind. I'll pull out her dinner chair, but I won't pull out of her until she's screaming and coming around my cock. I'll eat with the right fork at the table, but when I have her spread and wet before me, I only use my hands. And tongue."

Only the harsh rasps of her breath echoed in the silent room, reverberating like bellows in a fiery forge. *Jesus Christ.* The images he'd created with his carnal, raw, *exciting* words bombarded her with quick, jabbing blows not unlike those he'd delivered to her attackers earlier. How had he known? He'd described the men in her past with eerie accuracy. Boring. Average. Polite—in and out of the bedroom. Screaming and coming around his cock? She'd never had that, but *holy hell*, did she crave it now. Craved it with a fierceness that terrified her.

Terrified because he'd also omitted some characteristics in his sketch of her ex.

Dismissive. Uninterested…in her.

Controlling.

Phillip hadn't started out this way in the beginning of their relationship, but he'd eventually grown domineering, tired of her, critical of her flaws, rejecting her in bed and out.

Ciaran might not be polite, boring, or harmless, but inevitably, he would share the most hurtful traits with her former partner. But while Phillip's had injured her spirit, self-esteem, and heart, she suspected Ciaran—beautiful, strong, brave, dominant Ciaran—would crush her.

She stepped away from him. Then took another.

As soon as she placed enough space between them where a deep breath wouldn't contain his fresh, earthy scent, she halted and tipped her chin up. The illusion of courage, when inside she shook with desire and wariness, helped her meet his hooded gaze.

"This charade is going to include"—she paused—"displays of affection. We'll need to appear as a couple who—who—"

"I believe the words you're looking for are 'have sex.'"

Yes, that would be the phrase. And really, the matter-of-factness of the term shouldn't have heat barreling through her like a blow torch. And maybe uttered by another man, it wouldn't. But by him? She squeezed her thighs against the dull throb in her sex.

"Yes," she ground out. At this point, she would have lockjaw from all the gritting and grinding of her teeth. His derisive snort didn't help. "Do you have someone you're involved with?" Of course he did. Men who looked like him almost always had someone waiting on them at home—or in their bed. "Wouldn't she have a say or objection in your playing another woman's lover?"

Something flashed in his eyes, but the emotion vanished as quickly as it appeared. "No."

The one-word answer warned her not to walk in that particular minefield any farther. *O-kay.* "Fine. Still, can you maintain that pretense for five days?" Hell, Phillip hadn't been able to pretend he still cared for her toward the end of their relationship, and he'd been her actual partner, not a "pretend boyfriend."

"What is the difference between me and an employee I assigned to escort you, Sloane? He would need to act the part same as I would."

"Because it would be an employee's *job.* You're too close to Fallon, and I don't want to be your responsibility." God, she was reaching. She didn't even believe the reasons tumbling out of her mouth. But how could she say, *your need to control and watch my every move makes me want to break out in a panic attack?* Or even worse, how could she explain, *I wouldn't want to climb your employee like a kindergartner on a jungle gym*, and maintain her dignity?

"You were my responsibility the moment you walked through GDG's door. And before you try to come up with another excuse, let me save you the trouble, duchess. I'm. Going. With. You. No one else. Me. So what other conditions do you have?"

"No touching," she blurted. Fire surged up her neck and streamed into her face, but she held firm. Self-preservation kicked in, and her heart pounded in her chest like she was fighting for her life. In a sense, she was doing just that. A life not shattered by Storm Ciaran. "Outside of what's necessary to pull off the pretense."

"And?" he prodded, voice soft, eyes narrowed on her.

"This is a business arrangement. I'm a client, and I will pay you for your time."

Anger gleamed in his gaze, hardening it and his lips into a straight, grim line. "No."

"Yes." She nodded. "That point is non-negotiable," she said, lobbing his previous statement back at him. "Either I pay your firm for this job, or I don't go to the Hamptons." Christ, she could hear her mother now, but she refused to back down. She *needed* this to feel like she had at least a little power in this situation.

"This is ridiculous," he snapped. "You're a friend of Fallon's—"

"Which is serendipity, not a reason to turn down payment." She crossed her arms. "So what will it be?"

Silence throbbed in the room like a thunderous heartbeat. Even if the fireplace had been lit, the flames wouldn't have been able to dispel the deep freeze seeming to crystallize the air.

Finally, when her nerves stretched so taut they cried uncle, he dipped his chin in an abrupt nod. Quietly, she expelled the breath that had been trapped in her aching lungs, relief pulsing through her in overlapping waves.

Ciaran might believe her demand was foolish, but she needed the stipulation, or rather, the reminder the stipulation provided.

This was a business transaction—cold, necessary, an exchange of money for services. As long as she remembered this simple fact and didn't forget why he was there, she wouldn't lose her head or her heart...again.

Chapter Seven

For Ciaran, a fine line existed between a lie and a deception. As an ex-DEA Agent-turned-private-security specialist, he understood the distinction.

The difference all came down to motivation.

A lie was told to hurt, to hide, to betray. Most times it was self-serving and mean.

A deception, on the other hand, was employed to gather information, maybe to mislead, but also to uncover. It was often used for the greater good.

Not to mention "deception" just sounded better than "lie."

And while this charade of pretending to be Sloane's lover for five days to protect her from possible harm definitely fell into the "greater good" category, he suspected he would pay for this sin. He smothered a groan as he helped her climb into the passenger's seat of the luxury Range Rover. The skirt of her dress rode up her smooth thigh, and he briefly closed his eyes, shutting the door on the tempting, sexy sight.

Pay *dearly* for this sin.

Yet years of Sunday masses and acts of contrition would never atone for the lust that clawed at his gut and pounded in his cock every time he came within ten feet of Sloane. His only absolution was his refusal to act on the dark need. She was his client, his responsibility. History had taught him with bloody reinforcement that involvement with someone under his protection could only end up one way: disaster

All his focus needed to be centered and fixed on keeping Sloane safe...alive. Nothing—not even this inconvenient, greedy hunger—could come before that.

He clenched his jaw. Fuck, the next five days were going to be a special kind of hell. Touching her arm, back, or hair with the casual caresses of lovers in public, and in private, maintaining a firm distance he couldn't dare cross.

Maybe God hadn't really forgiven him for the time he'd substituted the communion wine with prune juice as an altar boy set on pulling a stupid prank to impress his friends. Maybe this was His divine punishment. Well played, God. Well played.

Jerking open the driver's side door, he nodded at Mark, who parked a discreet distance away in the hotel's underground lot. The ex-soldier would tail Ciaran and Sloane the entire four and half hours to Southampton, New York, to ensure they weren't followed. Spending that length of time cooped up alone with her seemed like a lesson in masochism. But he'd weighed the option of flying to their destination, and with strict TSA identification security measures, they would leave too much of an obvious trail if someone was tracking them. So nearly five hours of self-imposed torture had been the best, safest choice.

He climbed into the vehicle, and her light but sensual moonlight-and-sin scent immediately reached out with delicate chains, wrapping around him. It filled the interior, granting him a preview of what her skin—those shadowed nooks between her neck and shoulder, the tuck of that hour-glass waist, the crease where legs met torso—tasted like. Mysterious, fresh, sultry…decadent.

He twisted the key in the ignition and jammed the gear shift into drive.

Hell yeah. A long-ass five days.

"You look nice," she murmured, speaking for the first time since he'd guided her into the SUV ten minutes earlier.

Out of habit, he glanced in the rearview mirror, quickly surveying the Thursday morning traffic behind him before flicking a look to his right. Sloane stared out the side window. Good thing, too, because he couldn't suppress the sardonic twist of his lips at the compliment. Nor could he stifle the flare of irritation at the reminder of her assertion that her family wouldn't believe they were convincing as a couple—or squash the anger at himself for giving a damn.

My parents, sister, their friends. They'll never believe we are a couple. They'll never buy it.

That shit still bothered him like a pebble in a shoe that he couldn't shake loose. The fact that it bothered him fucking *bothered* him.

Maybe because he agreed with her.

Anyone with half a working brain cell could take one look at her thick, gleaming hair, pure, pampered skin, that polite aloofness that announced her fine, cultured breeding and recognize him for the former grease monkey, public servant, working-class plebian he was. Until he'd stood close to her on a covered, dimly lit patio, inhaled her alluring scent, and spied the latent sensuality deepening her forest green eyes, he hadn't cared about things as petty as money and social status. Hell, when the lights shut off, it didn't matter how far back a last name or ancestor could be traced to the Mayflower. Lust and sex were great equalizers with funny ways of leveling the playing field.

But he hadn't even had Sloane and instinctively understood and acknowledged she would be different. She *was* different. And standing next to her—within five goddamn feet of her—stirred the insane urge to go wash imaginary, long-gone car oil from under his fingernails or the grime from the streets off his body.

So yeah, that remark had struck a sore spot.

"Thanks," he said, replying to her compliment and trying like hell not to resent it even as a tiny, stubborn sliver of pleasure wormed its way into his chest. The lightweight summer jacket, white button-down shirt, and fitted khaki slacks had been Fallon's pick on the shopping spree she'd forced on him. Apparently, she'd taken exception to him showing up in the Hamptons looking like "fucking G.I. Joe"—her words, not his. He shot her another glance, dipping his gaze to the slightly frenetic twisting and clenching of her fingers on her lap. "What's wrong? Are you nervous?"

She stiffened, and he resisted the need to reach across the middle console and massage the tenseness from the back of her neck and shoulders.

"No." She shook her head. "Why do you ask?"

He snorted, but decided not to mention he'd overheard her low muttering about an ostrich's eye size being bigger than its brain. Though their association hadn't been long, he'd noticed Sloane seemed to recite nonsensical, but interesting bits of trivia when upset or nervous. Such as right now.

"Sloane, I know you still have reservations about this plan. But, I promise we're doing everything in our power to keep you safe. Shane and the others at GDG are working on finding out who's behind the stalking and attacks as we speak, and I'm not leaving your side the entire time. If someone does follow us to your parents' estate, they'll have to get through me to even come near you. I swear, sweetheart, that's not going to happen." Not again. Never again. Why he'd chosen

Sloane as his chance at redemption for failing Sam and none of the other female clients he'd guarded over the years, he couldn't explain. It just was.

"I don't doubt you, I don't. I mean, naturally I'm worried but that's not..." She flipped her palms up in a helpless gesture, emitting a low chuckle heavy with self-deprecation and frustration. "In the past few days, I've had my tires slashed, been attacked in my home and at my job. But right now, my stomach is a mass of nerves because in four too-short hours I'm going to be spending nearly a week with my family and their friends. How shallow and silly does that make me sound?"

He lifted a shoulder in a shrug. "Not really. My family drives me bat-shit crazy at least once a week."

Her head whipped toward him, and her fingers stopped their incessant twisting. The tension stringing her as tight as a guitar string almost evaporated. *Good.* Satisfaction hummed through him. He detested the nervous fidgeting and strain coloring her voice.

"Your family?"

He snorted, merging onto the exit for I-95 S. "Yes, duchess, I have a family. What? Did you think I hatched from an egg?"

"No." She paused. "I was thinking more like wolves were involved."

He loosed a bark of laughter. "Cute. But I'm not so sure my mother would disagree with you."

"How does your family make you, uh, bat-shit crazy?"

"Every Sunday afternoon, my parents expect my younger brother, sister, and me home for dinner. And more often than not, a daughter or niece of a neighbor, church member, or, hell, a grocery store clerk my mother met five minutes earlier, joins us. This is right after she's just browbeaten Sean and me about how she's not getting any younger and wants grandchildren before God takes her home." He shook his head at Sloane's low chuckle. The husky, delighted sound of it warmed him like a low slide of heated syrup. He mentally shook his head, focusing on the road and his story. "I've begged her numerous times to stop with the match-making ambushes, but she doesn't listen. And it annoys the hell out of me. Sometimes I consider skipping out on a dinner, but frankly, the woman scares me." He waited until her laughter died down and threw her a glance. The sight of her relaxed, soft smile simultaneously lit the kindling on the desire that never fully banked around her, and squeezed his heart. Both were trouble. "So what has you so nervous about seeing your family, duchess? Are you afraid they're going to have Quasimodo waiting for you when we arrive?"

The humor fled from her face as if chased, and that regal, aloof masked dropped back in place, shutting him out like a slamming door. The mask, too, he was learning, seemed to be as much of a defense mechanism as her trivia diarrhea.

"More like they're waiting to berate me for the one I've already let go." She chuckled again, but this time no humor laced it, no warmth heated it. Cold, brittle. Sad. "My parents and sister are…exacting. They have their ideas about what and who are acceptable, relationships, lifestyles. And if you don't conform to those ideas, they can be" — another long pause — "critical."

In other words, they were ball-busters just with a glossy, Brahmin veneer coating it.

Anger coalesced in his chest, gathering speed and heat. He didn't need a 900 number and psychic license to guess what her parents found "unacceptable" about Sloane. She moved in a circle where the women worshipped at the altars of Louis Vuitton and Chanel, spent more time at luncheons than they did at home, and considered "food" a four-letter word.

Sloane might be from their world, but with her understated

elegance and gainful, useful employment, he could see her garnering criticism. And then there were her curves.

Fuck. Those curves. When she'd opened the hotel room door that morning, he'd almost lost his shit, battling the urge to walk her back into that high-priced suite and press her against the nearest wall. The simple, sleeveless sheath with its gray and pink stripes was probably considered fashionable. Still, all he could think about was sliding the figure-hugging material up her legs, baring her sexy thighs until the hem cleared the triangle of cloth shielding her pussy. All he could imagine was cupping her gorgeous ass and nuzzling that damp material before tugging it to the side and tonguing the sweet, plump flesh until she came, hard, thighs trembling around his head, the sharp heels of those nude pumps stabbing his shoulder blades.

Yeah, he harbored all sorts of fantasies revolving around those beautiful curves her society peers most likely considered "unacceptable."

"So what's our cover story? Because we can expect the third degree over our...relationship," Sloane said.

Part of him objected at the obvious shift in subject; the need to assure her that she wouldn't have to put up with any bullshit while he was with her rode him like he wore a fucking saddle on his back. But it was also that same surge of protectiveness that shackled his tongue. He'd agreed to guard her body from physical harm, not her feelings. Getting involved in her family dynamics wasn't part of the job. Getting involved, *period*, wasn't part of the job. Best he remember that. Just a cover story. Just an act. Do the job, and then on to the next one.

"We keep it as simple and close to the truth as possible. Less chance of messing up that way," he said. "I work with Shane and met you through Fallon, except a month ago instead of one week. When we try to make it complicated is when we trip up." The pretense hadn't even started yet but all of this felt anything but simple. "Is there anything specific I should know about you and your family? Details they would pick up on?"

Sloane started relaying information about her parents and sister, Chelsea. Most of the surface facts he'd discovered on his own, but the smaller, more private tidbits couldn't be learned through the internet or Fallon. Such as what were her mother's pet peeves, guaranteed to prejudice her against him from the start. Or did her father enjoy sports, and if so, which teams? Or did she and her sister have a sibling rivalry?

Dramatic scenes and bad manners, golf and surprisingly, the Patriots, and yes. The sisters entertained a classical older sister vs. little sister competition. Nothing Cain and Abel-ish, but with her younger sibling married and with a family, he could read between the lines.

He shifted in his seat, angling his body away from her. Again that urge to comfort her, touch her, flared inside him like the flash of a newly lit torch. And again, he resisted.

"Anything else?"

"Yes." She sighed, and an "oh shit" knot clenched his stomach. "My ex-fiancé will be there."

He blinked. Shot her a stunned glance, certain he hadn't heard right. "What?"

"Since he was a business associate of my father's before he was my ex, my parents didn't see a reason to un-invite him just because our relationship ended."

Wow. The flat, even tone of her voice didn't betray her feelings about her parents' decision to invite a man whose presence would undoubtedly hurt their daughter. At the least make her feel uncomfortable and awkward in her own family home. Maybe the rich just did shit differently so he shouldn't—

"That's fucked up," he blurted.

Another sigh, so soft he almost missed it.

"Yes, it is." She turned and stared out the window, but not before he caught the grim line of her mouth.

Whoever this ex was…Ciaran hated the bastard already.

Chapter Eight

"Are you kidding me?"

Sloane barely caught Ciaran's grumbled question, but the awe, disbelief, and traces of disdain fairly emanated from his voice as he pulled the SUV to a halt in front of the opulent mansion in one of Southampton's most exclusive neighborhoods. Even by the wealthy elite's standards, her parents' estate—even as a little girl the place had never felt like *hers* or *home*—was luxurious…and huge. The eight-bedroom, eleven-bath Tudor-style house with its turret-inspired wings spread over two beautifully manicured acres. A traditional English Garden, tennis courts, huge patio for outdoor entertainment, lushly decorated pool, and lavish pool house sprawled across the immaculate grounds, each amenity declaring the ostentatious wealth of the owners.

She'd never been embarrassed about her privileged upbringing—it'd been all she'd known—but seeing the mansion and evidence of excess through Ciaran's guarded gaze, heat singed her neck and face. The *duchess* title never felt more appropriate than it did in this moment. Would he scoff at her if she confessed she'd never truly felt comfortable in this world? Like a child with her grubby hands pressed to the pristine window of a candy store, staring at the beauty and sweetness on the other side.

The passenger door opened, and a valet appeared, offering her his hand. She stepped from the vehicle, granting him a thankful smile—a smile that evaporated as soon as he released her. Ciaran appeared beside her, his large palm settling on the small of her back. Drawing in a deep breath, she climbed the shallow stone steps leading to the glass front door. Her stomach writhed with nerves, not even the soothing gurgling of the fountain was able to calm her. They stood, side by side, in front of the wide, tall doors, the handle awaiting her turn so they could enter the house.

In that moment, the twenty-six-year-old woman who'd forged a career path of her own and lived independent of her parents' largesse reverted to the chubby, shy, oldest child surrounded by a family of thin, glittering, beautiful people. It was here, in this mansion's open, airy rooms with their vaulted ceilings that she'd first learned to detest social situations. The luncheons, dinners, and parties had been torture for the little girl who'd hovered close to the refreshment table, more comfortable with the cucumber sandwiches and shrimp cocktail than the guests who were alternately cruel or dismissive. Years of endless social events had taught her how to pretend better, but mingling and striking up conversations with people had never been her forte. She left that *grand fete* to her younger, gorgeous, I-am-the-consummate-hostess sister. And here she was in for five days of her idea of masochism. Only worse. Ciaran would be right beside her to witness her insecurities…and failures.

"You're doing it again. Breathe," Ciaran softly ordered. Strong fingers slid under her hair and kneaded the nape of her neck.

"I'm doing what again?" *Step away from his touch. Don't lean back into it.* The warnings screamed through her head with blaring caution horns. Yet she remained still.

"You just told me ants stretch when they wake up," he said, voice dry with a hint of amusement. "Whatever we face, duchess, we'll do it together."

He probably meant to reassure her, and it did. But not how he intended. She straightened her shoulders, inching forward so Ciaran's hand fell from her neck. After Phillip, she'd vowed not to depend on another man for her strength. No one—not Phillip, Ciaran, or the next man she became involved with—could strip away her self-esteem, her power, her independence unless she permitted it.

Besides, it didn't matter a damn if Ciaran witnessed her social ineptitude or not. They were actors, pretenders. This was a business transaction between them. Nothing more.

Bullshit, her subconscious coughed. Flipping a mental bird at, well, herself, she opened the front door. And entered.

"Sloane." Mallory Johanna Sloane Barrett, one of Boston's and the Hamptons' most popular socialites—and Sloane's mother—sailed into the foyer. Sloane had always envied her mother's cool, blond beauty and composure. She'd never seen her mother falter in the face of any social situation...until today.

The welcoming, hostess smile wavered on her lips. The confident stride stuttered. The emerald green eyes, identical to Sloane's, widened as they shifted to the tall, broad-shouldered, and silent man beside her.

"Uh." Her mother blinked, for once speechless, but only for seconds before a lifetime of training kicked in. All traces of shock and confusion evaporated from her face, and her smile notched up its wattage as she resumed gliding forward, her arms outstretched. She clasped Sloane's hands within hers, and air-kissed both of her cheeks. Then she turned to

Ciaran, curiosity gleaming in her gaze. "Sloane didn't mention she was bringing company. Although I'm delighted she did. Mallory Barrett, Sloane's mother." She extended her hand. "And you are?"

Ciaran clasped her fingers and brushed a kiss over her knuckles. Sloane gaped as her mother—her never-shaken-never-stirred *mother*—blushed. Sloane cast a surreptitious glance around the entry, searching for a robed and bearded Jesus Christ. Surely He must've returned if Mallory had blushed *and* been flustered in the matter of minutes. That just didn't happen.

"Ciaran Ross, Mrs. Barrett," he drawled, releasing her hand. "I'm a friend of your daughter's." The "friend" was accompanied by a possessive grip of Sloane's hip. From the slight narrowing of her eyes, her mother didn't miss the gesture. *An act. That's all it is. Pretend.* But the heat branding her even through her dress felt like the furthest thing from a pretense. It felt entirely too real and…and visceral for a business deal.

"Please call me Mallory." He nodded, and she returned her attention to Sloane, brushing a kiss to each of her cheeks. "I was just about to call and see what was keeping you. Your sister is here, and our guests have already started to arrive."

Oh, joy.

"If we're late, Mallory, then it is my fault," Ciaran interjected, his deep voice smooth. "I asked Sloane to drive rather than fly so I could hoard more time alone with her since I imagine it will be in short supply in the next few days."

"Oh." There went that flush again, staining her mother's cheeks a light pink under her perfectly applied foundation. "I, uh, understand. That's sweet of you." She cleared her throat, her slim, bejeweled fingers fluttering around the base of her neck. "Let me introduce you to my husband and the rest of the family. I'm sure they will be delighted to meet you."

Ciaran inclined his dark head. "Thank you. I've heard so many good things about you from Sloane, I've been looking forward to it."

His hands slid from her hip to the small of her back, the weight of his palm a quiet, but stalwart reassurance. An assortment of emotions trickled through her: gratefulness at his quick defense of her; relief at his steady, strong presence; anxiety over…everything, and that ever-present desire flickering and pulsating in her stomach like a dancing flame on a candle.

The spinning coalescent ball of feelings whirled and whirled inside her as they neared the cavernous, exquisitely decorated formal receiving room. About twenty people milled about in small groups of three or four, sipping from glasses, their laughter and conversation like the drone of bees in a hive. The scene, so familiar yet dreaded, didn't ease the mass of nerves. Here, surrounded by her golden, beautiful family and their perfect friends, she'd never been more aware of being the "changeling Barrett." And Phillip had slid that point in as often as possible.

"If I can't get you to have some pride in how you look after two years, no wonder your family has given up trying after so long. God, you're an embarrassment."

"Your parents must wonder where they went wrong with you."

"Look at your sister's body. If you had an ass and tits like that, I wouldn't be able to keep my hands off you."

A big palm slid up her spine, under her hair, and circled her neck, much like the soothing caress on the front porch. She shuddered underneath Ciaran's touch, and unlike earlier, leaned into it.

For just a moment, she allowed herself to rely on it.

But not depend on it.

"John," her mother called out, entering the room. "Sloane

has arrived. Come greet her, darling."

Her father turned away from a group clustered near the fireplace, wearing a broad smile. Sloane flinched, at the last second swallowing a gasp. It'd been several months since she'd seen her father, having visited her parents at the beginning of the summer. In that time, her normally robust father had grown thinner, paler as if unwell. Though handsome in his casual jacket, shirt, and slacks, he seemed tired, worn. More salt peppered the dark brown hair he'd bequeathed her. *Jesus.* Fear thrummed through her, discordant and loud. Was he sick? Worry propelled her forward. Why hadn't anyone told her? Was this why her mother had been so adamant about her coming to the anniversary party?

"Sloane." He reached them, pulling Sloane into a tight embrace. Which did nothing to allay her concerns. John Barrett wasn't a hugger. She'd never doubted his love for her, but still, he didn't do public displays of affection. "I'm so glad you could make it with the school year beginning."

Mallory scoffed, waving away her husband's words. "Don't get me started on that job."

"Then don't, Mother," a dry voice drawled. Chelsea Barrett Winters, her younger sister by two years, joined their circle. Petite, slender, blonde, and gorgeous, she was a reflection of Mallory—a wife, mother, hostess, socialite. The opposite of Sloane. "Good to see you, Sloane." Chelsea brushed a kiss over her cheek. "And who's this?" she practically purred, slanting a glance at Ciaran.

"Dad, Chelsea, I'd like you to meet Ciaran Ross, my…"— Sloane hesitated—"friend. Ciaran, this is my father, John Barrett, and my sister, Chelsea Winters."

Her father moved forward, his hazel gaze steady and assessing. "Nice to meet you, Ciaran. I would say we've heard so much about you, but…" His eyebrow arched high, his scrutiny shifting to Sloane.

Though the need to fidget wormed through her, she arched a brow in return. "Message received, Dad."

"Well he's certainly a vast improvement over the last one," Chelsea grumbled.

"Chelsea!" Mallory hissed, her frown forbidding.

Her sister rolled her eyes, and Sloane struggled not to gape at the other woman. What the *hell*? What alternate universe had her figurative Kansas farmhouse plummeted into? This one, where her father hugged her and her sister muttered under her breath, was as strange as one with a gold brick-paved road, talking apple trees, and munchkins.

"Fine," Chelsea said, green eyes wide and blinking in a façade of innocence. "So, how long have you two been"—the corner of her mouth quirked—"friends?"

"About a month." Ciaran's palm slid down her back, over her hip, and he tangled her fingers with his. "A mutual friend, Fallon Wayland, introduced us."

"Ah, Fallon." Her father nodded. "I know her father. He's a good man." To John, that meant he was a good *business man*. "He recently told me she was engaged."

"Yes, sir. To my friend and partner, Shane Roarke."

"Partner?" Mallory tipped her head to the side, studying him. "You own your own company, Ciaran?"

"Yes. A private security firm in Boston with Shane and two other partners."

Sloane waited for one of her parents or her sister to call bullshit, but her father seemed impressed, her mother intrigued, and her sister...gleeful. God, this day was weird.

"I can't wait to get to know you better over the next few days," her mother said. "John, why don't you introduce Ciaran to the others while I borrow Sloane for a moment."

Oh shit. Here it comes.

"You good?" Ciaran murmured in her ear, his lips brushing against her hair.

She nodded, and with a squeeze to her fingers, he released her, following his father.

"Chelsea," Mallory bit out, when her sister didn't follow the men. "I need to speak with your sister. Alone."

"Oh. Sure." Chelsea shrugged. She backed away several steps, but as soon as Mallory turned to face Sloane, Chelsea mouthed, *he's hot*, pointed in Ciaran's direction, and then popped up a thumb.

Sloane blinked. Seriously, who was this woman, and what the *fuck* had happened to her stuffy, snobby sister?

"Your sister," Mallory *tsked*, shaking her head. "I swear, this separation must be taking its toll. I don't know what's gotten into her lately. But anyway, young lady." She peered at Sloane, curiosity and speculation rife in her eyes. "When I talked to you last week, why didn't you tell me about this new man in your life? Why didn't you mention him the last few times we spoke?"

"The relationship is new, Mother, and I didn't feel comfortable asking him to a family function so soon," she recited the excuse she'd readied in preparation of this question. "But Ciaran wanted to finally meet you and Father, so…" She trailed off, and to her relief, her mother seemed to accept the explanation.

"That's understandable. He's certainly…handsome, isn't he?" She glanced at Ciaran, who stood with her father, talking with a small group of men. Ciaran fit right in—no, that wasn't exactly true. The…magnetism and vitality that radiated off of him overshadowed the others. Like a powerful, sleek panther among harmless housecats. "Did Fallon tell him who your family was before you met?"

Right. Because a man as stunning in masculine beauty as he had to possess some ulterior motive for being attracted to her. Such as connections with her successful, rich father.

"I don't know. She could have."

"Hmm." Mallory tapped a French-manicured fingertip against her bottom lip. "Just be careful, honey. I don't want you hurt. But he's here, so that speaks very well in his favor. So we'll see. Anyway..." She clapped her hands together. "Given the turn of circumstances, I'm glad I took the liberty of selecting a dress for tonight. I think it will be lovely on you. I hung it in your room."

"Thank you, Mother."

"You're welcome, darling." She looped an arm through Sloane's and steered her farther into the room. "Also, since I didn't know you were bringing someone, I didn't reserve an extra room. Ciaran will have to share your room." She arched a dark blond eyebrow, a gleam in her eyes. "Will that be a problem?"

Holy hell. She hadn't foreseen this. Would dressing, *un*dressing, and sleeping in the same room with Ciaran Ross for the next five days be a problem? Would inhaling his male scent, glimpsing his virile body, and trying to shield her lust for him without any kind of break be a problem?

"Sloane?"

She forced a smile to her lips and wondered if it appeared as pained as it felt. "No. No problem."

Chapter Nine

Ciaran tipped his face back under the steady stream of the shower water and moaned. Pleasure pulsed over his body, relaxing his muscles, granting him seconds of contentment. God, it felt so fucking good. He shivered, but stifled another groan. One moan slipping free had been bad enough. Two? Shit, he might as well check in his Man Card. Because no self-respecting man gained this much pleasure from a shower unless his dick was in his fist.

With a snarl, he twisted the shower faucets and stepped out of a tub the size of his bed at home. Which was apropos since the bathroom was roughly the size of his goddamn bedroom.

Shaking his head, he grabbed a towel and rubbed down his body before wrapping the soft, luxurious cloth around his waist and ignored the almost sensual caress of the material against his skin. Damn. At some point in the shower, he'd grown a vagina.

Still, this kind of wealth—he huffed out a breath. The house, the people, the lifestyle… Jesus. True, he'd guarded plenty of high-end clients through GDG, but this was a whole different level. He called Sloane "duchess," but how could he have guessed the house she'd grown up in was damn near a palace?

A job. An assignment. He jerked open the closet door and removed his pants from the hanger. He could protect her in a castle just as well as he could in a hovel. And if anything, the sight of her world solidified the differences between them. Reminded him why he was here. As a hired contractor pretending to be her man, but not her man. Not a part of this opulence that would have funded a Third World country.

No matter how strongly the urge to protect her stalked inside him like a newly awakened, circling beast. But a real partner did those things, not a fake one. His focus was protecting her, keeping her safe…alive.

He fastened his pants and removed his shirt from the closet, resolve firmed. With a mental nod, he opened the bathroom door. If it came down to a choice between her life and her feelings, hands down—

"What the hell do you have on?" he snapped.

Sloane whirled around and the voluminous folds of the red *tent* she wore swirled around her body. The long, dark strands of her hair were swept over her shoulder, the curled ends brushing her breasts. Breasts barely visible underneath the knee-length muumuu she wore.

"Sloane?"

"Yes?" She stared at him. Blinked. Slicked the tip of her tongue over her parted lips. Blinked again. "I'm sorry, what?"

"What the hell are you wearing?" he demanded.

"Oh." Her pretty mouth twisted into a wry smile. "My mother bought me a dress for tonight's dinner."

He snorted, slipping his shirt on. "Are you sure she didn't just grab it off one of the tables downstairs?" The deep crimson was pretty against her golden skin and chocolate hair, but goddamn, clowns and acrobats could have performed under the thing.

She plucked at the sides. "In her defense, I think she believes it's flattering to my figure."

Loosing a short bark of laughter, he started buttoning his shirt. "Sweetheart, there is no defense for that thing. And flattering, hell. You can't even see your figure in it."

Another humorless curve of her lips. "I think that's probably the point. Fashion rule number one. Emphasize your assets and conceal your flaws."

His fingers froze mid-fasten. What. The. *Fuck*.

He studied her, and this time noticed what he'd initially missed. The light stain of color tinging her high cheekbones. The faint smudge of hurt darkening her green eyes. The restless clenching and relaxing of her hands against the dress.

Anger flared in his chest like a struck match. He dropped his arms to his side, curling his fingers into fists. Either that or stride across the room, grab her by the shoulders, and haul her close. Crush his mouth to hers, thrust his tongue hard past her lips, and take what he'd been fantasizing about since the night of the engagement party. Show her in explicit detail just how beautiful she was.

With a snarl, he stalked past her and toward the huge walk-in closet where an unseen maid had hung their clothes. He knew fuck all about women's clothing, but as a man, he could narrow the choices down to ugly, pretty, and take-that-off-so-I-can-fuck you.

Rifling through the dresses, shirts, skirts, and pants, he flipped to a black dress with a similar style to the one she'd worn earlier. He studied the sleeveless sheath with the small slit on the side. Hell yeah. This fell between pretty and take-that-off-so-I-can-fuck you. Perfect.

Glancing up, he met Sloane's curious yet wary gaze. He could just imagine how he appeared in her eyes, a grown-ass man going through her clothes. Humor infiltrated the anger, lessening it, but not abolishing it. The anger wouldn't disappear until that uncertainty in her eyes did.

"Here." He extended the dress toward her. "Put this on. And take that shit off. Use it to wallpaper this closet, spread it on the floor as a rug, or upholster the couch"—he nodded toward the small sofa in the corner of the closet—"but just take it off."

"Is that an order?" she whispered.

"Do you want it to be?" he whispered back.

The thought of directing her, rendering a command and watching her obey stroked his cock like a tight fist. Blood pumped hot and heavy in his veins, pulsing in his gut, throbbing in his flesh. He liked to be in control in the bedroom but didn't need it like some men. And with her overwhelming family and asshole ex, he would give free rein to Sloane, allow her to take her pleasure, own it. Fuck, he would love to witness that. Still…watching her sink to her knees just at the pressure of his hand on her shoulder or from a simple word, and her *want* to be there… A growl rolled in the back of his throat. Yeah, he may not need it. Damn sure didn't stop him from craving it.

Silent, she stepped forward, reaching for the dress. For a moment, they both grasped the hanger, the tension between them like a living, breathing entity. Sex vibrated in the room, humming against his skin, stoking a need he was finding harder and harder to fight.

"I'll change in here and leave you the bedroom to finish getting ready." Her gaze dropped to his bare chest before jerking back to his face. "I should only be a minute."

With a sharp nod, he exited the closet, closing the door shut behind him. Closing her in. Keeping him out.

"Shit," he muttered, jerking the lapels of his shirt together, and with rough movements, buttoned up his shirt.

Minutes later, as he tugged on his suit jacket, his cell rattled against the dresser where he'd tossed it before showering. His mouth flattened as he shot a glance toward the walk-in closet and hurried to grab the phone. A cursory peek at the caller's name had grim satisfaction settling inside him. Good. He'd been waiting on this call.

"Yeah?"

"Hey, Key-Key" his best friend and partner, Maddox Wright, greeted in his usual laid-back manner, complete with irritating-as-hell nickname. "I have some intel for you."

"Fuck you, and what is it?"

Maddox *tsked*, and Ciaran could just see the other man shaking his blond head, wearing his trademark smart-ass grin. "Do you kiss your mother with that mouth?" Before Ciaran could snap out a reply, Maddox barreled on. "Through the tracer on your girl's cell, I tracked down that number." His voice lost the lazy affectation and hardened, revealing the tough, ex-police officer who'd served seven years as a beat cop and detective with the New York City Police Department. "It led to a burner phone. I was able to determine where it was shipped to and what store received and sold it, which is a convenience store in Dorchester. Other than that, without knowing what timeframe the phone was bought, we pretty much have a dead end. Especially if it was purchased more than a week ago—which is as long as the store keeps the video feed before the footage is recorded over."

"Damn." Ciaran frowned. He wasn't surprised about the burner phone, but dammit, he'd hoped Maddox would've had better news.

"Yeah, but if this bastard switches phones and calls from a new number, we'll have a better chance of tracking it and him down since we'll have a tighter timeframe along with the location. It's a long shot, but…" Ciaran detected the shrug in his friend's voice. "Also, Jake traced the IP address on that yourenext Yahoo email account. I saw the pictures this guy's been sending Sloane, Ciaran," Maddox murmured. "It's some sick shit. And the fucker is smart enough to cover his tracks. The account and emails originated from an internet café on High Street. And get this: they don't have video surveillance cameras to protect their customers' confidentiality." He snorted. "It's all fun and privacy until your ass gets robbed," he grumbled. "Doesn't matter, though. I paid them a little visit last night. They have surveillance now whether they want it or not. If this guy returns to the café, we'll have an image of him."

"Shit." Ciaran shoved a fist into his pants pocket. More ifs. "What about the two assholes from Monday? Did Jake find anything from the ID I gave him?"

"Benjamin Russell and Ronald Anders. They're not talking, just like we figured. And they've lawyered up," he added, disgust dripping from his tone. For Maddox, criminal defense attorneys ranked right above shit on a stick but under flaming shit on a stick. "According to Jake, their rap sheets would put Baby Face Finster to shame, but nothing having to do with kidnapping. Assault, robbery, drugs, even fucking shoplifting, but no kidnapping."

"Confirms my suspicion that they were working for someone else." Someone else who was still out there, most likely with pockets deep enough to hire another to carry out the plan Russell and Anders had failed to execute. "Kind of makes you think someone who wouldn't verify if the people he's hiring possessed more credentials than common street thugs isn't an amateur himself."

"Exactly what I was thinking," Maddox agreed. "But then again we all know novices can be more dangerous than the professionals. Anyway, I asked Tristan to see if he can hit up one of his friends on the force. Let us know if anyone comes to visit them in county, and if they make calls, who they're to."

"Thanks, that's a great idea."

Tristan Scott, a childhood friend and newly ex-Boston

police officer had joined GDG about a month ago after resigning from the department. Though his departure had been under less-than-stellar circumstances, Ciaran didn't doubt that as a once highly respected detective, the other man would still have connections he could tug if needed. Especially since they'd pulled the school's security footage before Ciaran had left town. It'd revealed what they already knew. Two assailants had approached Sloane after she'd exited the building for the evening and accosted her. Even though he'd been there, watching the attempt and Sloane's struggle to escape on video had sent ice cascading through his arteries.

If he hadn't followed her... He shoved the stomach-churning thought aside and focused on Maddox's continued report.

"Also Dodger retrieved the information from the computers and laptops in Drake Morriston's home. She passed the flash drives on to Jake."

"Good." It was a long shot, but Sloane had seemed adamant about her former student being involved in this somehow. So, though he didn't necessarily agree, Ciaran had instructed Willow to infiltrate the Morriston's home and copy their computers so Jake could examine them for incriminating evidence. "You'll let me know if he finds something?"

"Will do. If anything at all develops, I'll hit you up."

"Thanks, Maddox."

"No prob, Key-Key." The line *clicked* in Ciaran's ear before he could snarl out a comeback, picturing that motherfucker laughing at getting in the last word.

He tossed the cell on the mattress as the closet door creaked open behind him. He turned. "I'm just about—"

And the breath stalled in his lungs. God*damn*.

On another woman, the simple, clean lines of the sleeveless dress would've been...nice. Safe. But not Sloane.

Beautiful, firm breasts, that small waist, and feminine, sensual flare of hips transformed the black sheath into an accessory that accentuated the gorgeous body beneath. Jesus Christ, she could tempt a saint into throwing aside his halo, Bible, and salvation just for a sip from the shallow bowl at the bottom of her collar bone. Just a lick of nipples he instinctively knew would be a dark, lovely cinnamon. Just a taste of the liquid heat between her soft thighs.

And he was far, far from a saint.

"Sexy as hell."

He hadn't intended to vocalize the thought or for the hoarse rumble to reflect the lust tightening his gut and balls. But when her eyes widened and her lips parted on a gasp, he couldn't regret his outburst.

"I need your help," she murmured.

All his flesh computed was "I need," and it leaped in joy behind his zipper. He couldn't admonish his dick. Not this time. Because, dammit, he needed, too.

"Would you mind?" She pivoted, presenting her back to him. With her hair brushed to the side and over her shoulder, the slice of honeyed skin in the V of the unzipped dress called to him like a siren calling sailors to their watery doom. Like those entranced seamen, he crossed the distance of the room toward the siren who offered heaven and hell. Because touching her would be both.

Anticipation and dread coiled inside him, so entwined, he couldn't separate one from the other. As if from a distance, he watched his fingers pinch the tab and slowly drag it up. His knuckles skimmed the petal-soft skin, and he caught the fine tremble of her body. A corresponding shudder rippled over his skin.

He tugged the zipper to the top, and unable to help himself, he leaned forward, inhaled the graceful column of her neck. Moonlight and sin. Fresh, welcoming air and sultry, hot sex.

She shivered, loosing a soft, muted sound that was abruptly cut off.

But too late, he'd caught it.

Dropping his hands to rest on her hips, he waited. Waited for her to shift out of his hold. A desperate part of him screamed at her to do just that. Because as he studied the back of her dress and the sexy, sheer panels of material that revealed the elegant line of her spine, he could easily imagine dragging his tongue over every vertebra before nipping the indention at the base.

Nipping, hell. Corrupting. The duchess looked like she'd never been dirtied, used—or invited to use in return. God, he wanted to be used, taken, *fucked*. Maybe in the hot, milking clasp of her sex, the black, yawning hole surrounding his soul wouldn't feel so, so…desolate. Maybe just once sex wouldn't be a physical release, but an exorcism of guilt and pain-riddled memories. Maybe he would finally find forgetfulness. Even if only for one night.

"Ciaran." She moved forward. Thank God. But his relief was short-lived as she turned around. And laid her pretty, *hungry* gaze on him. The same hunger that clawed at him. She eased forward, resting her slim hand on his forearm. "I—"

He inhaled a deep breath, abruptly moved back a step. And then another. Distance. He needed distance. "We should go," he said, tone flat.

Damn, she was dangerous.

Sloane Barrett, with her regal bearing, lush curves, and simmering sensuality, was dangerous. Forgetfulness was a fairy tale, an urban legend as elusive as rainbow-shitting unicorns and sewer-dwelling gators. Yet, for a moment, she had him believing in it. Believing she could offer it to him.

He didn't deserve to forget.

The stains on his soul couldn't—and shouldn't—be erased.

The blood painting his hands shouldn't be washed away. He'd earned every blemish, every splash of crimson. Nothing could absolve him.

Not even a duchess with the seductive promise of oblivion in her haunting green eyes.

"I was just about to come look for you two. Mother is getting anxious. Thank God I popped a Valium a couple of hours ago, or she would be tap-dancing on the last good nerve I have left," Chelsea grumbled by way of greeting as Sloane and Ciaran descended the staircase into the entry. "Oh my God, you look gorgeous." Her sister grinned, changing conversation tracks with headache-inducing speed. She leaned forward, green eyes twinkling. "I've always loved your boobs. I had a full C while pregnant with Madison, but after she was born? Right back to the itty-bitty-titty committee." Chelsea sighed, glancing down at her cleavage.

Holy shit, Sloane mused not for the first time in the last twenty minutes. The first time being when Ciaran emerged from the bathroom—shirtless. Good God, the man was ripped. Muscles on top of muscles adorned his deceptively lean frame, and he possessed an eight pack. An honest-to-God eight pack. Up until then, she'd believed abs that defined were the product of over-sexed female imaginations or air-brushing.

She'd seen him in what she labeled his battle gear—cargo pants and long-sleeved shirt. She'd glimpsed him in casual wear like what he'd worn to his office and the dressier slacks and shirt he'd worn today. But Christ on the cross, none of those compared to Ciaran Ross half naked. Even with the wrapping of clothes, she'd sensed the sexual, male animal beneath. Wearing only his taut, golden skin, the trappings and pretense of civility had been stripped bare, leaving the sleek, beautiful predator unadorned.

Then there'd been the tattoos. Warmth poured between her legs, moistening her sex, setting up a faint but erotic pulse in her clit. She squeezed her thighs against the sweet ache. Red, blue, green, and black swirls of art inked into skin, covering his right arm, shoulder, and pec. She'd never been one who found tattoos sexy; it seemed like every Tom, Dick, and Harry had one. Like some ridiculous, frat boy rite of passage. But there'd been nothing ridiculous or juvenile about the mural of swirls, geometric shapes, and pictures staining his skin. Art. He'd been a breathing work of art like the erotic frescoes that had once decorated the walls of the doomed city of Pompeii. Stunning, hedonistic…forbidden.

And then he'd called her *sexy as hell*…

"I wanted to catch you before dinner." Chelsea clasped Sloane's hand, pulling her down the last step, and to the side. She paused, and the laughter evaporated from her gaze, leaving it hard, glacial. "Phillip is here."

The warm slide of heat in her veins congealed into a thick, sickening sludge.

"Is that the ex-fiancé?" Ciaran murmured from behind her.

Shit, she didn't want him to overhear this. But she suspected, even if she asked him to let her speak to Chelsea alone, he wouldn't budge. Dammit.

"Yes, the smug bastard," Chelsea replied to Ciaran, her mouth puckered in a disgusted moue that still managed to look adorable. "I have no idea why Mother and Dad didn't kick his ass off the guest list," she grumbled, shocking the hell out of Sloane. Never—*ever*—had she'd heard her sister disagree with or criticize their parents. At the risk of sounding like a scratched CD…*What. The. Fuck*. "I didn't want you to walk in there and be caught unaware. Especially since he brought his *girlfriend*," she sneered. "What a prick."

"Mother said he was bringing her with him." That shouldn't hurt, because as all the nasty, hurtful insults he'd hurled at her on his way out the door echoed in her ears, she could admit that, yes, Chelsea had nailed it. Phillip was a prick. Yet, he'd gone to the next woman as if their relationship had meant nothing, hadn't impacted him at all. As if *she'd* meant nothing. Acknowledging that she'd been so inconsequential to him stung.

Chelsea snorted, eyes narrowing. "Yeah, you can't miss her. She's the chick in serious need of a cheeseburger and a dress all the way up to her See You Next Tuesday."

Behind her Ciaran sounded as if he were choking.

"See you next Tuesday?" Sloane repeated, even as part of her shouted *don't ask!*

Chelsea rolled her eyes. "See"—she drew a C in the air— "You"—sketched a U—"Next—"

Sloane snatched her sisters hand mid-N. "Okay, damn. I get it." She scowled. "No, really. Who are you, and what have you done with my sister?"

"She woke the hell up and realized what a blind, self-centered, vapid bitch she's been." A grim smile curled her mouth, resembling a sharp blade. "Not that being a bitch is bad. I'm just choosing to use my powers for good these days. Speaking of which"—she squeezed Sloane's hand—"I need to go run interference. See you in there."

Sloane watched her sister sail off in stunned silence.

"I thought you said the two of you weren't very close." Ciaran's hand cupped her hip, and his fresh, earthy scent enveloped her. Embraced her. She stiffened, but at the last moment remembered they were supposed to be a loving couple.

"We weren't. Or aren't," she said, deliberately relaxing into his touch

"I like her."

Sloane arched an eyebrow, staring after her sister's retreating figure, picturing the funny, blunt, and sarcastic woman she'd met since arriving at the house.

She woke the hell up and realized what a blind, self-centered, vapid bitch she's been.

"I think I do, too."

Chapter Ten

"Sloane. Come here, darling."

Smiling, Sloane stepped out onto the wide, covered porch, slipping her hand into her father's. John Barrett pulled her into his side, pressing an affectionate kiss to her hair.

"Don't hog her, John. After all she's my goddaughter, and I haven't seen her in months, it seems." Matthew Daniels arched an eyebrow, and Sloane chuckled at her father's best friend's not-so-subtle admonishment. Sliding out from under her father's arm, she crossed the short space to hug her godfather.

"Months, huh?" She snorted and placed a kiss on his cheek. "I was just over for dinner a couple of weeks ago."

So thin. She held on to Matt a moment longer as worry for both men clenched her heart. While she didn't understand the change in John's appearance, she fully comprehended why Matt's cheeks were gaunter, his dark hair more liberally sprinkled with gray, and his tall, slender frame even more spare. Even when she'd spent the evening with him and her aunt, Sloane had noticed the transformation in both of her godparents. Their son's suicide had exacted a heavy toll on them, physically as well as emotionally.

Maybe concern for his oldest friend explained why her father seemed so tired and...old. The thought of losing either man... She cleared her throat of the knot of emotion tightening it.

"Well, that was my subtle way of telling you we want to see you more often. Not for me, you understand, but your Aunt Grace. She misses you."

"Un-huh." She laughed again. "Funny, because not ten minutes ago, Aunt Grace told me the same thing about you."

"In thirty years, that woman has never met a piece of gossip she didn't love or spread," Matt grumbled.

Her father shook his head, smiling. "So," he said, shifting his attention back to her, "getting ready for the new school year?"

She nodded. "We had our open house earlier this week. When I return home, it'll be time to go back."

She studied her father, the need to tell him about the charter school hovering on her tongue. She longed to discuss the career option with him—especially since the day before she'd been offered the opportunity to teach there. Excitement and nerves quivered in her chest, like a baby bird on the edge of its nest, yearning to take flight but terrified of the fall. She hadn't accepted yet, but like that hatchling she desperately wanted to, even if the unknown scared the shit out of her.

John Barrett was considerably less, uh, high-strung than Mallory, but the knowledge that his oldest daughter planned on teaching in inner-city Roxbury wouldn't go over well no matter how laid-back he was. Though he'd hoped Sloane would join him in the family's investment management company, he'd conceded to her dreams and even commandeered the Kennedy-Lewis position for her. Leaving would seem like an ungrateful slap in the face. God, she hated disappointing him.

Inhaling a deep breath, she briefly closed her eyes. "Dad, I need to—"

"Hello, John. Matthew." A pause. "Sloane."

Oh shit.

The last time she'd heard that voice it'd been spouting spirit-destroying vitriol.

I can't even pretend to get my dick up for you.

Men put cows out to pasture, not marry them.

No self-respecting man is going to want you.

Inside, deep inside where the razor-sharp words had left wounds barely scabbed over, she cringed. Nausea roiled and churned in her stomach, scalding her like acid. She'd managed to avoid Phillip all evening, but her luck had apparently run out.

Slowly, she turned and faced the monster.

On the surface, he appeared as handsome as ever. Close cropped, neat blond hair. Pleasant features and a charming smile. Tall, fit body. At one time she'd considered herself lucky to claim him as hers. But that had been before he'd systematically tried to chip away at her esteem and heart, trying to mold her into who and what he wanted. And when she'd refused, he'd become mean. Not physically—never physically. But the verbal and emotional jabs had still been torture...and the bruises had yet to fade.

And her parents, oblivious to what skulked beneath the polite and charismatic facade, had welcomed the bastard into their home. Of course Phillip had never, ever been less than the perfect, solicitous boyfriend in front of them. And Sloane had never said anything to contradict their perception of that image.

Her father extended his hand to Phillip, greeting him with a smile.

"Have you come to join us for some fresh, gossip-free air, Phillip?"

A shiver tripped over her skin at her ex's chuckle. This one was warm, amused. It was scary how he could appear so damn *nice*.

"Actually, I came out to finally catch Sloane. I haven't had the chance to speak with her all evening." His gray gaze shifted to her. Why couldn't anyone else see the icy sleet in his eyes? Or was his contempt reserved solely for her?

"Well, you two don't need us old men listening in." John nodded, and after brushing a kiss across the top of her head, disappeared inside the house with Matt.

"Aren't you the hard one to pin down?" Phillip purred, sauntering closer until mere inches separated them. Recognizing the intimidation tactic, she resisted the urge to backpedal, but stood her ground. His signature Armani cologne enfolded her, causing the bile in her belly to inch toward her throat. The cloying fragrance differed from Ciaran's earthy, woodsy scent like the sticky, sour aroma of a fading, aging beauty couldn't compare to the fresh, vibrant scent of brash youth.

"Not really," she said, proud of her steady voice.

"How have you been, Sloane? You're looking"—he scanned her in a slow, long perusal, the corner of his lip curling into a faint smirk—"well."

She remained silent, and his mouth slightly thinned.

"I was surprised to find out you were attending the party this weekend," he continued, voice silky and at odds with the ice chips in his gaze.

"Really?" She tipped her head to the side. "Why is that? They are my parents."

"True. But once they informed you they didn't intend to un-invite me, I expected you not to show up. I'm sure Mallory told you I was bringing Tammy." Tammy would be the gorgeous teacher's assistant with the dress all the way up to her—how had Chelsea put it?—See You Next Tuesday.

"Mother did mention you were bringing a date with you." She curled her fingers around the porch railing. Why in the hell were they doing this? Ah, yeah, of course. Phillip needed to gloat, to carve out his pound of flesh. "I don't understand why that would keep me from celebrating my parents' anniversary, though."

"No, I guess you wouldn't, but you had knowledge I didn't," he murmured, his eyes narrowing. "I underestimated you, Sloane. You aren't as slow and innocent as you pretend." He inched closer, further violating her personal space. The curl of his lip deepened, became darker, more sinister. "You had a ram in the bush, huh? So what's the truth? Were you fucking this guy behind my back the entire time? Are you that good of an actress, Sloane?"

"Are you kidding me?" *The. Fucking. Nerve.* "Are you really asking me that? You walked out, remember? And you arrived here with someone else. But because I did, too, I was cheating? I don't owe you an answer. I don't owe you anything."

"And I don't want anything from you. Now. The only thing I wanted from you back then you must be giving to this guy now. So is that it, hmm? Did you promise him Daddy's connections?" he mocked, shoving his face closer to hers. The ice had melted from his eyes, leaving a roiling, furious storm. "That must be it. Otherwise why would he be interested in a fat, boring—"

"You have five seconds to back the fuck away from her, and four and a half of them are already gone."

The flat, arctic tone sent shivers racing down her spine, somehow the utter lack of emotion menacing. And one look at Ciaran's face ratcheted the shivers into quakes.

Here was the DEA agent who'd seen the worst humanity had to offer and waded in to the morass to defend the defenseless even if he was tainted by the muck. Here was the guard who willingly put his body and life on the line to face threats on behalf of clients. Here was the man who had kicked the shit out of two armed assailants in a dark school parking lot, regardless of the danger and the fact that he'd been outnumbered.

Here was the defender, the fighter…the predator.

Ciaran shifted, and in one movement, stood in front of her, shielding her from Phillip.

"Excuse me, Mr. *Ross*," Phillip sneered, his derision plain. *Idiot*. His arrogance didn't even allow him to recognize the danger right in front of him. "But Sloane and I are having a conversation that doesn't include you, and I'd like to finish our discussion without you."

Phillip's hand appeared to the right of Ciaran, reaching for her.

She stumbled back a step at the thought of him touching her… But he didn't have a chance to. Ciaran's arm shot out, his fingers locking around Phillip's wrist, and from her ex's whimper, the grip probably wasn't gentle.

"Anything you have to say to her, you can damn well say it in front of me. As a matter of fact, I fucking insist on it. Now, because it's her parents' party, I won't cause a scene by planting your ass on this floor, but, Phillip? Are you listening, Phillip?" A pained gasp was Ciaran's only answer. "Good, because I need you to hear me." Ciaran's voice dropped to a menacing growl. "You touch her, even brush by her on accident, and I'll snap this hand in two. Are we clear? Nod, goddammit."

Phillip must've obeyed, because Ciaran freed the other man. And when he finally moved from in front of her and turned, they were on the patio alone.

"Are you okay?" The rumble like an ominous roll of thunder hadn't evacuated his voice, yet. The harsh lines of his face and the hard slash of his mouth hadn't softened, and she almost lifted her hand to smooth the furious strain from his features. But mortification mixed with a profound mixture of gratitude and humiliating seed of hero worship kept her arm locked to her side.

"Yes. Thank you."

He dipped his head in acknowledgment, the just-this-side-of-tamed black curls grazing his sharp cheekbones and clenched jaw. Shoving his fingers through the strands, disheveling them further, he glanced to the side, but she doubted he was admiring the shadowed garden and tennis court. Not when a low gravelly rumble emanated from his chest like a disturbed lion denied the gazelle it'd been stalking for dinner.

"Sloane." He returned his attention to her, and the fierceness in his hooded scrutiny scalded her. "I know this is your parents' event, but if you need me to take you out of here, all you have to do is ask."

A trembling breath escaped her lips as her eyes slowly closed.

Save her. Is that how he saw her? An insecure weakling who couldn't stand up to the big, bad wolf of her ex-fiancé?

Hell, how could he not?

And wasn't that just damn humiliating?

She jerked her chin up, praying the shadows concealed most of the heat flooding her cheeks.

"I appreciate you stepping in with Phillip, but I'm not some damsel in distress in need of rescuing." She'd survived a childhood of bullying, a fractured engagement to an abusive jerk, and taught entitled trust-fund babies. Fuck Prince Charming and the white horse he rode in on. Two months ago, she'd learned to rescue herself. "I'm a big girl." Her mouth twisted into a bitter smile. According to Phillip, she was a *real* big girl. *Bastard.* "I can take care of myself."

"Did I say you couldn't?" Something shifted in his

expression, and if possible it harshened until the planes could've been carved from unforgiving rock. "That asshole must've really done a number on you."

Again, his words struck way too close to the truth. And she backpedaled, as if the physical space could insert an emotional gap.

"I don't know what you're talking—"

He snorted. "Don't bother. You wear your pain as clearly as your sexy-ass curves. And for the record, Sloane?" He lowered his head, his gaze capturing hers, his lips so close she could almost feel the movement of them. "They are sexy. As hell. It's a damn shame you don't seem to realize it—or that someone made you doubt it."

She blinked, her whirling mind unsure which of his revelations to grab onto first. Her obvious pain? The embarrassment of that. Sexy-ass curves. God, she would never get tired of hearing him, who resembled some long-forgotten pagan sex god, utter those words.

And that she clutched on to them with greedy desperation only fired the shame and disgust for herself from simmer to conflagration.

"Is this the part where I swoon in appreciation? Does that usually work with woman? You play hero, assure them they're pretty, and they fall to their knees in gratitude?" God, she was such a bitch. But she couldn't shut up, couldn't halt the pain from rolling out of her mouth and lashing out.

Not a muscle moved in his face or big body, but she didn't miss the flare of heat that flashed in his eyes like dry lightning at the mention of her going to her knees. Nor could she ignore the spasm in her sex at the image of grasping his hard flesh in her hand, guiding it toward her mouth as he stared down at her, lust stamped on his features.

She sucked in a breath, shifted backward. But he stalked forward, claiming the space she placed between them as his own.

"Duchess," he growled, his hand pinching her chin and tilting her head back. "When you get down on your knees in front of me, it won't be out of gratitude. It'll be because you want to be there. Because more than anything else you want my cock in your mouth."

The gasp became tangled in her throat. Outrage—she should feel outrage at his raw, crude words. Men of her acquaintance didn't speak to her like that. Hell, even in bed Phillip's dirty talk had been limited to grunts and a self-satisfied "That's it" as he rolled off her. The only thing missing had been a congratulatory pat on his own back. And it'd been okay, she'd never considered herself a woman to be turned on by a man growling an f-bomb or uttering "cock" or "pussy." But just like before when he'd drawn the vivid, sexual picture of what he did to women who found themselves in his bed, her sex quivered at his blunt, erotic words.

What was he doing to her? Anger, mortification—those were the emotions that should be flooding her. Not desire. Not need and an aching emptiness that begged to be satisfied, filled.

He angled her chin higher until the back of her neck ached in protest, sank his fingers into the hair at the base of her skull, and tugged. She whimpered, the gesture like a lever that connected directly to her clit. Squeezing her thighs against the throb, she clutched his shirt in one hand and wrapped the other around his thick wrist, simultaneously holding on and trying to push him away. It mirrored the same indecision waging war inside her. Her mind screamed a warning to walk away while her body issued a silent plea for him to give her everything he described. Everything she pictured in her head.

"Let's get one thing straight. I'm no hero." Something dark and tortured flashed in his hooded gaze, but it was there and gone before she could claim for certain she'd seen it. Then he lowered his head, nipped her bottom lip, and she almost forgot her damn name much less what she'd glimpsed. "You're my client." The tip of his tongue soothed the pleasing yet painful sting. *Oh Jesus.* "My sole purpose in being here is to make sure you're not harmed." He drew on her upper lip, sucking lightly. "And yet all I want to do is go in there and break that motherfucker in half for daring to talk to you. Fucking breathe the same air as you."

"Ciaran," she whispered, in protest...encouragement? She shook her head—or tried to. His grip on her chin prevented the movement. And the show of dominance shouldn't have been sexy. Shouldn't have triggered a series of flutters in her sex or dampened her panties. But damn, it did. *He* did.

"I need to concentrate on who the hell is terrorizing you, but instead, all I can't think about is this." He pressed a thumb to her mouth, the inner skin grazing her teeth. "This is what I've been thinking about since the night you entered that restaurant. This mouth. This beautiful, sinful mouth. And not only is losing my focus dangerous, but I don't do clients. I don't get involved with them, and I damn sure don't want to spread them out on their pristine beds and fuck them until we dirty up their sheets."

Not hardly sonnets or flowers. But from the clenching in her belly it might as well as have been the most romantic thing ever uttered since Cyrano de Bergerac. Her lashes fluttered, then lowered, her breath breaking against the pad of his thumb like waves on a rocky shore. Was the hunger burning inside her really reflected in her gaze for him to see? Probably. She wasn't used to experiencing this kind of snaking, curling heat much less used to hiding it. She was a novice, an amateur, while Ciaran had undoubtedly been dodging desperate women for years.

"Ciaran," she breathed, shaking her head.

"Shh," he hushed, the pressure of his thumb silencing her

protest. Then the sensuous sliding of the digit between her lips, parting them to penetrate her mouth, made her forget any objection she'd been about to voice. Instinctively, her tongue curled around the invader, sucking lightly. His dark, carnal groan rumbled above her, and her moan mingled with it as his flavor—bold, dark, rich—exploded over her taste buds. Suddenly ravenous, she drew harder, tighter on his thumb.

"Damn it," Ciaran snapped and replaced his finger with his tongue.

She shook against him, helpless to the fury of his kiss. Kiss, hell. It was a marauding, a plundering, a conquering. He didn't ease her into passion, he flung her into it with a ruthlessness that should've scared her, but instead thrilled her. Made her crave more. Stretching her mouth wider, she switched her grip to his arms, hanging on for this ride. Ciaran angled her head to the side, dove deeper, demanding she get wilder with him. The meeting—or clash—of lips and tongues was wet, uninhibited, and explicit. She had no problem imagining sex with him. His kiss let her know it would be messy, untamed, fierce, and primal. No holds barred.

And she wanted it with a strength and need that had her wrenching free of his grip.

Even with the chatter and laughter flowing out of the open patio doors, all she could hear was her harsh breathing and the pounding of her heart. Her pulse seemed to *thump* in time to the throb in her tingling, tender lips. Unbidden, she lifted her fingers toward her mouth, but dropped her arm at the last moment.

But Ciaran had caught the aborted motion, his narrowed perusal flicking to her hand before lighting on her face.

"Sloane," he said, voice low, rough. He moved forward, but her hand shot up, palm outward, warding him off.

"We should go back inside," she murmured.

She didn't wait for him to reply, but turned and headed

back toward the dining room and the relative safety in numbers.

Ciaran wielded some kind of super power that caused her to transform into a woman ruled by her emotions instead of her head. She'd been there, done that.

And had the wedding registry, china pattern, and ex-fiancé to prove it.

Chapter Eleven

Sloane slid the glass door open, the soft *swoosh* almost imperceptible. Still, she glanced behind her to ensure a tall, wide-shouldered bodyguard hadn't exited the bathroom early and followed her downstairs. Not that she was running. Again. Just that after the kiss earlier…she needed space.

Jesus Christ, that kiss.

Okay, yeah, maybe she was running.

But any woman with common sense, tough layers of scar tissue on her heart, a resolve to avoid relationships like the plague, and oh yes, a stalker on her ass, would've made tracks as fast and hard as possible. She and relationships went together like Ike and Tina—a big, flaming disaster with its own soundtrack. And she'd sworn relationships off, instead focusing on finding her way career-wise, seeking happiness and contentment with herself, not with a man.

Not that Ciaran wanted a relationship with her. He'd made that abundantly clear by stating he didn't "do" clients. And though his actions had contradicted his words, she believed him. He didn't become involved with clients, and a kiss, though hot as hell itself, didn't constitute a *relationship*.

So she let her guard down that once. But she couldn't afford to do it again. Because if she did, if she allowed him to touch her again, she would cave. Without a doubt she knew she would. The insane desire that had consumed her when he'd parted her lips with his would convince her she could surrender and not face consequences. Not become emotionally entangled. Not want more. Denial was not pretty—neither was ugly-crying into a pillow at three o'clock in the morning.

Trusting men—loving them—had only led to pain and betrayal. And perhaps worse, loss of self. And Ciaran was more "man" than most. She couldn't allow passion to blind her to the ultimate outcome waiting for her at the end of that pitted, pot-hole-ridden road.

Loneliness. Hurt. Shame.

Powerlessness.

Only an idiot would hit her turn signal to head down that street again.

Sighing, she stepped out onto the limestone patio and descended the two steps to the pool area paved in beautiful, smooth sandstone. Her parents had spared no expense in transforming the huge pool area into a tropical oasis. LED lights illuminated the deep blue waters while lush trees and overhanging flowers and plants created the illusion of paradise and privacy. A small waterfall spilled from the second level where hedges concealed a Jacuzzi spa. This was the one area that deviated from the clean, elegant, New England style. It was different, vibrant, exotic. Maybe that explained why she loved it so much.

She climbed the winding steps to the Jacuzzi, strategically placed floor lamps guiding the way. The tension that had strung her tight since arriving that morning slowly bled from her shoulders and spine, the knots in her belly loosening. This part of the house had always been her favorite spot. Peaceful and secluded, she could disappear here. No prying, critical eyes could scrutinize her here. Even the generously appointed pool house that was a mini-me version of the main home had provided her with a sanctuary. It didn't surprise her that once again she'd run here.

Anticipation weaved through her as she slipped from her cover-up and set the clothing and towel on the bench next to the bubbling spa. With a sigh, she eased into the hot, gurgling water and couldn't contain her moan. The water streaming from the jets massaged her back and feet. The remaining strain in her body evaporated along with the rising steam, and closing her eyes, she sank down until the gently waving water lapped at her chin.

Her mind blanked of emails, phone calls, career choices, attacks, asshat exes, and kisses—okay, maybe not kisses. But here, she could pretend an erotic tangle of lips and tongues hadn't leveled her. Here she didn't have to make any decisions about her future or whether those choices would disappoint those she loved.

Here, she could just be—

Click.

She opened her eyes, but stygian darkness greeted her. The LED lights from the pool and the surrounding lamps no longer illuminated the area, and her oasis suddenly became a menacing, shadow-filled jungle with plenty of hiding places for predators.

A chill trampled over her skin despite the hot, bubbling water.

Don't be silly. Someone just shut off the lights by mistake. Nothing to be scared of...

"Hello?" she called out, hating the tremble in her voice. "I'm out here." Silence. "Hello?"

When more silence, thick and heavy, met her words, she

slowly straightened. She tried to listen for a hint of sound that would be amplified in the complete darkness, but the frantic slamming of her heart roared in her ears, deafening her to anything else.

Forget this. Foolish or not, I'm out of here.

Palming the shallow ledge in the Jacuzzi, she pushed herself up...

Hard, bruising hands clamped her shoulders. Shoved her down. Underneath the water.

Oh God!

She screamed, but the garbled cry only resulted in a mouthful of chlorinated water. Shutting her lips, she struggled, twisted, trying to free herself of the iron-hard grip. She clawed and pinched at the thick wrists and hands, but the hold didn't loosen, the implacable fingers digging into her muscle with evil, deadly intent.

Terror filled her, surging from her belly and pressing against her sternum. Her shrieks bounced off her skull like a horrifying cacophony. Pressure built in her chest, her lungs burning, beginning to scream from the lack of air. Fear pumped in her veins, stealing precious oxygen.

Desperate, she continued to scratch at her attacker, but her wild movements slowed, grew more sluggish.

No! God, no.

She cried, her mouth stretched wide as she wrenched and jerked, but even her fight weakened as her brain seemed to register the imminent danger and clicked into survival mode. Every bit of energy poured into her lungs, clinging to the last scrap of breath. She scraped her wet nails down tough skin once more, the attempt to damage feeble...

Then the pressure disappeared.

She launched upward, coughing up water before dragging in a noisy, greedy lungful of air. Followed by another. And then another. Pain seared her chest but she didn't care. Jesus, she was alive.

Dread and panic pounded in her head, throat, and body as she whirled around, searching the obsidian shadows for her attacker. She whimpered, terrified that he still lurked, enjoying the sight of her fear before grabbing her again.

"Sloane!"

Ciaran.

"Ciaran," she shouted. Or tried to. It emerged sounding more like the croak of a bullfrog. "Ciaran, up here." She tried again, and though her voice cracked, it was louder.

Seconds later, firm but gentle hands clasped her upper arms. Even in the dark, with his frame and face hidden in shadows, she recognized his touch. Recognized *him*.

He lifted her from the spa and cradled her close.

And she let him.

John Barrett shot up from the stool at the kitchen island as Ciaran shouldered his way through the glass door that separated the kitchen and the back of the house, Sloane cradled in his arms. Matthew Daniels, Sloane's godfather, rose more slowly, shock slackening his features.

Damn. He'd hoped to enter the house undetected.

"What's going on?" her father demanded, striding toward them.

"Sloane? Is everything okay?" Matthew asked.

Sloane's body trembled against Ciaran. He'd wrapped her in one of the heavy, white towels on the spa bench, but her bared shoulders, arms, and wet hair soaked his T-shirt. Not to mention shock was probably kicking in like a motherfucker. He had to get her upstairs and dried out. Had to make her feel safe. But first he had to get her past her father and Matthew.

She lifted her head from his shoulder, and offered her

father a shaky smile. Warmth and admiration for her streamed through him.

"Nothing, Dad, Uncle Matt," she rasped. "I'm fine. I caught a cramp and panicked a little. Ciaran is just being a little overprotective." Her pale pallor and tremulous voice lent credence to her story.

"Overprotective, romantic. To-may-to, to-mah-to," Ciaran drawled even as he tightened his arms around her. "I'm going to get Sloane upstairs. So pretend we didn't interrupt," he added with a pointed glance toward the half-eaten thick sandwiches on the island that the two men had obviously been sneaking and eating before Ciaran and Sloane had barged in the kitchen.

The concern slowly eased from John and Matthew's faces.

"If you're sure," John said, sinking back onto the stool. Chagrin entered his expression. "And what you saw here stays between us."

Dragging up a rough chuckle, Ciaran nodded and escaped the room, forging a quick path to Sloane's bedroom.

Thirty minutes later, he replaced the screen in front of the fireplace, the low dancing and swaying flames emitting a mild warmth that toasted his skin. Under normal circumstances, lighting a fire in late August would seem absurd. But under normal circumstances, a woman wouldn't be sitting on the rug, wrapped in a blanket after being attacked and almost drowning in a Jacuzzi.

Balanced on the balls of his feet, arms braced on his thighs, he glanced over his shoulder to Sloane. Her dark, damp hair hung over her shoulder, the normally straight strands wavy and loosely curled. She appeared so young with the white comforter draped over her shoulders and drawn-up legs, her bare, painted toes peeking out from under the edge.

Young and vulnerable. And scared.

It was the "scared" that alternately ate him up and had

him impatient to go on the hunt, locate the bastard who'd dared touch her, and break the hands that had held her underwater.

He should've been there. No one should've been able to come near her, much less grab her, terrify her, hurt her. Her eyes, usually so vibrant like the emeralds her mother wore on her fingers, were dull with residual fear. He detested seeing that fear.

For a moment another pair of eyes wavered in front of him. Brown instead of green, but containing the same horror…before they went blank with death.

He inhaled a deep breath, returning his attention to the crackling fire and away from the guilt that gnawed a hole in his gut. She didn't have to confirm it, but it'd been the kiss that had propelled her from the safety of his protection as soon as his back had been turned.

Fuck. His fingers curled tight until two fists hung between his thighs. He'd known better. From the beginning his number one rule had been keep his hands off. That when the choice came between her life or his dick—there wasn't a choice. Failure wasn't an option. And yet, all it had taken was seeing her asshole of an ex cornering her and that annoying, inconvenient possessive streak had reared its irrational head. Once Phillip walked away, that should've been it. But no, the overprotectiveness had only morphed into something darker, something almost primal. This need to claim her, brand her as his own surged in him, and he'd surrendered to the impulse.

He could still taste her.

And even now, realizing what a colossal mistake he'd made, he hungered for more.

"Can you tell me what happened?" He didn't glance at her again, but kept his gaze riveted on the bob and weave of the flames.

"I came downstairs while you were in the shower…" She

relayed the narration in a halting voice, and it required every ounce of ragged control he possessed not to go to her and stroke her hair, smooth his thumbs over the trembling mouth. Replace that blanket with his body.

Fury thickened his blood so it permeated every cell, every organ, so he breathed it as she recounted how someone grabbed her and shoved her under. How she struggled but couldn't get free. How she believed she was going to die.

Silence hung in the room like a shroud, the only sound the *pop* and *snap* of the flames.

"If the switch for the LED and halogen lights are located in the pool house, then there had to be two people behind this. From your account, you were attacked seconds after the lights were cut. There's no way this person could've been in two places at once." The house stood at the far end of the enormous pool, only the fucking Flash could've made it that distance in moments.

"I honestly thought I was safe here," Sloane murmured, drawing his gaze. He rose to his feet, thrusting his hands in the front pockets of his jeans. Stalking across the room, he paused at the arched set of windows and stared out into the darkness. If he'd emerged from the shower even a minute later, or had waited to go searching for her, she wouldn't be sitting there on the floor but floating face-up in the Jacuzzi.

He squeezed his eyes shut, trying to dispel the image that was entirely too crystal clear in his head.

"Tell me again," he ordered, his tone quiet. She didn't argue or question his request, but complied. And as she spoke, the visual of it materialized on the back of his eyelids like a silent movie. When she finished, he turned to her. "When you scratched him, did you notice if he wore a watch, if there were cuffs around his wrists?"

"No watch, and no, no shirt cuffs either." Even with the distance between them, he could spy the hope lighting her eyes. "Do you think we'll be able to find someone with scratches on their hands and arms?"

"It's a long shot with the guests and the staff, but if it takes me until we leave, I plan to search every man here." He would, dammit. And heaven help the bastard when he found him.

Getting too personal.

Like the fucking kiss wasn't?

Well, shit, now he was arguing with himself.

Shaking his head, he frowned. "Sloane, from now on I'm by your side wherever you go. You don't move unless I'm with you. This won't happen again." Not on his watch. His hands weren't big enough to be stained by more blood.

Her mouth firmed as if she wanted to argue with him. After a long moment, she nodded. "I don't want my parents, Chelsea, or Matt to know about this. I don't want them to worry." Squeezing the bridge of her nose, she said, "Especially Matt. He's already lost his son, I can't add to his burden right now."

They damn well should worry. Their loved one was in trouble. If his mother or sister's lives were in danger, he would hate being left in the dark. But the security specialist charged with guarding her life, unfortunately, agreed.

"Fine. But only because I don't know who to trust," he said.

Disbelief slackened her features. "You can't possibly believe they have anything to do with this," she snapped. "What about Drake Morriston? He makes more sense than my family. Are you even looking into him?"

"We're pursuing all angles, Sloane. And no, I don't believe your family is behind this. But I don't know if anyone they're associated with is. Your parents or Chelsea could inadvertently pass on information and not realize they were assisting whoever is stalking you."

The incredulous outrage ebbed from her face. "That

makes sense." She sighed. "I'm sorry. I didn't mean to snap at you. I'm just"—she lowered the blanket a fraction and rubbed her shoulder, wincing—"I'm just tired."

The flinch snagged his notice. Before he could warn himself to keep his damn distance, he was already stalking across the room toward her. He knelt behind her and gently brushed her hands aside. Folding the edge of the comforter down, he exposed her shoulders and the upper portion of her back.

God. Damn.

Bruises. Just forming under her pale honeyed skin, but there. Under the base of her neck like a loose chain and marring the front of her shoulders. By tomorrow, and especially in a couple days, the marks would darken to a mottled purple, black, and blue. A constant reminder to her that someone wanted her life. A constant reminder to him that he'd almost let them have it.

With the utmost care, he trailed his fingers along the discolored skin below her neck. *So fucking soft.* How sick did it make him that even with her sitting there in front of him, vulnerable, the evidence of her ordeal marring her body, and probably more than a little bit in shock, he could think about how silky and beautiful her skin was? The bruises seemed sinful on her skin, blasphemous.

He brushed the contusions on her shoulders, and she flinched slightly, her breath hitching.

"Hurts?" he murmured.

"Yes...no."

Her chest rose and fell below his fingertips. Quick pants burst past her lips, the harsh, rapid breathing echoing in the quiet room. He smothered a groan and shifted his hands to her upper arms, gripping them over the blanket. Sloane wasn't terrified—at least not only terrified. Desire, lust, need. Sloane was turned on by his gentle strokes.

Jesus Christ. He'd meant to soothe, not arouse. To calm, not stir. To comfort, not awaken. *Move*, his haloed conscience ordered. Get across the room. Take another cold shower. Anything but remain sitting there, inhaling her sex-and-moonlight scent, cataloging each shallow breath that was a wicked solicitation to take and satisfy the hunger in both of them. He leaned forward, burying his nose in her still-damp hair. His fingers flexed on her arms, careful not to hurt her, but unable to release her. But the longer he sat there, the more frayed his resistance and resolve became. All the reasons—valid reasons—for not touching her, for keeping a professional distance steadily seemed less important than kissing her pain away, than tasting her lips and skin and reassuring himself he'd made it on time.

He eased a hand up her arm, over her shoulder, and into her heavy, dark hair. Curling his fingers, he grasped the strands in a firm but gentle grip. She tensed and he paused, waiting for the demand to let her go. But it didn't come. Instead, she exhaled a small gust of air and relaxed into his hold.

Damn. His flesh swelled, hardened, the zipper of his jeans doing its damnedest to stencil itself onto his flesh. Did she understand what the small sign of surrender did to him? Not only was it as erotic as fuck, but it signaled trust. She trusted him with her vulnerable femininity, her pleasure…trusted him to not hurt her. To protect her. After the events of this night, God, he needed that. He craved it.

Tugging on the mass of waves and curls, he tipped her head back. Long black lashes hid her eyes from him. But the flush coloring her cheekbones, the parting of her pouty, sensual lips revealed what he couldn't glimpse from her gaze. Still, he needed to see. Needed to confirm that the lust riding rough-shod through him tormented her as well.

"Look at me. Let me see those pretty eyes." For just a moment she hesitated, but in the next instance, she lifted her lashes, and...*hell yeah. Right there.* Desire clouded the bright green, and his gut clenched, his hand flexing in her hair and tugging on her scalp. With a gasp, she arched into the hold, loosening her clasp on the comforter and flattening her palms to the floor on either side of her hips. The cover fell around her, and damn if she didn't look like sex on a platter.

"Goddamn, Sloane," he growled, scanning her breasts, thrust up under her top in silent offering and down past her stomach to the area between her thighs. Loose pants of the softest material covered her hips and drawn-up legs. But the shimmering silk undoubtedly couldn't compare to the wet velvet of her pussy. The starving hunger inside him demanded he find out.

Settling behind her, he bracketed her legs with his, pressed his chest to her elegant spine, wedged his dick against the small of her back. And groaned. A perfect fit. *Too fucking perfect.*

He lowered his head. And took. Angling her head farther back, he thrust his tongue between her lips, sweeping in, tangling, and sucking. Consuming.

Christ, she tasted just as good as the first time. Better. Like earlier, this kiss wasn't tender or hesitant. No, it was wild, carnal, ravenous. This could've been their hundredth kiss instead of second. He dove into her, and she met him in the erotic duel, meeting him stroke for stroke, lick for lick, greedy moan for greedy moan. And when he lifted his head for air, she followed him with a needy whimper. *Shit.* He crushed his mouth to hers again. *Breathing was way overrated.*

Unfolding his fingers from around her upper arm, he splayed them wide over her stomach. Her muscles contracted under his palm, the tell-tale flinch telling him without words how he affected her. Pride, fierce and heady, and a sense of power barreled through him like a tidal wave. This gorgeous woman—this duchess—ached for his touch, panted into his mouth, begging for what he could give her.

He slid his hand up her torso until he cupped the delicious weight of her breast. Twin moans echoed in the room, drenched with pleasure. She ripped her mouth from his, bowed into his hand, her head pressing into his shoulder.

For a second, he closed his eyes, savoring in the warm, firm flesh in his hand. But fuck that. He had to see what his fingers gloried in. Even though a top composed of the same silk as her pants covered her breasts, the taut bud of her nipple poked through the material, an erotic invitation he couldn't turn down. He swept his thumb over the tip, and she cried out, her arms lifting and encircling his neck, her fingers tangling in his hair. The tiny stings against his scalp only fired the molten need in his veins, pooling in his cock.

"Beautiful," he praised, lust roughening his voice like gravel. He pinched the rigid peak, tugged, and tweaked, over and over, testing her, determining what she liked and what made her hips circle in a slow grind. Oh, hell yeah. The duchess seemed to crave a little bit of bite with her pleasure. A slightly hard pinch and she whimpered, those sweet thighs parting wider, her ass almost leaving the floor. He lowered his other hand to the neglected breast, shaping the flesh before treating the nipple to the same caresses as its twin.

"Ciaran," she breathed, sinking her teeth into her bottom lip, and he licked the curve, tasting her low, serrated groan. Her lack of inhibition floored him...delighted him. She was already a beautiful woman, but passion stamped on those regal features transcended her to something indescribable. Something he couldn't walk away from right now even if doing so was the smart, professional option. Now that he'd seen arousal straining her features, darkening her eyes, quivering through her body, he couldn't stop until he witnessed her coming apart. Until he observed what she looked like with ecstasy stamped on her face.

He abandoned one breast and retraced his path down

her torso and belly. The band of her sleep pants barred his way, but he slipped beneath, not stopping until he slid through slippery, plump folds.

"Fuck, you're wet." The low, hoarse words were barely legible even to his own ears. Had another woman gotten this hot and drenched for him before? If so, he couldn't remember. Hell, with his fingers burrowing through her slick folds, he could barely remember his own damn name. He lifted two fingers, glistening with her moisture, to his mouth. Sucked them clean. His moan rumbled up out of him, long and low. He'd savored her mouth, but the sweet, sultry essence of her... Christ, he could feast on her all night and still want more.

Drawing his fingers from between his lips, he glanced down and caught her staring at him. Lips still swollen and damp from his kisses, she couldn't hide her arousal. Still, a tiny frown creased her brow as if she wanted to ask him...

"Delicious." He answered her unspoken question, then captured her mouth in a hot, quick kiss, sharing her flavor with her. "Addictive."

He slipped his hand back underneath her pants, cupping her, grinding the heel of his palm against her clit. The humid heat of her bathed his hand, and with a keening cry, her thighs widened, granting him more access to her sex. He gritted his teeth, fighting the almost animalistic urge to lay her down on the nest of blankets and thrust his tongue into the clenching entrance his fingers teased.

Still plucking and rolling one taut nipple with one hand, he eased one finger of the other inside her and swore at the perfect tightness. Tiny, feminine muscles fluttered and rippled around him. Too easily he could imagine the same muscles milking his dick. Pulling at him, urging him to bury himself deeper and harder...

"Wider," he ordered, this time not waiting for her to comply but lowering his other hand and pressing it against her inner thigh. Once she was spread for him, he thrust another finger inside her core and strummed her clit with his thumb. A wild cry burst past her lips as she clung to him, her hips writhing and pitching under his hands.

He maintained a hard, steady pace. A thrust. A tight circle over her clit. Thrust. Circle. Thrust. Circle. Moisture coated his fingers, so the only sounds in the room were her constant stream of mewling pleas and the wet suction of her flesh receiving and releasing his fingers. She shook like a wind-tossed leaf in his arms, but he was ruthless as he pushed her toward orgasm. He had to see it. Had to have it. Had to cause it.

"Ciaran." His name cracked on a wail, and his only reply was to give her another finger inside her, stretching her. "Oh God, please." Nails bit into his scalp. Hot flesh squeezed him until he wondered if he would carry bruises the next day.

Another stroke. Another firm massage of her clit. Her sleek walls clamped down on him.

And she broke.

Shuddering, twisting, screaming. She came for him so hard her body mimicked a seizure with the sharp jerks and undulations. Clenching his jaw, he continued to thrust past spasming flesh. Continued to rub that convulsing bundle of nerves at the top of her folds, determined to grant her every ounce of the orgasm she deserved, and he was honored to give her.

Gradually, she quieted, her body calmed, loosened, her breath like blasts of heat against his neck. He eased his fingers from the still-quivering clasp of her core, and she whimpered in weary protest.

"Shh," he soothed, lapping at the perspiration dotting the slim column of her neck and beading her shoulders. "I got you. It's okay."

Liar, his conscience taunted.

Things would never be okay—the same—again.

Chapter Twelve

Okay, it was time to come out the closet.

Not the proverbial, hey-family-I'm-gay closet, but her literal closet. But *Jesus Christ*. Sloane twisted her fingers, staring at the closed door. She sympathized with the gay population. Because part of her would rather walk downstairs and announce to her firmly Catholic parents that she was sexually attracted to Christina instead of Christopher before emerging from the sanctuary of her walk-in and confronting Ciaran the morning after the hottest, most mind-blowing finger-fuck she'd ever received.

She squeezed her thighs together against the phantom ache still pulsing in her sex, and flattened her palms against her lower belly. She closed her eyes, but immediately opened them as flashes from the night before flashed across her lids. Ciaran's hand tugging and plucking her nipples. Both of his big hands between her widely spread thighs, filling her, rubbing her. Her back and hips arching and twisting to the erotic tune he played on her body. Coming like she'd invented the damn phenomenon.

Heat razed her cheeks until she probably resembled a sunburned tomato. Hanging her head, she smothered a mortified groan. She'd been so…uninhibited. Sexual. No man had ever elicited that kind of unrestraint from her. Granted, no man had ever touched her with such patience, passion, and skill like Ciaran had. No man had ever kissed her with the tangy taste of her…her desire still on his tongue. Still… She hadn't held back, instead had bucked and sweated and been freaking *noisy*. God, she'd never been *noisy*.

But her total sex-starved-kitten act hadn't been the ultimate humiliation. That honor belonged to the moments after the glow of orgasm had faded.

When Ciaran had laid her on the bed and then retreated to the small sofa to sleep.

She ground the heels of her palms against her eye sockets. He'd chosen to fold his ridiculously tall frame on that Lilliputian couch rather than sleep beside her. Yes, that had been the crowning glory. Logically, she should be grateful he'd distanced himself. Last night had been a…cataclysmic event…*mistake*. A mistake. One she would be an idiot to repeat. The kind of passion and lust she experienced with him would chain her to him tighter than the most Houdini-proof cuffs. And he hadn't even been inside her, yet. No. No way. She'd just discovered her freedom; she refused to sign up for another tour of duty.

Still…he'd treated her like one of those coyote-ugly chicks…

And now she had to walk out of this closet and face him like she was wrecked by cataclysmic orgasms every day. Yawn.

Pearls dissolve in vinegar.

She inhaled. Exhaled. Shit, even her usual calming mechanisms weren't working. Swiping her damp hands over hair and down her high ponytail, she straightened her shoulders and…

"Grow a pair," she ordered herself. For God's sake, she couldn't remain hidden in the damn closet for the rest of the morning, no matter how much appeal the idea held. Tilting her chin up, she stalked toward the door and pulled it open before she could do a backward shuffle toward the evening wear.

She skidded to a halt as if an invisible brick wall sprang up in front of her.

Oh for the love of...

Ciaran sat on the sofa he'd slept on, studying the screen of a laptop perched on the coffee table he'd pulled up. Skin. Miles and miles of taut, golden skin etched with reds, blues, greens, and black ink. Not an ounce of fat in sight, just intriguing, sexy dips and ridges that called for a woman to run her fingertips and tongue over. Her gaze latched on to the thin trail of dark hair that bisected his unbelievably ripped abs and disappeared beneath the waist of his gray pants. Last night, what lay underneath those pants had pressed against her back. Even now she could feel the rock-hard column nudging and grinding against her. Moisture fled her mouth as she jerked her gaze back up to his face. Safe territory.

Or not.

Ciaran had noticed her standing just outside the closet, and his gaze was fixed on her. Unlike last night, his bright eyes didn't burn with desire. Instead the blue reminded her of ice — cold, hard, flat. She shivered and smoothed her palms down the wide, flowing legs of her dark green jumpsuit, fighting not to wrap her arms around herself.

"Do you think Phillip could be capable of attacking you?"

That quick, images from the attack bombarded her. Heart thudding against her sternum, she absently massaged one shoulder and then the other. This morning, the bathroom mirror had revealed the bruises had started to darken and mottle. She'd purposefully chosen the jumpsuit with its wide straps to hide the violence marring her skin. Sticky, obsidian remnants of fear tried clawing their way up her throat, but she shoved them back down. Focused. And frowned.

"You think he could be responsible for last night?"

"I don't know," he admitted. "I can't rule anyone out. That's why I'm asking for your opinion."

"Phillip has always been"—she twirled her hand as if trying to conjure up the accurate description for her ex— "arrogant. In the beginning of our relationship, I saw it as confidence, and it was part of his attraction. Only later did he devolve into a condescending, verbally abusive asshole."

"Abusive?" Another shudder tracked down her spine at the quiet, but ominous tone.

"Verbally," she hurried to assure him.

A dark eyebrow jacked high. "And that makes a difference?"

"No, it's just…" She waved a hand. "I got through it. I'm over it."

"Really?" he drawled.

Warmth flooded her face as his words from the night before haunted her.

You wear your pain as clearly as your sexy-ass curves… It's a damn shame you don't seem to realize it—or that someone made you doubt it.

"I thought we were talking about whether Phillip is capable of coming after me," she said, voice devoid of the hurt and shame rioting through her. "The answer is no. He broke up with me. He has no reason to hate me enough to break into my house, have people attack me, and come after me himself."

"Normally, I would agree with you on that." Ciaran leaned back against the couch. She forced her gaze to remain above his neck to keep from leering at the stretch and pull of all that muscle. "But last night, that wasn't a man with no hard feelings. There was anger there. And if he didn't care about you, he wouldn't have called you those ugly names. No, he followed you out on that patio for a purpose, and he was going to see it through if I hadn't interrupted."

"I don't know what he wanted." She held out her hands, palms up. "When he walked out he was very clear"—*Fucking you is charity work*—"that we were over."

He watched her with narrowed scrutiny. "You've just reaffirmed my opinion that he's a stupid motherfucker but not convinced me he's innocent." Returning his attention to the laptop, he started tapping on the keyboard, his dark brows drawn down in a V over his eyes as he continued to peer at the screen.

"What are you looking at?"

"Phillip's phone and bank records," he murmured.

Wait...*what*? "Did you request a subpoena for that?" She crossed the room, perching on the arm of the couch and leaning over to glimpse at the laptop monitor. *He couldn't really be...nope, he was.* Phillip's name, address, and service provider jumped out at her as if blinking a neon red.

"Do you really want the answer to that question?"

Yeah...probably not. "What are you looking for?"

His glanced at her. "Phone calls that are a break in his usual pattern. We know whoever is behind the stalking and attacks hasn't been working alone. We're checking the calls that have nothing to do with family, friends, or are business or social-related. The same goes for his finances. Outside of his usual pattern of expenses, we're searching for unusual payouts or even payments. Has he been receiving money from someone that is out of the ordinary?"

A fist of emotion—disbelief, sadness, anger—wedged in her throat. "Have you found anything?"

"Not yet," Ciaran said, his gaze narrowing as if he could peer inside her and see the tumultuous clash of feelings. "Do you want it to be him?"

She stood, evading his too incisive stare on the pretense of retrieving her jewelry from the dresser. "No," she whispered, choosing a diamond stud and rolling it between her fingers. "Because that would mean I slept with, gave my heart to, and intended to marry a man who hated—and hates—me enough to terrorize and kill me." And she'd been too blind or naive to see it. Maybe even hadn't *wanted* to see it. Inhaling a deep breath, she slid the first post into her pierced lobe. "Who else are you looking at?"

"The student you told us about, his parents. Your father."

Jesus. She flinched. *The man needed to wear a bell or something.* Without her detecting him, he'd crossed the room and stood behind her. Close behind her. God, she swore pure animal heat emanated from his bare skin, sending flames licking her belly and lower south. *Focus, dammit.* She wouldn't make a fool of herself again with him like she had last night.

"My father?" She frowned.

"He's a very wealthy man, Sloane. And that alone makes him a target for enemies or those who envy what he has."

"I don't know," she murmured, picking up the back of the earring. "This whole thing has felt kind of"—she lifted a shoulder—"personal."

"I agree. But we have to examine every angle." Long fingers reached around and plucked the jewelry from her hand. He gently fixed the earring back to the stud with an ease and skill that had her tamping down an irrational surge of jealousy. *Not my business.* He retrieved the matching diamond and, with a gentle, expert touch, slid the gem into her lobe. "If it is Phillip, not recognizing the darkness he hid doesn't make you stupid or blind or any of the other names I know you're calling yourself."

"How about needy?" she scoffed, regretting the slip when his hands stilled on her.

"If he couldn't appreciate the passion and beauty in you than that's his shame, not yours," he said, the rumble in his voice low and gravel-rough.

"Says the man who couldn't get away from me fast enough last night," she drawled, going for nonchalant and sarcastic and, to her own ears, falling somewhere between hurt and miffed.

Silently he finished fastening her earring, then backed away, taking his body heat with him.

"You don't understand," he murmured.

"Understand that you would prefer to sleep on a cramped couch rather than a bed big enough to fit the entire Patriots' defensive line because I was in it." She turned around and offered him her best don't-bullshit-the-bullshitter smile. "Don't worry. I received your message loud and clear. You regret last night, and it won't happen again."

"You don't get shit, duchess," he growled. His full, sensual lips hardened into a grim line. He shoved his fingers through his black waves, and she couldn't help but notice the delicious dance of muscles and tendons under his inked skin. He glanced away for a moment before pinning his laser bright gaze on her. Part of her wanted to step back, retreat from the glint of steel in his eyes, but she held her ground, squaring her shoulders. "I haven't slept with a woman in four years."

She stared at him. Snorted. "Okay."

"Not fucking." His shadowed eyes dipped to her mouth before returning to meet her scrutiny. "Sleeping. I haven't slept beside a woman in years."

The implications of his quiet statement slammed into her like a sledgehammer. At face value, the words could sound like those uttered by a man-whore. But underneath... underneath the admission something dark, painful— something haunting—lurked. *Christ.* What had happened?

She moved toward him. "Ciaran—"

A knock reverberated on the bedroom door. Frustration and relief poured through her. Frustration because whatever she'd been about to say had been interrupted. And relief because whatever she'd been about to say had been interrupted.

"I'll get it." Clearing her throat, she crossed the room and opened the door to reveal Chelsea on the other side.

"Hey," she greeted. Leaning around Sloane, she waved at Ciaran. "Good morning, Ciaran. Oops, didn't know you still were still in the middle of dressing. I apologize." She straightened with a sweet smile, but as she withdrew from Ciaran's view, her eyes rounded comically wide, and she mouthed, *Oh. My. God.*

Oh, if she only knew the half of it.

"No problem," Ciaran said from behind her. "I'm going to finish getting ready."

"You don't have to on my account," Chelsea grumbled.

"Stop!" Sloane hissed. slapping her sister on the arm as the *click* of the bathroom door closing reached her.

"What?" She lifted her hands, palms up. "You did good. I'm just saying."

"Come in." Sloane stepped to the side, granting Chelsea room to pass by her. "I've been meaning to talk to you, anyway," she said, shutting the door behind her. "Mom told me about you and Greg divorcing. Are you okay?"

Chelsea tossed back her thick mane of blonde hair and beamed. "Nope. Not in the slightest."

"Oh honey…"

She extended her arm toward Chelsea, but a beat of indecision pulsed within her, holding her back. Their relationship had never been close. Hell, cordial would be putting a nice face on it. There had always existed this tension between them—competition, sibling rivalry—and, it had prevented them from forming a close bond. Not to mention that though Sloane was the older child, she'd always felt like she'd forever been in Chelsea's shadow. And it wasn't a comfortable or enviable place to be. Still, as she stared into her sister's overly bright smile and glistening eyes, none of that mattered. Especially when Chelsea met her halfway and grabbed her hand, hanging on as if Sloane were her only lifeline in a raging storm.

"I feel so stupid." Chelsea chuckled, the abrupt bark of laughter water-logged though she didn't allow a tear to fall. "Right in our bed. With his secretary, too. How fucking cliché is that?"

Before Sloane could reply, could assure her that his cheating didn't reflect on her, Chelsea clasped Sloane's hand, squeezed it, then dropped it just as quickly. Flipping her hair over her shoulder, she groaned and frantically waved a hand in front of her face. "Ciaran, you caught us at a bad moment."

"No problem," came his deep timbre from behind Sloane.

Slowly she turned around and found herself pinned in place by his searching regard.

"I came up here with a purpose, actually," Chelsea continued. "Mother has an excursion planned for today and sent me to fetch you two. Golf."

Jumping on a reason to evade Ciaran, Sloane pivoted to face her sister. "Golf?" A boulder of dread sank to the bottom of her stomach. Not only did she hate the boring sport, but surely Ciaran hadn't received his big, rangy build by putting a tiny white ball across an immaculately manicured green. He seemed more the physical, football type. She didn't want him to feel awkward or out of place. "I don't know— "

"We'll be there shortly," Ciaran interjected, moving up beside her and sliding an arm around her waist. The simple touch rocked her more than it should have. But considering the last time his hands had been on her, they'd been finger-deep inside her, she could be forgiven her reaction.

"Golf?" Sloane repeated, doing a God-awful job of lassoing the skepticism in her voice. "Are you sure?"

He nodded, and Chelsea grinned. "Great! See you there."

As the bedroom door closed behind her sister, Sloane arched an eyebrow and stepped to the side so his fingers fell away from her hip. She'd set the rules after all: No touching outside of what was necessary to pull off the pretense.

Yes, they had failed spectacularly with that one so far, but if she were going to emerge from this long weekend with her sanity and heart intact, she had to get it together. Stand her ground on the no-contact rule. Stop being a sex-starved wuss.

"You can play golf?"

He returned her arched brow, the gesture rife with arrogance. "Of course."

Well, of course. How silly of her to ask.

Chapter Thirteen

"This isn't what I meant, and you know it," Sloane muttered.

"What? You asked me if I could play golf. I can't read your mind," Ciaran said, swinging his club back and then forward. The iron connected with the bright pink ball, and it sailed down the green—and disappeared through the mouth of an enormous hippopotamus squatting in the middle of the course. He circled the hulking, purple monstrosity, and with another stroke of his gold club, sank the ball into the hole. "Two strokes," he bragged, retrieving his ball and stepping off the green.

"Bragging that you finished in two strokes. Just like a man." Sloane lined up her shot.

Ciaran grinned at the smart-ass comeback, and as she drew back to swing, he drawled, "It's not the quickness that matters, sweetheart. It's what you do with the time you're given that counts."

"Damn!" She swung, barely clipping the ball.

"That counts," Ciaran pointed out.

"Shut it." Scowling, she jabbed her club in his direction. "I didn't try to distract you when you were up." Resettling herself, she swung again, and three strokes later, landed her ball into the hole.

"Hmm." Rubbing his chin, Ciaran gave her a mock frown as she straightened from picking up her ball. "I thought you were supposed to be good at this."

"Now who's making assumptions?" she shot back. "I never said that. And for the record, slick, I'm pretty decent. There's a big difference between aiming for a hippo's intestines and hitting a shot across a green."

"Point taken." He paused. "Aaand yet, I'm winning."

"Bite me."

He arched an eyebrow and leisurely surveyed her from her dark brown ponytail, over the green one-piece jumpsuit that cupped her gorgeous breasts, slid over her hips, and flowed around her long, lovely legs. "Is that an invitation?" he teased, but the rough note in his voice—all too damn real.

"Oh no you don't." She scowled. "Sexual innuendoes are hereby banned from this course."

He inclined his head, grinning. "Understood." Waving his hand to the next stop, which included a big-ass bunny with disturbingly huge eyes and teeth, he said, "After you." Pause. "Which is my motto in most things."

Throwing him a glare, she marched ahead of him, and he didn't bother holding back his laughter this time. An hour and a half and two more games later, they turned in their golf clubs and multi-colored balls.

Fun.

He'd had more fun in the last two hours than he'd enjoyed in… God, he couldn't remember the last time. She'd done that—given him pleasure that didn't include a bed, sweaty and straining bodies, and orgasms. The usual ways he found pleasure with a woman. For four years, he'd avoided relationships, attachments. Which included allowing a woman close enough to make him feel anything more than physically satisfied. But Sloane… Since the moment he'd met her she'd been eliciting emotions from him: curiosity, hunger, fear, this increasingly alien joy. Her ability to do so only made him want her more.

And scared the shit out of him.

He longed to draw her close…and shove her far, far away.

But right now, with the early afternoon sun highlighting the scattering of gold freckles over the bridge of her nose and along her cheekbones, he ignored the warning blaring like a foghorn inside his head. Instead, he decided to bask in the moment.

Too shortly they would return to her parents' home and resume their charade and their boundaries. But not here, with eight-feet-tall grinning animals and the shouts and laughter of children and adults surrounding them, he was going to… enjoy himself.

Enjoy Sloane.

"How about a hot dog and ice cream?" He extended his hand and couldn't contain the swirl of delight in his chest when she slid hers in his. "Loser pays."

"I'm already paying an astronomical bill for your services," she protested. "And now I have to pay for your lunch? Aren't expenses included in that fee?"

"A: You were the one who insisted on paying said bill." Of which they weren't accepting a dime, but pointing that out right now might ruin the mood. "And B: This is completely separate from the job. Loser always pays. It's a universal rule."

"A man must've invented that so-called rule."

He lifted a shoulder in a half shrug. "Probably."

She snorted. "Definitely."

Ten minutes later, they sat on one of the bench-table combos outside the clubhouse, Nathan's hotdogs in hands.

Sloane bit into hers, and eyes closed, moaned. Ciaran averted his gaze, jaw clenched. Wicked, pleasure-drenched sounds like that should be reserved for sex, not a hotdog. He should know since the same groan had reverberated in his ears last night while he'd stroked her to orgasm. Damn good thing he was sitting down and the picnic table hid his lap—and the erection tenting his pants.

"I haven't had a Nathan's in years," she murmured, plucking up an onion and popping it into her mouth.

"You don't say," he said, voice dry. "When I was in New York, I had one at least three times a week."

"I didn't know you lived in New York." She sipped from her soda, and again he found himself needing to adjust the fit of his pants and averting his stare away from the sight of her pretty lips wrapped around her straw. Hell. He needed to smack a leash on his mind. "You're from Boston, though, right? I thought you and Shane grew up together."

"I am, and we did. I joined the DEA straight out of college and worked in New York City for four years before returning home." *Please don't ask why. Please don't spoil this day by making me remember...*

As if she'd heard his silent plea, she didn't continue down the path of what had brought him home. Instead, she sighed, set her half-eaten food on the table. "Straight out of college?" She shook her head, a small wistful smile barely curving her lips. "I can see you knowing what you wanted and going for it. I envy that."

He released a short bark of laughter, not entirely devoid of humor, but tinged with a hell of a lot of self-deprecation, earning him a look of surprise from Sloane. "Being an agent wasn't my first choice for my career. Since I was in grade school, all I wanted to be was a football player. The dream of most boys, right? But I was damn good. So good I went to school on a scholarship and had coaches—college and NFL—

scouting me by my junior year in high school." Memories of those days filled with grueling practices, Friday night games, and the incomparable high of knowing you left everything you had on the field and it paid off in a win filled him, warmed him. "But my sophomore year in college I blew my knee. There I was, no scholarship, no NFL career, and no idea what I was going to do with my life. I had to reevaluate everything, and turned out I loved my criminal justice classes. And when the opportunity came to apply to the DEA, I took it."

Now, the disappointment of seeing his dreams of playing professional football didn't carve out a hole in his chest like it used to. As his mother had been so fond of telling him, "Everything happens for a reason." And now, with years' distance from that bleak time, he could agree with her. But not everything. Just some things. Because he still couldn't reconcile why God would allow a woman as loving and beautiful as Sam die in such a violent manner. Why she died and pieces of shit like he used to arrest still lived and breathed.

"And the rest is history," she murmured.

Not quite. "Something like that." He dipped his chin in her direction. "I got the feeling you loved teaching," he said, veering the discussion away from him. "Education wasn't your first love?"

She didn't answer right away, and though her face had adopted that shuttered expression he was growing to detest, he didn't push her. Finally, she glanced down, fidgeting with the paper boat her food rested in.

"No," she replied softly. "I've always wanted to teach. Even when my parents 'urged'"—she curled her fingers in air quotes—"me to major in something I could use like communications or business, I didn't back down. For once."

"But," he gently pressed when she paused.

"But, I'm not happy. Doesn't that sound so ungrateful?" She scoffed, shaking her head.

She lifted her head, meeting his gaze, and he bet if she realized how much of her heart resided in those emerald green eyes, she would duck her head once more. As it was, he fought the need to reach across the table, and smooth away the wrinkle between her eyebrows. Stroke her jaw, mouth. Comfort her. But instead, he maintained his stranglehold on his empty hotdog container, crushing the paper until the edges pricked his palm and fingers.

"Ungrateful because you've changed your mind?" he asked.

"No. Even though Dad didn't agree with my decision, he arranged the teaching position for me at Kennedy-Lewis, which is a prep school for the wealthy. But I've been so"—she straightened and curled her fingers as if attempting to grab the answer out of the air—"unfulfilled. Not because of the kids, although there are those like Drake Morriston—except maybe not as destined to be on America's Most Wanted. Most of the kids are great, but they don't need me. Not really. They have the best education and resources money can buy, including teachers. I want more. I want to feel like I'm making a difference. Instead I'm making everyone else happy but myself. No," she objected, frowning. "That's not exactly right. I feel like I'm failing myself."

Shock ricocheted through him. When a person first glanced at Sloane, they would see a statuesque, reserved, beautiful woman—never guessing the passion that smoldered beneath the aloof exterior. He'd been burned by that fire last night and witnessed it today. It was intoxicating to be on the receiving end of it, and exhilarating to see. "It's hard to believe you could fail at anything, duchess."

Surprise flared in her eyes, and moments later, a smile quirked the corner of her mouth. Small and wry, but it was a start. "There is an opportunity…"

"It stays here," he promised when she trailed off. He

sensed she hadn't told anyone of this opportunity yet. While she might not be able to trust his increasingly ragged self-control when it came to her, she could believe he would protect her with his life and anything she said to him didn't go any further. He needed her to believe it. "Me and you."

"I have a chance to teach at a new charter school in Roxbury."

He whistled. "That's a big difference from your prep school."

"I know," she agreed, leaning forward, eagerness brightening her gaze, fairly vibrating in her body. "But to be in on the ground floor of structuring and planning the curriculum? Being a part of something important and lasting? This is what I've always dreamed of doing."

The excitement and the joy shining in her eyes struck him hard in the chest. This was the true Sloane. Passionate, animated, confident.

"What's holding you back, then?"

The light in her expression dimmed the slightest bit. Her smile faltered. "Me," she murmured. "I can say I'm afraid of disappointing my parents. Or I could say that after years of being the flawed Barrett, I cringe when I think of adding one more black mark against my name. But those are the simple answers." She shook her head. "The truth is I'm scared to screw this up. Being the perfect daughter, the perfect socialite, an engagement—I've failed at those, and yes, they hurt. But this—teaching, working with children—is my heart. It's my passion. I'm terrified of failing at my passion."

Silence pulsed between them like a heartbeat. He, more than anyone, understood fear of not being enough, of letting others down, of fucking up when it meant the most. His cost had been horrific. Because of him the woman he'd loved was gone. The price of losing her was his to bear, to suffer, to always remember like a penance that could never be absolved.

But Sloane didn't have to pay that same price.

She deserved happiness, peace, and her dreams. And it was his job to protect her, keep her safe so she could have that future at the school.

"Sloane." He waited until he had her undivided attention before continuing. "We conducted a background search on you when we took your case. Mainly to discover if maybe you'd encountered disgruntled employers or acquaintances that you might've forgotten to tell us about." At least on the surface, that had been the purpose. If he were truly, I'll-only-admit-it-in-the-darkest-hours-of-midnight honest, he'd wanted to know more about her. The need had only intensified in the days since. "All your co-workers, your reviews, and reports had certain words in common. Dedicated. Hard-working. Cares for her students. Kind. Need more like her. Sweetheart..."

Even as his mind blared a "back the hell up" warning, he submitted to the desire to touch her. Even as his brain taunted him with what happened the last time he crossed the line with a woman he should've been guarding, he reached across the table, clasped her hand in his, and trailed the backs of his fingers of the other down her soft cheek. "You won't *be* great, because you already *are* great. I can think of no greater crime than to see you lose the light you have when you talk about doing what you love. Don't let fear hold you back."

"Thank you," she whispered, cupping her hand over his.

Turning, she placed a gentle kiss to his palm. And the sweet gesture bolted through him like lightning, throbbing in his veins. Shutting down the shudder that tried to work its way down his spine, he withdrew from her. He couldn't afford to forget how dangerous she was to his self-control.

"That's becoming a habit with you," she murmured.

"What is?" He met her steady, too incisive observation.

"Pulling away. I could be offended," she said, her lips

twisting into a faint, wry smile. "But something tells me it has more to do with whatever makes you zone out sometimes. Whatever—or whoever—causes your eyes to darken with pain."

Ice spread through him, and he allowed it to infiltrate his voice. "I don't know what you're talking about." No way in hell he was going there with her. He could barely think of Sam and her death—and his part in it—without curling in on himself. Damn if he would have a *kumbaya* moment about it. Especially with Sloane.

"You do that often, too. Shut me down." Her gaze roamed over his face as if searching for answers that he refused to give her. Couldn't give her. "Control is that important to you, isn't it, Ciaran?" she whispered. "What happened that made you crave it so badly?"

Flashes of a dirty back room, of a blank stare, of blood flashed before his eyes. Death, pain, fear—they all made him desperate for control. They were ruthless masters that demanded it. And he was their bitch.

He rose from the table on the pretext of gathering their trash and crossing the few feet to toss it away. The task granted him physical and emotional space and time to still the whirlwind her questions had stirred.

"You know what I just realized," he said, returning to her and infusing a teasing note in his voice. "Not once today have you recited one of your weird facts."

Red stained the curves of her cheekbones, but she chuckled. "Weird to you, but they work."

"Work how? And how in the hell do you know all that anyway?"

She shrugged, slipping her half-eaten hotdog into its bag. "Being the chubby, shy kid provided me with a lot of time to read. And besides reading *Charlie and the Chocolate Factory*, learning things I figured no one else would know made me feel smart."

He absorbed what she said—and what she hadn't said. Since she felt she wasn't the pretty sister, she could be the smart one. He could only imagine the pain of feeling being constantly compared to a popular, thin, beautiful, younger sibling. And always coming up short.

He picked up his drink and sipped from it, studying her. "Snails can sleep for three years without eating."

A slow grin spread over her face. "Maine is the toothpick capital of the world."

"The average human eats eight spiders in their lifetime while sleeping."

She scrunched her face up in disgust, but shot out, "An ostrich's eye is bigger than its brain."

"Turtles can breathe through their asses."

"Snakes—" She straightened. Blinked. "You made that up," she accused.

He folded his arms on the table, arching a brow. "Google it."

"Hold on." She pulled her cell from her pocket. Tapped the screen. Tapped some more. She lifted her head, eyes narrowed. "Damn. They really do breathe through their asses."

Chapter Fourteen

Sloane stood outside her bedroom door, her hand grasping the knob.

For the second time in a day, she found herself staring at a closed door, wary of facing the man on the other side. Unlike this morning, it wasn't embarrassment about stolen, erotic moments in front of a fire that had her heart imitating a drum line. No, the honor belonged to a day of miniature golf, smack talk, hotdogs, and sharing dreams and hopes she'd never revealed to anyone.

The honor belonged to stripping away one layer of the man guarding her—because she didn't fool herself into believing there weren't many more.

The honor belonged to discovering that man had secrets, pains, and wounds hidden under his hard exterior, and she wanted to mine those depths.

And therein lay the reason she hovered outside her room. She wanted.

His softly whispered confidences in the middle of the night. His trust. Hell, him. She wanted him.

A line had been crossed today. Last night could be relegated to high stress and nerves after a traumatic event, and him offering her comfort and relief through physical release. Happened all the time. Especially in romance novels.

But today... Those moments on the miniature golf range and afterward had been more intimate than the pleasure he'd brought her. More vulnerable.

Part of her craved being completely honest with someone, the freedom to let her walls down and be *seen*. But another part—the more cynical, experienced part—shied away from that need. The past had taught her nothing good came from lying physically and emotionally naked before someone.

Not that any of this mattered. Not the hunger to touch and taste and be taken by Ciaran. Not the need to know the man and not just the security specialist.

Because Ciaran was here with her for one reason—to catch her stalker and would-be kidnapper and determine who and why someone wanted to hurt her. As soon as those tasks were accomplished, they would go their separate ways, maybe occasionally seeing one another at parties like Shane and Fallon's wedding.

She inhaled a deep breath. Exhaled it slowly, deliberately. Turned the door knob. And it was better that way. She didn't confuse a passing attraction with feelings. Didn't complicate business with sex—

Jesus Christ, the man was trying to kill her.

Ciaran turned to face the door, his cell phone pressed to his ear, an arm raised and fingers buried in his black tumble of hair. He must've answered the phone while in the middle of undressing because the sides of his dress shirt flapped around his bare, hard chest. His blue eyes locked on her, but she couldn't tear hers away from the sight of his bare chest... again. This was the third time she'd seen his inked skin, so she should be used to the size and beauty of him.

But then again, after visiting the Louvre three times, one didn't say, "Oh, you've seen one Leonardo da Vinci, you've seen them all."

"So nothing on their computers? Okay," he said to the person on the other end of the phone. "She hasn't received any more calls, but some more emails came through. Anything on that?" He quieted, listening, eyes narrowed. "All right, good. Keep me posted." Pause. "Yeah, thanks."

"One of your partners?" she inquired as he lowered the phone from his ear, trepidation curling in her stomach. Worry and fear were two very effective killjoys of lust.

"Yeah." Ciaran set the cell on the small table in the sitting area. "Several days ago, Maddox set up eyes on the internet café where the emails originated from. He traced the recent emails you received back to the same café and is going to view tape on the place tonight. Maybe we'll have a picture of the person sending you the messages."

Relief tumbled through her in an avalanche. She pressed a palm to her belly as she crossed the room and lowered to the couch. "That's great, right?" She frowned, taking in the rigid lines of his face, the unsmiling, firm mouth. "Why don't you look like that's great?"

"Because the last email came through at 12:08 last night when we were here in the Hamptons. Which means whoever is sending the mail is in Boston and not here trying to drown you."

Realization dropped on her like an Acme anvil. "Damn," she whispered. "I didn't think of that."

He nodded. "We've been working under the assumption that these are several perpetrators working for one person. But something doesn't fit. A couple of things don't fit."

"Such as?"

"First, the tire slashing, the vandalism, and attempted kidnappings, I can see the mastermind behind this hiring people to take care of that for him. But the emails? The phone calls? Those are personal actions most stalkers use to get close to their victims. To either hear, see, or know they're touching them in some way. I can't see someone letting a hired thug carry that out. Which brings me to my next issue."

He stuffed his hands in his pockets, the motion drawing his shirt open wider. *Jesus, girl. Focus.* "Boston is hours away from here. If the person who attacked you last night intended to knock you out—which I'm not too certain about—wouldn't the person they were working for be close by? If what we assume is true—that the purpose is to abduct you—then why would they attack you here and transport you hours away? Wouldn't it make more sense to wait until you returned to Boston? Or better yet, for the mastermind to be in the Hamptons?"

Her brain whirled with his questions, and she pressed the heel of her palm to her forehead as if she could press them into submission. "Wait, wait. What do you mean you're not too certain about the attack last night?" she asked, latching on to one thing at a time.

His frown deepened. "It doesn't fit. Even the assault in your home, we don't know what his intentions were. It could've been to subdue you and remove you from the scene. At your school, I'm almost certain the goal was to move you to a secondary location. But last night..." A muscle along his jaw flexed. "It seemed as if the goal was to hurt you, render you unconscious at the least, drown you at the worst. Which doesn't fit the MO. It sounds like two different offenders."

She shook her head. "What are the odds of two different people harboring a vendetta against me? I know I'm not Miss Popularity, but that's kind of stretching it."

"True," he agreed. "But that leaves us with three options. One, our first assumption is correct, and one person is behind the entire thing. Two, there are two different perps involved.

Or three, one person behind the emails, calls, and assaults in Boston. And the attack last night was a completely different assailant."

She absorbed his assessment. "You're still thinking Phillip might have something to do with it."

"I'm just not ruling him out." He tilted his head, studied her in that silent, piercing way he had that reminded her of a scalpel. "Does that bother you?"

"Does it bother me?" she repeated, scoffing. "Of course. It *bothers* me that anyone wants to kill me."

"You know that's not what I'm asking," he said, voice quiet but firm, demanding an answer.

She surged to her feet, dragging both palms over her hair. "Didn't we discuss this already?" She didn't want to talk about Phillip. Especially not with Ciaran.

"No. Earlier I asked if you thought he was capable of coming after you. That's not what I'm asking you now." Again with the unsettling scrutiny. "Are you still in love with him?"

She flinched, shock almost rocking her back on her heels. "What?" she rasped.

"Are you still in—"

"No!" she shouted, then sucked in a breath, shook her head. "No," she reiterated, softer this time. "We're over. Been over. He's moved on."

"You wouldn't be the first woman to still love a man after the relationship has ended, even if he has started dating someone new."

"Really? Are you speaking from experience?" she shot back. "I can imagine a few of the women you 'don't sleep with' have a hard time letting go."

Ciaran stared at her, and his features could've been carved out of stone, a sexier, fiercer addition to Mt. Rushmore.

God, she was such a bitch. Throwing something he'd confessed back at him like a verbal bomb was low. And beneath her. Or so she'd believed.

"I'm sorry. Forget I said that," she whispered. Bowing her head, she pinched the bridge of her nose. "But I don't know what you want from me. It's almost like you need to hear me say I'm holding a torch for my ex."

"Maybe," came the rough, muttered response.

She jerked her head up, eyes widening. "Why—"

"You said he's moved on. You didn't mention yourself, Sloane."

Frustration welled up in her, and she glanced around the room as if searching for an escape route from his relentless pursuit. Only instead of chasing her, he cornered her, prodded her with questions she didn't want to think about, damn sure didn't want to answer. Because they weren't simple. What Phillip had done, had stolen from her, wasn't black and white. But Ciaran, with his overwhelming masculinity and exuding confidence, wasn't her idea of a Mother Confessor.

"You don't understand. You don't know," she murmured, pushing her arm out, palm up as if the gesture would physically halt his inquisition.

"Then explain it to me, Sloane," Ciaran urged, low and insistent. "It's only been two months since your engagement ended, and he shows up here with another woman. He might be enough of an asshole to move on that quickly, but you?" He shook his head. "I don't think so. You even admitted you'd given him your heart, your body. You were prepared to marry him. It has to feel like a betrayal. Especially if you still lo—"

"I don't want to talk about it," she pleaded. "Stop." *Please stop*.

He quit speaking. But it didn't stop the emotional pressure from building inside her like a hot spring geyser. It built. And built. And…

"He hurt me," she blurted, her chest rising and falling on harsh, rapid breaths.

Silence boomed in the room like a bass drum, deafening, its heavy beat pulsing through her. A deep, menacing growl rumbled across from her, and seconds later it vibrated under her palm. Ciaran had moved so fast, she gasped, blinking as his hard, bare chest filled her vision. Her hand flattened between his pecs, the heat from his skin branding hers. Jesus, did a furnace burn inside him? Or was the heat all her? The arousal that had flared to instant life like a struck match as soon as his body came into contact with hers?

"He. Hurt. You," he bit out. "I thought you said he didn't lay a hand on you."

"He didn't." She sighed and dropped her hand, but his shot out and grasped her wrist, holding it to him again. "Ciaran…"

"Explain." Pause. "Please." Another pause. "Sweetheart, I won't bully you into talking to me, but I'm here. I'll listen. No judgment."

When she didn't immediately start talking, he kept his promise. He didn't press her, but waited.

"He…" She averted her gaze to the bank of windows over his shoulder. If she glimpsed pity in his eyes… "I've never been naive about my looks. I have a pretty face. That's what most people say, including my mother. What they really mean is 'if only you'd lose weight so your body could match your face, you would be perfect.' The men I've dated in the past claimed I was pretty, and that they weren't bothered by my size-two-challenged body, but eventually they were. And those men were never shy about telling me. But Phillip was different, at least in the beginning. He called me beautiful, was charming, solicitous…until he wasn't. There were little signs, but so tiny and subtle I didn't pay attention to them, when I should have. 'Let's eat healthier.' 'Do it for me.'"

Her voice trailed off, and she became submerged in the memories of her slow, two-year descent into a controlling, emotionally abusive relationship.

"But soon, the criticism became more overt. Especially after the engagement. And the insults didn't stop at my weight. I was too uneducated or stupid to understand his work. I was obviously weak and lazy because I couldn't lose twenty pounds. I was a needy bitch. In front of my parents, he was the perfect future son-in-law, but behind closed doors…" She shook her head. "I don't know why I stayed so long. Maybe I was as weak as he called me."

"Fuck that," Ciaran snapped.

She shifted her attention back to him, a smile breaking through the shroud of sadness and shame that had wrapped around her since she'd started airing the dirty laundry that had been her relationship.

"He was fond of telling me no other man would ever want me or put up with me, and at some point, I suppose a part of me started believing him. But after dinner with his co-workers where he said one of his snide comments in front of them, I suddenly had this vision of what life would be like with him. It was the first time he'd criticized me in front of other people, but something inside me knew it wouldn't be the last. So I told him I refused to put up with it anymore. That if he didn't love me for me, didn't accept me for the woman I was—the woman he'd supposedly fallen in love with—then he could walk. And he did. A couple nights later, he left, but not before calling me names, telling me I wasn't good enough for him, and informing me of the great disappointment I was in bed and out."

Those last few moments rolled through her head like a horror movie. Only scarier because it was based on true events.

"Phillip made me believe in the possibility of the future my mother and sister had—husband, family, happiness. Before him, I didn't think I would have that, it's why I put my all into my career. But he gave me hope, and then he took it from me. When he walked out that door, he carried every dream with him. My pride and self-esteem. And I'm so damn mad at myself for giving it to him in the first place. I can't forgive myself for that."

"Sweetheart," Ciaran murmured, cupping the nape of her neck with his big hand.

"I don't want your pity," she said, pushing back against his hold on her.

His dark eyebrows arrowed down over the bridge of his nose as his fingers tightened. "Good," he countered, voice flat, deliberate. "Because you don't have it. The defenseless, the helpless, the fragile—they deserve pity, not you. Nothing about you is weak."

His words penetrated her protective shields, infiltrating her head, her heart...her spirit.

"Phillip is a bastard. A small-minded, manipulative bastard with a yellow streak a mile wide running down the middle of his back. Some people are so terrified that others will look closely at them and see their own insecurities and imperfections, they try to rip up someone they perceive as a scapegoat. That's Phillip. A coward who probably never felt smart enough, strong enough, successful enough, so he tries to tear down someone who is what he's not. What he desires to be. You, Sloane. Since he couldn't be you, he tried to smother your spirit, your fire. And when you stood up for yourself, and he saw he failed, he left, leaving you to believe you were the failure when the exact opposite is true." He drew her forward, pressing his lips to her forehead. "God, you're beautiful," he whispered.

She huffed out a laugh, but not an ounce of humor filled her. This time when she pushed out of his grip, he let her go. Avoiding his gaze, she crossed the room to the dresser. A sense of *déjà vu* tripped over her. Just this morning, she'd stood at the same dresser, in the same outfit, having the same conversation.

And as she started to remove her earrings, the same body crowded her and the same hands gently shoved hers out of the way. Silently, he took over the task of taking out the diamond studs. Once done, he leaned forward, planting his palms on the dresser, his arms and chest caging her in. They stood there, neither of them moving. Hell, she was *afraid* to move—afraid to stay there in his embrace, afraid to leave it. And Ciaran...

His earthy scent enveloped her, and she closed her eyes, inhaling it so he filled her as well as surrounded her. God, she hungered to be filled by him. And not just with his fragrance. She'd had his fingers inside her. Even now, she could feel the thrust and press, the slick caresses. Her thighs trembled before she firmed them. But there was nothing she could do about the heat rushing through her veins, the sweet ache beading her nipples, the blood pounding in her sex. Jesus, all he had to do was glance over her shoulder to catch the effect he had on her. She cringed at the thought...and yet a part of her wanted him to. Wanted him to see it, do something about it.

Not that he would. He'd made that clear last night when he hadn't finished what they'd started in front of the fire, and confirmed it when he told her he didn't sleep with women. He fucked them, but didn't sleep with them.

He hadn't done either with her.

"Ciaran," she said.

"I wish you knew how much of a temptation you are." He shifted closer, and his lips grazed her earlobe and the sensitive skin beneath. The rigid, unmistakable length of his cock nudged her ass. She sucked in a breath. Held it. "I take that back. No, I don't want you to know. Because if you did, you would run right now. Run hard and fast in the opposite direction."

Don't ask, dammit. Keep your mouth shut and just. Don't.

Ask.

"Why would I run?" *Damn.*

His fingers curled into the wood top. "Because right now I don't want to protect you... I want to fuck you. Your mouth, your hands, your tight, sweet pussy." He growled, and the vibration hummed through her back, eliciting a twin response from her. "I want to drown in you so when I walk away, I can still smell you on my skin, still taste you on my tongue, still hear your screams in my ears. I want to corrupt you, get dirty and rough with you because I know this sexy-as-hell body can take it. Can take *me*. Right now, Sloane, someone needs to protect you from *me*."

A shudder quaked through her. She could barely catch the air she sucked into her lungs. A moan escaped her before she could drag it back in. Behind her, Ciaran stiffened, going still as a statue.

"Walk away, Sloane," he warned, the deep timbre of his voice rolling over her like a molten caress. "Now. I don't have control anymore, so sweetheart, you need to walk away for both of us."

Yes, she should turn around, escape out the bedroom door. She knew herself. Casual sex wasn't her thing, and there would be nothing "casual" about being with Ciaran. He would mark her, and when he left, she would be forever branded. Yet...

Just once she longed to be selfish, to grab a hold of what she desired, needed. Just once she could be the reckless, damn-the-consequences one. Just once she wanted to be *wanted*.

She'd never been with a man like Ciaran—beautiful, strong, sin incarnate. And he craved *her*. The long, thick column of flesh nudging her ass attested to his need. Just once she could be on the receiving end of such passion, such hunger...

Just once...

She slowly turned and faced him. He watched her, his

hooded stare studying her, waiting. Shivering under the heat of his scrutiny, she pushed past him, slipping out of his embrace. Something dark flashed in his blue eyes. Resignation. Maybe disappointment. Not relief. And the absence of that emotion bolstered her courage even as her heart thundered in her chest like a jackhammer.

On knees threatening to give out, she crossed the room until she stood next to the bed. Pivoting, she lifted a hand to the wide strap of her jumpsuit and eased it down over her shoulder, down her arm. Then repeated the action with the other.

A loud inhalation of breath reached her seconds before Ciaran did.

He leaped on her.

And God, was it hot.

His mouth crashed down over hers just as her back hit the mattress. Greedy. Wild. Raw. The kiss was all those and more. She whimpered beneath the sexual onslaught even as she opened wider for him. Met his tongue thrust for thrust. Angled her head for a deeper penetration. Sex. The clash of lips and tongues was pure sex. A prelude to a deeper, more carnal connection. One her sex already wept for.

Without breaking the erotic contact, he gripped her hips and slid her higher across the bed. Crouched over her like a sleek, dark predator, he consumed her as if starved. Which seemed appropriate since she was ravenous for him, for his taste, for the hard, solid weight of his body pressing down on hers. She craved all of it, and yet none of it was enough.

As if he could read her thoughts, Ciaran reared up, and shrugged out of his shirt. The air rushed out of her, leaving her momentarily breathless. It was like being up close and personal with a wild, dangerous cat and being allowed to pet and stroke it. Even knowing the animal could bite...even knowing she would relish that bite.

She placed trembling hands on the ridges of his tight abdomen. Gloried in the feel of him, sighing at the heat that seemed to emanate from him. Slowly, fingers splayed wide, she slid her palms up his torso. And when a shudder ripped through him, she hoarded the pleasure and knowledge that she—her touch—was responsible for the reaction from this beautiful male animal. A sense of power she'd never experienced in bed before blossomed inside her, mushrooming like an atom cloud. Moaning her pleasure, she roamed higher, stroking his small, dark brown nipples, and up, over his firm pectorals and the first swirl of blue, black, and red ink...

Tough, raised flesh abraded her fingertips.

She paused. Brushed over the anomaly of smooth, taut skin. A scar a little bigger than a quarter. Round. A bullet hole. And another just over it. Shock and horror tore through her, shoving aside the pleasure. *Jesus*, Ciaran had been shot.

Firm, implacable fingers cuffed her wrists and shoved her arms down to the mattress on either side of her head. She stared up into his narrowed gaze, sadness and fear for him a metallic taint on her tongue.

"Ciaran," she whispered.

But he shook his head once, then swooped and claimed her mouth in another fiery, carnal kiss that swallowed her question and refused to give her answers. In seconds, the desperate need returned in full force, submerging everything else beneath a deluge of passion.

Calloused fingers pushed her bra straps over shoulders and down her arms, leaving them just below her elbows. His lips abandoned hers, but she didn't protest because they brushed over her cheek and jaw. His teeth scraped her neck and collar bone, forging a scalding path lower. Once more he rose, his strong, muscled thighs straddling her hips. As if unable to resist, she dropped her hungry gaze to his cock. She swallowed, an embarrassing, low sound of lust escaping her throat, and her fingers curled into the covers, longing to shape themselves around the hard flesh. The clear outline of his intimidating, rigid length pressed against the front of his pants. God, he seemed so huge. No possible way he could fit all of that inside her. Her sex clenched, spasmed with an empty ache as if volunteering to give it the old college try.

"You want to touch my cock, duchess," he murmured, lowering the cups of her bra and baring them to the cool air and his hot stare. "You'll get to. I want you to wrap your hands around me. Or better yet, that sexy mouth. But after…"

After… She bit back a scream as his big hands cupped her breasts, pinching her nipples. Oh God. *After.*

The previous night must have taught him what she liked, because he didn't treat her like fine china. He rolled the tips between his fingers and thumb, tugging and flicking them into stiff peaks. She arched toward him, offering more, begging for more. *Needing* more.

He shifted between her legs, his stomach pressing against her swollen, throbbing sex and pulsing clit. She cried out, widening her thighs, rolling her hips, and grinding herself against him. *Oh Christ.* So good She lifted her arms, encircled his shoulders, and bucked against him again. And again. Pleasure radiated inside her, originating from her sex and spreading outward. God, she could come from just rubbing her clit over his washboard abs…

"You need to come, sweetheart?" He rose, settled his cock right over the top of her sex, and circled his hips right where she needed it. Fire raced through her veins before culminating in a heavy, thick swirl between her legs. "I can take the edge off if you need me to." Another cry-inducing circle of his hips, his dick dragging over her clit. She gasped, digging her nails into his shoulders, holding on for damn dear life. "All you have to do is ask," he whispered, licking the top of her breast. "I'll give it to you."

Temptation. He was temptation, wickedness, and sex wrapped up in one six-foot-plus package.

"C'mon, sweetheart," he purred against her skin. "I can feel you trembling beneath me. I bet your pussy is wet, needing just a quick release. I'll take care of you. Just ask."

He must've known vocalizing her request was torture for her. Sex had never been noisy, filled with cries, groans, and this dirty, so-fucking-erotic talk. She'd never asked for what she wanted, and no man had ever asked her either. The words crammed together at the back of her throat. Desperation kept them ready to trip over her tongue, but fear of rejection or ridicule kept them trapped.

"Sloane, look at me." Eyes she hadn't even been aware of squeezing shut opened at the hard demand. "Nothing we do in here is wrong. I'll never shut you down. Whatever we do in here stays between us, in these walls. You're safe, sweetheart." He nipped at her bottom lip, and the sensuous sting caused a flutter in her belly. "Now, tell me. What do you want from me? What can I give you?"

She stared up into his lust-sharpened features, the blue of his eyes that burned brighter, hotter. And trusted what she saw. Slicking her tongue over lips, she whispered, "Get me off. Make me come. I need it." The flare of lust in his gaze emboldened her. "I need you."

He shot off of her as if blasted from a gun. With quick tugs, he removed the jumpsuit and her panties, leaving her naked except for the bra tucked under her breasts. She didn't have time for modesty or embarrassment, because in seconds he covered her again, his hand tucked between her legs and his mouth latched to her breast.

"Ciaran," she cried out, driving her fingers through his tumble of curls. The silken strands, so much softer than they appeared, caressed her flesh as he sucked her nipple deep between his lips, drawing on her, tugging, licking. Desire lashed her as hard as his tongue, and she couldn't prevent the pleas and tiny screams that rolled out of her in a sensual litany.

He switched breasts, and thrust two fingers deep into her. Another scream ripped out of her at the fullness, the pleasure. Again, he wasn't hesitant; last night had introduced him to her sex, and he filled it like they were old familiar friends… or fuck buddies. He set up a fast tempo meant to launch her into orgasm. Just as he promised. The heel of his palm rubbed her clit with each stroke. Electrical sparks sizzled at the small of her back, crackled and coalesced in her core. So close. God, so close.

Ciaran pinched the nipple he wasn't sucking. Withdrew his hand…then drove high and hard into her sex.

She splintered, a high, keening wail on her lips. She couldn't breathe, couldn't speak. Couldn't do anything but shatter and shake in orgasm.

"Fuck, that was gorgeous. You're goddamn gorgeous," Ciaran growled above her. She blinked, her fuzzy vision revealing the stark lines of his face. Blue fire gleamed down at her, and his golden skin was pulled tight over his facial bones, making the carnal curves of his mouth even more pronounced. A flush stained his cheekbones as he studied her with a lust that reignited the sated heat inside her. No man had ever looked at her with such…hunger. Like if he didn't have her he might lose his mind. "I want more of that. My fingers have fucked you twice. Now it's my dick's turn. You're going to squeeze me tight just like that, you understand?"

All she could do was numbly nod. Whatever he said. As long as he again took her to the place she'd just tumbled from.

For the second time, he left her. He backed off the bed, reaching into the pocket of his pants. His gaze never left hers as he removed his wallet and plucked a small, foiled square free and tossed it on the bed. In moments, he'd shoved his pants and underwear down his hips and thighs, standing naked before her like that pagan sex god she'd often compared him to.

Holy shit.

This is what he hid beneath the veneer of civility with his clothes. Wide shoulders and chest. Narrow hips. Muscled thighs. And his cock. She crossed her arms over chest, and the protective gesture wasn't lost on her—or him, if the wild flicker in his eyes was any indication. He tracked the movement, his hand rising to the huge, thick column of flesh angling out and upward from his body, fisting it. Stroking it. The bulbous head almost reached his navel, and a flash of feminine anxiety quivered inside her sex. She'd thought his fingers had filled her, stretched her. No. Not like that almost brutal-looking shaft of flesh would.

He settled a knee on the mattress and picked up the condom, continuing to roughly pull on his cock while he ripped the packet open. Her palms itched with the need to replace his hands with hers. She could imagine the silk-over-steel heaviness in her fist, savor the throb of it.

"You're going to make it hard for me to go slow if you keep looking at me like that," he warned, gliding the protection over his length.

"You promised you'd be rough with me," she reminded him, not recognizing the hoarse, throaty tone as hers.

"Yeah, I did." He crawled back over her, captured her mouth in a burning kiss. "I also said you could take it. Tell me I'm right. Can you take it, sweetheart? Take me?"

"Yes." She wrapped her arms around his neck, and this time she took his lips, nipped the corner. "Don't hold back."

He didn't answer, but a tiny muscle jumped along his jaw, telegraphing he'd heard her. She glanced down between them as he guided his cock to her entrance. At the first nudge of the head against her flesh, she jumped, even though she'd expected it.

"Shh," he soothed, rubbing the tip back and forth through her folds, slickening himself in her wet heat.

She moaned when he bumped her clit, and nearly bowed off the bed when he circled the flared crown around the nerve-packed nub. When he pressed the head against her again, she whimpered, needing him to enter and ease the ache he'd created deep inside her. He didn't make her wait.

Oh. *God*. The burn. The stretch. The bite of pain that mingled so closely with pleasure, she couldn't decipher the blurred tangle of it. Like he vowed, he didn't stop his relentless surge forward. He burrowed past resistive muscles, taking, claiming, branding. She released a long, low, greedy groan, clinging to him as he carried her along on an erotic ride she couldn't have possibly prepared herself for. He filled her and filled her until she almost believed she couldn't take any more of him.

"Yeah, you can," he assured her. Had she spoken the thought aloud? She must have, because he leaned back on his knees and palmed her thighs, spreading them wider, pushing them back and higher. "Fuck." He groaned as he sank deeper, staring at the place where he penetrated her. "So beautiful how your pussy opens up for me, sucking me in, squeezing me. A little more, sweetheart. A little more." He shifted her hips, angling her, and with one more thrust of his hips, was fully seated inside her.

She writhed beneath him, trying to get away....trying to get closer. Lust had grabbed her in its teeth, ravaged her, tossed her back and forth like a rag doll. She couldn't think past the pleasure and pain that seemed to tear her in two and stitch her back together as this new, wild, carnal creature.

Ciaran fell over her, his palms bracketing either side of her shoulders. "That's it, baby. Ride my dick. Use me to get there." He loosed a soft chuckle. "Take it."

She didn't need his urging. Locking her heels behind his

back and digging her nails into his shoulders, she bucked and undulated underneath him, crying out his name, demanding he move, demanding he fuck her.

"Dammit," he growled, and she swore she could feel the snap of his control. He proceeded to ride her hard, his hips slamming down, plunging into her over and over. And she rose to meet every pounding drive. He gripped her behind the knees, shoving her legs wider and toward her chest and God, dug deeper, rocking higher inside her. He didn't give her any mercy. And she didn't want any.

Their harsh breaths, their groans, her whimpers, the slap of sweat-dampened flesh, the wet suction of his cock withdrawing and burying inside her—it filled the air, the symphony of dirty, rough sex. She twisted in his grip, grasping for the orgasm that loomed just within reach.

"Ciaran," she cried, begged. "Please. I need..." she breathed, gasped, unable to finish the plea. But she didn't need to. He dipped his hand between them, slid his thumb over her clit, once, twice. Thrust, and hit a place she hadn't known existed deep and high within her.

And she imploded. Detonated from inside out. This orgasm was harsher, more cataclysmic than its predecessor. Darkness closed in on her, winking at her, even as she continued to shudder and quake as Ciaran rode her into the mattress, extending the rapture, shattering her in pieces. Dimly, she heard his muted growl and hoarse roar. Felt him stiffen over top her. Savored the pulse of his cock within her spasming sex.

Slowly, the black veil shrouding her senses ebbed, receded. She cataloged the tiny aftershocks still rippling in her core, noted the heaviness of Ciaran's body on top of her, cherished the hot expulsions of his breath against her neck.

Minutes—an eternity—passed as their bodies cooled, relaxed. Silence crept in, and so did cold reality and the inevitable doubts.

She closed her eyes, trying to hold on to the rapidly fading, sensual lethargy. No, dammit. She didn't want to think. Didn't want to see the recriminations and regret in his face. God knows, she hated to see that...

The vibration of a cell phone on the bedside table seemed discordant and deafening in the suffocating quiet. Carefully, Ciaran eased out of her. And in spite of the whirlwind of thoughts rioting through her head, she bit her lip, moaned as her muscles reluctantly released his flesh. Her lashes lifted, and she caught the sexual glint in his gaze and the firming of his mouth before he turned away from her and snatched up the phone.

"Yeah," he said, voice brusque, so unlike the sensual, lazy tones of moments earlier. "You're kidding," he barked, tension entering his body and any semblance of the fierce, focused lover from moments ago evaporated. "Shit. We're leaving now. We'll be there in a few hours."

He tossed the phone on the bed and got to his feet. In seconds, he'd pulled on his pants and shrugged into his shirt.

"You need to get dressed," he said, no traces of warmth remaining in his face or voice. Suddenly, an inexplicable cold crept through her body, and the modesty that had been missing before made its presence known in full force. She sat up, folding her arms over her breasts, crossing her legs. Hiding from him and maybe from the unknown words he would utter next. "We have to leave and head back to Boston."

"What's wrong?" she whispered, searching the floor for her discarded clothes.

"That was Maddox. The surveillance team we had on your house just caught someone trying to break in." He paused, and she shivered as his expression hardened, transforming him into the lethal ex-DEA agent and security specialist. "It was Drake Morriston."

Chapter Fifteen

Ciaran pulled his SUV outside the District A-1 station of the Boston Police Department. Even at nearly ten o'clock at night, the station teemed with life. As the station that served the downtown business district, Financial District, Charlestown, North End, Beacon Hill, and Bay Village, where Sloane lived, this place was never really quiet.

He hated bringing Sloane here; he hated that she had a reason to be here. He glanced to the passenger side where she sat, back as straight as a poker, fingers clenched together in her lap, the cool reserved mask firmly in place. She stared straight ahead through the windshield, and a casual person would presume she was composed and calm. And that person would be mistaken. Ciaran had only known Sloane for a week—damn, had the engagement party only been last Friday?—but he could decipher the tell-tale signs signaling stress. The flattening of her pouty lips. The slightly elevated rhythm of her breathing. The pale knuckles from the tight clasp of her hands. He lifted his arm, almost reached out to her. But at the last second, he lowered it. Hell, hadn't he *touched* her enough tonight?

No. The answer was immediate, loud, vehement inside his head. Even now he could still taste her kiss, could feel the sensual abrasion of her pebbled nipples grazing his palms, pressing against his tongue. He could hear her plaintive whimpers and moans in his ears…could sense the chokehold of her tight sex on his cock. His heart thudded in his chest, and that quick need thickened his blood, pounded in his dick. That kind of pleasure was mind-blowing.

Worse. That kind of forgetfulness was addictive.

He didn't deserve the gift of forgetfulness. He should *always* remember.

Briefly closing his eyes, he inhaled a deep breath, grabbing for his control. Desperate, he grappled for an image of blank eyes, blood, and pain. The consequences of losing focus, of not maintaining control at all times. How the hell he could disregard that, or allow himself to ignore it for one second, he couldn't explain. Couldn't reason or rationalize.

He'd fucked up.

But he had to try to undo the damage. She'd already been attacked on his watch. And now, as he prepared to walk her into this station to possibly face the person at the helm of this coordinated assault, he couldn't afford to think about how good—no, goddamn amazing—the sex had been. He had her life to protect.

That was his number one, his *only*, priority and purpose.

"Ready?" He palmed his car keys, his hand on the handle. She nodded, and he pushed the door open. "Okay, wait while I come around to get you."

Again, she nodded. Seconds later, they headed toward the station, his hand pressed to her back as he scanned the parking lot and surrounding area out of habit. Just because they were at a police station didn't mean shit. Hell, the building was full of criminals.

"Hey, Ciaran." The tall, broad-shouldered man straightened from his lean against the stair railing. "You made good time."

Ciaran shrugged a shoulder. He'd made the four-and-a-half-hour drive in a little under four, anxious to get to the station before they released Drake Morriston. Because Ciaran didn't doubt the little shit would be released. After all, he was a rich, well-connected little shit.

"Tristan, this is Sloane Barrett." Turning to Sloane, he waved a hand toward his friend and new employee of GDG Security. "Sloane, this is Tristan Scott. He works with us."

Tristan nodded. "Nice to meet you, Ms. Barrett."

"Sloane," she corrected. "It's nice to meet you, too. And thank you for calling us about"—she paused, and the tremble that quivered through her vibrated against Ciaran's palm—"Drake."

Ciaran shifted closer to her, silently offering his body for protection and heat. The temperature had fallen to the mid-seventies, and in her haste to leave, she'd neglected to grab a sweater. Tristan glanced from her to him. Though he didn't say anything, Ciaran knew the ex-cop hadn't missed the gesture.

"We should go in. They're questioning him now. I had to cash in some favors, but they've agreed to let us watch the interrogation," Tristan said, pulling open the station door, and Ciaran and Sloane followed.

Ciaran could only imagine the price in pride Tristan must've paid to call in those favors. Just three months ago, his friend had been a detective on the Boston police force at this very station. But he'd quit after Fallon and Shane had almost been killed, and his fiancée had been implicated in aiding the murderer after them. Returning here, facing the men he'd served with, had to be difficult, even though Tristan had been blameless. Didn't matter, the other man wore his guilt like a shroud.

About ten minutes passed before Tristan, Ciaran, and Sloane stood in a small room with recording equipment and monitors. With the three of them and two more detectives packed into the room, it was crowded and quickly grew hot. But the comfort was negligible. Every bit of his attention belonged to the monitor and his first glimpse of Drake Morriston.

The kid lounged in the uncomfortable-looking folding chair as if he were at a party instead of hemmed up in an interrogation room. Handsome, well-dressed, and even through the monitor he contained an entitled air that rubbed Ciaran raw.

"The smug little bastard hasn't copped to anything," Detective Carson, an older black man with salt-and-pepper hair and a build like a bull, muttered. "Your people caught him red-handed with a damn lock-picking kit, and still he denies it. Excuse me, ma'am," he apologized with a glance toward Sloane. "It's like he's playing with us. He keeps hinting he should ask for an attorney, but won't do it. Like he's enjoying this."

"He probably is," Sloane murmured, staring at the screen. "He's arrogant."

Detective Carson snorted. "Don't we know it. Our guy just went back in there with the IP address info and the video footage from the Internet café. We may not be able to use that in court, but Morriston doesn't know that. We'll see what he does once he's confronted with it."

Ciaran nodded. Tristan had already informed him that Maddox had provided the police with the footage from the café video feed. Because of the cameras being installed without the café's permission, chain of custody, and other regulations and procedures, the evidence could never be used in court against Drake. One of the perks about the private sector. They didn't have all the red tape public servants did.

From experience, Ciaran knew how strangling they could be, even if they were necessary.

"I don't know how many times I have to explain it, Officer. Oops, I mean, Detective." Drake grinned, insolence dripping from the gesture. "I was just going by my former teacher's home to see if she was okay since I'd heard about the troubles she'd been having. I always have the kit on me in case I lock myself out of my house."

What ridiculous bullshit.

"And how did you hear about her 'troubles' again?" the detective in the interrogation room asked, leaning back in his chair. Tristan had mentioned his name was Lawson.

"Here and there. Gossip. Nothing stays secret in our circle very long." The kid's tone implied the detective couldn't understand considering he obviously wasn't included in Drake's "circle."

"And so you were just dropping by? Even though you've left threatening voicemails on her phone, and your parents have tried to have her fired? You just stopped by her house unannounced because you care."

"Exactly, Officer." Drake spread his hands wide, palms up. "And granted, I might have been upset when I left the voicemail, but that's all. There's a big step between a message and vandalism and breaking and entering."

"Jesus Christ, can you believe this kid?" Detective Paul, the other detective in the room with Ciaran and Sloane, snarled.

Yeah, he could, Ciaran almost said. Money, privilege, and no morals were a toxic mix.

"You might be right about that," Lawson continued, cocking his head to the side as if really considering Drake's point. "But what about harassing emails and phone calls. That's not a far leap at all, is it?"

Drake smirked. "I don't know what you're talking about,

Officer."

The detective didn't fall for the bait. "You don't?"

"Nope."

The detective reached into the pocket of his suit jacket and set a small device on the table. One of the newer models of the handheld cameras and recorders GDG employed.

"Funny," Lawson mused, pressing a button on the camera and tilting it toward the kid. "This sure does look like you at this computer in the internet café. And since you seem to know about coincidences, you'll certainly appreciate this one. The emails that were sent to Ms. Barrett originated from the IP address of the computer you're on. At that specific time. And the café's records show you signing in for this particular computer. What are the odds, Drake?"

Shock flickered in the kid's face before his smirk made an appearance. "That doesn't prove anything."

"But this is the thing about coincidences, Drake," Lawson drawled. "One, like you showing up to your teacher's house with a burglary kit in hand is serendipity. Two, like you sitting at the same computer at the same time those emails were sent is dicey. Three, like the convenience store footage of you buying a burner phone from the same store where the cell that those late-night calls originated from is guilty as hell." Drake opened his mouth to interrupt, but the detective shot up a hand, forestalling him. "Now, we can play this as an asshole kid who's mad at his teacher and decided to play a prank and took it too far. Or we can look at this as an eighteen-year-old adult stalking, assaulting, and terrorizing a woman. Which one is it gonna be, Drake?" Lawson leaned forward, a mean, hard as flint note entering his voice.

Drake froze, and maybe the full implication of the detective's accusations penetrated that smug exterior and thick head, because he thrust his fingers through his hair, his demeanor cracking for the first time. Huffing out a breath, he crossed his arms, a scowl darkening his brow.

"Okay, dammit. I sent the emails and called her. But I was just playing, letting her know she can't treat me like shit. But I didn't break into her house. Yeah, I was going to go in tonight and throw some things around, but I didn't do it the first time. And I don't know shit about an assault. That's all I'm saying. Get me my attorney."

And that was that.

Chapter Sixteen

"Do you believe him?" Sloane's soft question halted Ciaran, his arm in the air. The four words were the first she'd spoken in the half hour since they'd left the police station and arrived at Ciaran's condominium. Arms crossed, her hands clutching her elbows, she appeared younger, so vulnerable. The simple ponytail, sleeveless shirt, and jeans solidified the impression of bruised innocence.

After a second, he switched on the lamp, bathing the living room of his Charlestown condo in a soft, golden glow. The open floor plan with rooms that flowed into one another, couches, tables, and flat screen that shouted Man Cave didn't near the luxury of her parents' home, but it suited him. "You didn't get a chance to eat. Are you hungry?"

He didn't answer her question...yet. She seemed two seconds away from crashing, and discussing the topic of Drake Morriston, his crimes, and the threat still unresolved would probably speed up that timeline.

"No," she murmured, moving farther into the room. "But I need you to answer my question and stop treating me like

I'm about to break. I'm not fragile, Ciaran."

Hell, he knew that…intimately. But damn if he didn't want her to endure any more ugliness tonight. Tomorrow they would head back to the Hamptons. That would be soon enough. Should be. Obviously, Sloane felt differently.

"All right." He shoved his hands in the front pockets of his pants. "I do believe him. Unfortunately." Because he'd hoped all this would end tonight. Drake Morriston was immature, spoiled, and a criminal-in-the-making, but he wasn't sophisticated enough to coordinate the assaults. "His whole demeanor changed when confronted with that video. And why admit to that and not the rest of it? He seemed justified in terrorizing you. If he'd committed the attempted kidnappings and assaults, he would've blamed you for it. Add in, an idiot isn't behind the rest of these crimes. An amateur, maybe. But not an idiot. And that kid is a flaming idiot."

Her shoulders sagged like a deflated balloon, and for several seconds she seemed to curl in on herself. But only for seconds. Before he could make a move in her direction, she straightened, tilted her chin up, and dropped her arms to her sides.

"Okay," she said, the same strength in her body coloring her voice. "What now? Where do we go from here?"

"The two who tried to kidnap you at the school are still in custody. The police are tracking their calls and visiting logs. Tristan has a friend who promised to let him know who they call and shows up to see them. We're looking into the records and history of your co-workers. We've even added your brother-in-law to the list."

Her eyebrow hiked up. "Greg? Why?"

He shrugged. "You said your sister is divorcing him. This could be retaliation. I've seen more far-fetched reasons. It doesn't matter if the person's motives don't make sense to us. All that matters is that they make sense to the perp."

A beat of silence passed where she rubbed her arms, her attention focused on the bank of windows. "I wanted it to be him," she admitted. "When we left the house, I hoped all this would end tonight."

"I did, too." His fingers curled into fists inside his pockets, battling the urge to circle her arms and pull her close. "At least if we went back to your parents tomorrow with the truth of what's been going on, your mother might not rain down the holy hell I saw in her eyes," he teased.

A ghost of a smile touched her lips, then disappeared. "True." Sighing, she smoothed a hand over her hair. "I need a shower. Is it okay if…"

Her voice trailed off as the memories of why they both would need a shower plummeted in the room, as tactile and real as the furniture between them. Neither had had time since Maddox's call had come before the sweat had dried on their skin. Tension throbbed like a heartbeat, a subject they couldn't ignore, but neither wanted to address.

What the fuck could he say without sounding like a grade-A douche? *Sloane, you are the sexiest, hottest women I've ever met, and the sex damn near rendered me blind and deaf, but it was a mistake. One we can't repeat. Sorry.* Yeah, douche walking.

It was the *why* of the mistake. He'd told himself from the moment she'd walked into GDG's offices that he couldn't touch her, couldn't have her. The last time he'd allowed his feelings, his needs interfere with his training, the woman he'd loved had lost her life.

Sam didn't have seconds or minutes. She didn't have a life any longer. While he, who'd caused her life to be so viciously and violently snatched, drew breath, existed. If every moment of his life was devoted to paying for his terrible mistake, then he would pay that price.

And he couldn't allow the temporary oblivion he found in

Sloane's body make him forget that. Because it was temporary. Hell, he couldn't even sleep next to a woman.

Not as long as he continued to think of that intimate place beside him as belonging to Sam.

And how screwed up was that? Holding the spot for a dead woman who would never return like a fucking shrine.

Yeah, he could try to explain all this to Sloane. Then watch as she tried to get as far from him as possible, placing herself in even more danger.

Not going to happen.

"Of course it's okay," he said, leading the way down the hall. The condo boasted three bedrooms, one of which he'd turned into a home office. He pushed the door open to the guest room. "You can sleep in here. The bathroom is across the hall. I'll leave a T-shirt and sweatpants out on the bed for you to sleep in. They'll be big, but…"

"Thank you." She entered the bathroom and quietly shut the door behind her. He stood and stared at the door for several moments, guilt pressing down on his chest like a dumbbell without a spotter to relieve it. The interrogation wasn't the only thing culpable for the tired wariness on her face. "Jesus," he muttered, scrubbing a hand down his face and stalking farther down the corridor to his bedroom.

After depositing the clothes he'd promised on her temporary bed, he jumped in the shower in the bathroom off his room and changed into a clean T-shirt and jeans. When he heard the guest room door open, he already had a cup of coffee waiting for Sloane on the kitchen bar that separated and connected the dining room.

She appeared on the opposite side of the bar, and he paused, his mug halfway to his mouth. Scrubbed free of makeup with his clothes baggy on her tall, curvaceous build, the impression he had of her earlier returned full force. Young. Vulnerable. Not fragile, but strength that had taken a beaten and needed time to recharge, to become indomitable again. Because that's how he saw her, even though she couldn't perceive it in herself...yet.

Sloane didn't see a lot of things in herself. Such as her innate sensuality that was as natural as her dark hair and brilliant eyes. Though his shirt hung off her shoulders, the firm thrust of her breasts were unmistakable, the feminine flare of her hips drew his gaze as did the alluring sway when she walked. A man had to be dickless, gay, or dead to not notice her, be tempted by her. And he questioned the first two.

"Thank you." She picked up her coffee, sipped, and hummed in appreciation, the pleasure in the sound reminiscent of the moan she made when he thrust a finger inside her.

Shit. His fingers clenched around his cup, and he completed the coffee's journey to his mouth. The dark brew scalded his tongue, and he welcomed the burn. It distracted his mind from the other burn in his body.

"I was thinking about not returning to Southampton tomorrow, and staying here in town," Sloane said, setting her drink on the bar top.

"That's not going to stop the attacks." As this person had proven, they would follow her.

"I know," she agreed. "But with me gone, the threats are removed from my family."

"And you'll also miss out on their anniversary party," he added, frowning. "Sloane, don't allow this person to start dictating your life. Caution and awareness are smart, but once you begin to live like a prisoner with fear as your warden, he wins."

"I am being cautious," she insisted. "And practical. If I stay in Boston, the responsibility of guarding me isn't all on you. There would be a team, and you could have your life back, too."

Ciaran stared at her, hearing everything she hadn't said.

"Say it, Sloane," he ordered, voice quiet.

She gave him one of her patented duchess smiles, cool, aloof. It lit his temper like a match to dry kindling. "When you took on this assignment, you didn't expect complications."

"Complications being sex," he stated.

"Complications being sex with the person you're charged with protecting. You can't exactly walk away from me, can you? Keep your distance? Leave afterward?" She studied him, the smile fading and leaving a sadness that scraped at his skin. "Who was she?" she murmured.

He flinched before he could control the reaction. "What?"

"You didn't think I'd put it together?" She shook her head, wearing that same sad expression. "I don't believe you are a man who can't love or who doesn't want it. Just the opposite. I think you're one of those who love hard…and once. So much that even after four years you can't sleep next to a woman. Who was she?"

Fuck. He couldn't have this conversation with her. The need to escape crawled over him like a hundred marching ants.

"Sloane." He pushed away from the bar and circled it. "We're not going to do this. Not tonight."

"Did she leave you?" she pressed as if she hadn't heard his warning.

"She's dead," he snapped.

Shock widened her eyes, parted her lips for the soft gasp that echoed in the room. Shit. He hadn't meant to say anything, hadn't meant to stay in the goddamn room. Sam, their relationship, her death, getting shot…the images rolled through his mind, tumbling over each other as if they were in a race to flash before his eyes first. To remind him of the woman he'd loved, the grief of loss, the agony of failing.

Before Sloane, he could compartmentalize the emotions, not let them interfere with his job, his daily life. But she had entered his life, and the memories, the fear, guilt, and pain refused to remain contained. She poked and aggravated the wounds, made him fucking *feel*.

He flexed and straightened his fingers, flexed and straightened. As if reaching for something, then pulling back at the last moment. As if craving something, then repudiating himself for the need.

He dragged both hands over his head. *Get away. Leave.* Before he did something they would both regret...again. Too much roiled and spun inside him like a tornado sweeping up everything in its path and spewing them out in utter disarray and chaos. That's what he was right now, an emotional natural disaster.

Pivoting on his heel, he stalked toward the dining room entrance. If he stayed in this room with her, she would be his next casualty.

"I'm sorry, Ciaran."

Her whisper halted him mid-step. *Keep going, keep walking*, the tattered remnants of his control shouted. But he slowly turned, faced the woman who he'd seen as his chance at absolution and had become his ultimate test, his temptation. His redemption.

"For?" he asked, the restraints on his discipline resembling a quickly unraveling rope.

"For hurting you. I should've left it alone," she whispered.

"Yeah, you should've," he growled, reclaiming the distance he'd placed between them with deliberate, long strides. He didn't stop until he caged her against the bar, slapping his palms down on either side of her hips. Lowering his head, he studied her plump, bare mouth, the faint smattering of golden freckles across the bridge of her nose and cheekbones, and last, her densely lashed emerald eyes. "You want to make it better, duchess?"

Even as he drawled the words, he cringed inside. She

didn't deserve to be the whipping boy for his anger, guilt, and pain. Others had committed the same sin against her, and shame that he could now count himself among that number clawed at his chest. Dammit—

A soft palm cupped his face, and he shuddered at the gentle touch. Rage at his offensive question didn't harden her gaze. Instead, understanding, desire, and something else he couldn't identify warmed her gaze.

"Is that what you want?" She brushed the pad of her thumb over his bottom lip.

He shook his head. Taking advantage of her selflessness, releasing his confusion and emotions on her, her body? No, he couldn't do that, couldn't ask that of her. "Yes," he rasped.

She rose on tip-toe, erasing the last centimeters separating them, and, burying her fingers in his hair, covered his mouth with hers. For a moment, he didn't respond, but closed his eyes and reveled in the sensual glide of her lips, the shy but needy sweep of her tongue, the quickening of her breath. But just for a moment.

With a groan, he opened his mouth wider, snagged control of the kiss, delved harder, deeper into her. Their tongues tangled in an erotic duel, both seeking and battling for dominance. A quiet pressing of mouths erupted into a clash for carnal ground. He licked, sucked, plunged, and she parried and thrusted, meeting him, challenging him, seducing him. Her teeth sank into his bottom lip, tugged, and he growled at the nip of pain, loving it.

Grasping her waist, he hoisted her on top of the bar and moved between her thighs. But her palms slapped on his chest, preventing him from crowding closer.

"Wait," she breathed with an underlying vein of steel. He paused, his chest rising and falling, his cock throbbing with the need to ride the slick V between her legs. Before he could ask what was wrong, she inched down, landing on her feet and slipping around him. Like invisible strings connected them, he turned, already reaching for her. But she evaded him, circling his wrists and lowering his arms to his sides. "This is for you."

And she slid to the floor.

Oh. Fuck.

A shiver quaked through him. "Sweetheart, you don't…"

She shook her head, her fingers already busy at the front of his jeans. "I want to. I've dreamed about it. Let me," she said.

Like he would deny her—deny himself, the selfish bastard he was—this pleasure. How many times had he imagined her kneeling before him, her eyes, dark with arousal, fixed on him, her hands unbuttoning his pants? Her pretty lips parting for his cock? Too many to count. And now… Only one thing was missing.

He tugged on her ponytail. "Take it out."

He didn't trust himself to remove the band from her hair. With his big fingers and greedy need, he would make a mess of it and probably hurt her. She complied, abandoning his zipper to remove the restriction on the thick, heavy strands he had developed a secret fetish for.

"Let me," he murmured after she tossed the band aside. With a groan, he dug his fingers into her long, dark hair, the strands falling over his hands and wrapping around his wrists like silken cuffs. He drew it forward, over her shoulders, then contradicted himself by clutching the locks in a fist at the back of her head. As much as he loved tangling his fingers in her hair, he couldn't have anything hinder his view of this beautiful, sexy woman taking his cock into her mouth for the first time.

As if perceiving his thoughts, she lowered his zipper, the metallic sound reverberating in the air like an electrical current. And when she reached inside his jeans and fisted his cock, the current sizzled through him, replacing blood and filling him with static. Moans rose in the room. Hers. His. A sensual blending of the two, impossible to separate.

She squeezed him. Then she released him, and he almost begged her to put her hand back on his dick, to finish what she'd started. But when she tugged his pants lower, giving herself more access to him, he thanked God. Which seemed damn near sacrilegious, but he couldn't bring himself to care. Not when her fingers were wrapping around his heavy, aching flesh once more, and the other hand was freeing his balls and cupping them.

He'd once told her that he wanted to corrupt her. How ironic that now she was the one doing the corrupting. Forever changing him so he would never think of this act without picturing her, on her knees, her regal, slim hands pumping his cock as she stared at him with hungry eyes. Fuck, he didn't think he could allow a woman to touch him like this again. Not after this. Not after her.

"Take me, duchess," he pleaded, voice rough with lust, with need. "Suck me deep into this pretty mouth like I've fantasized about." He trailed his fingertips along her jaw, chin, the corners of her mouth. "Make it better," he whispered.

Her lashes fluttered along her cheekbones as she arrowed his cock down and toward her mouth. The breath trapped in his lungs as she brushed a kiss along the head, her lips becoming glossy with the pre-cum already beading at the slit. Christ, he tightened his grip on her hair. The tip was swollen, ruddy, aching to be introduced to the hot, moist depths of her mouth.

"Don't tease me, duchess," he said, covering her hand with his so they both gave his dick a couple of lush pumps. He gritted his teeth against the gut-tearing pleasure. "Please."

God. That first push into her wet heat—not unlike first penetrating her sex. He closed his eyes, but immediately opened them again, not wanting to miss a moment. His cock disappeared inside, her mouth spread wide as she took more and more of his length. On a long, low moan, she withdrew, her tongue bathing the underside, polishing the tip. She swallowed him down again, her puffy lips bumping her fist. Another sound of greed—this one a hum—vibrated over his flesh. Pink stained her cheeks, desire gleamed in her hooded eyes. She was *loving* it.

She set up an enthusiastic, healthy suck. Not skilled, not rhythmic. And all the more beautiful and perfect because of it. His other hand joined the first in her hair, held her head steady.

"Please," he murmured, asking for permission as he nudged her lips. She opened for him, sweetly, willingly, and let him sink inside. "Jesus, that's pretty. Open up wider for me, Sloane." He fucked her mouth, loving the sight of him shuttling in and out, of her lips stretched to accommodate him. And God, did she accommodate him, give to him. Let him take his fill.

His cockhead bumped the back of her throat, and she gagged. He retreated, crooning to her. A fierce pride and blast of possessiveness that could probably be tracked to the caveman surged within him. His. No man had ever breached her throat before. He was the first. *And the last*, that until-now-repressed caveman snarled. But the few brain cells that hadn't evacuated his brain for his dick, shied away from that thought. Instead, he rubbed the pad of his thumb along the front of her throat, soothing her.

"Relax for me, duchess. Breathe through your nose, and let me in," he instructed continuing his caress of her neck, willing her to trust him not to hurt her. Though his body screamed at him to thrust, to take, he waited. And when she uncurled her fingers from around his cock and flattened both palms on his thighs, he couldn't contain his growl of relief, of arousal, of gratitude.

Deliberately, he glided forward along her tongue, his pace unhurried. And damn, he didn't want to rush this—not this first for her, not the pleasure for both of them. When he bumped the channel to her throat this time, she didn't fight him. Soft exhalations escaped her nose as she permitted him entrance to the narrow opening.

Lust, need, hunger—there weren't any words to describe the power and ecstasy that ripped down his spine, that tightened his balls to the point of pain. *Again*. She nodded, and hell, he must've been so caught up, he'd uttered the word aloud. She took him again. And again. Jesus, she was going to kill him. But could you kill a willing sacrifice?

He couldn't last. The need crackling through him, gathering strength and speed with each race up and down his body wouldn't allow this head-long plummet into rapture last. He cupped her jaw…groaned when her mouth tightened around his flesh in an eye-crossing suck.

"Sweetheart, I'm too close," he rasped. "I'm about to come," he groaned, withdrawing, "so fucking hard. But I don't want to come here. I want to be deep in your pussy, drowning in it when I do. But first…"

Clasping her shoulders, he dragged her to her feet and yanked the sweatpants down her legs. In seconds, he'd grabbed her waist, lifted her to the bar again, and knelt between her thighs. Spreading her wide before him, he pressed his lips to the crease that connected her torso and legs.

"Ciaran." Sloane clutched his hair, tugged on it, but at the same time tried to move his face away from the swollen, wet sex just a breath away. "I don't…this doesn't…"

Shoving aside the need to dive into her, he flicked a look up, meeting her flushed face and the uncertainty that shimmered through the desire in her eyes. That hint of insecurity yanked at his heart. Someone as sexy and gorgeous as this woman should never suffer a moment of doubt about her sexuality. She was everything feminine, beautiful, and so selfless.

Not releasing her from his scrutiny, he traced her slit, and gathered the evidence of her desire that glistened on her folds. Without hesitation, he slipped the finger in his mouth and sucked it clean. Her taste—fresh, tangy, and her—exploded on his tongue like the rarest treat. God, he craved more than this sample. He wanted to dine, to feast on her. He'd wanted it from the moment he first saw her.

"You're so pretty here," he praised, gently circling her clit. She emitted a whimper, her teeth sinking into her bottom lip. "Shh," he hushed, gripping her hip with one hand to control the reflexive buck. "So soft." He caressed a plump fold. "So sweet." He licked a path from the top of her sex to the fluttering, tiny entrance of her core. "Hmm. Addictive."

Then he devoured her.

Her cries and pleas rained down on him as he lapped, sucked, stroked, and savored. He couldn't get enough of her. Stabbing at her clit with the tip of his tongue before soothing the pulsing nub with careful, slow flicks. He didn't leave an inch of her undiscovered, dined on her. And when he thrust two fingers inside her, more of her delicious cream was his reward. That, and the orgasm so strong, he wouldn't be surprised if tomorrow his skin boasted bruises from the tight clamp of her muscles. She came for him, wept for him, and he reveled in it.

The shudders hadn't ceased wracking her body before he ripped his wallet from his back pocket, removed a condom, and sheathed himself. With movements roughened by the lust writhing inside him like a living thing, he jerked his T-shirt over her head, baring her completely to his hungry gaze. Cupping her hips, he dragged her forward until her ass was balanced on the bar's edge.

"Hold on to me," he ordered, his tone harsher than he

intended. But the need to get inside her… "Tight, sweetheart." As soon as her arms encircled his neck, he plunged inside her, burying himself inside her clenching, wet heat. "Fuck," he rasped, pressing his face to her wild tumble of hair. "You're so goddamn good. I can't get—" He ground his teeth together, trapping the admission that would reveal too much. Would doom him. But he couldn't stop them from rebounding against his skull like a ping-pong ball. *I can't get enough of you.*

Pulling from her grasping core was torture, driving back in was masochistic. Her hot flesh sucked his cock, coaxing him deeper, higher with every thrust. Hard, short digs. Slow, long strokes. Each hurtled him toward the oblivion he craved— the oblivion he feared. But as he pounded into her…as she unwound her arms, planted them behind her and arched, offering him more of herself, he didn't think of guilt, shame, or penance. As his lips closed over a rigid nipple, and he rolled the tip on his tongue before drawing on it, he didn't think at all. She consumed him. He filled her body, but she filled his head, his senses. Only her. Only Sloane.

Her plaintive whispers bathed his ear, her convulsive trembles vibrated against his body. Reaching between them, he rubbed her clit, not gentle, because she didn't want gentle. This fucking wasn't gentle but hungry, fierce, wild. She writhed against him, demanding release. And he acquiesced. Her scream echoed in the room as her slick walls clamped down on him, rippling around him. She shook with the power of her orgasm, and he rode her through it until her cries softened to whimpers.

Only then did he let himself go. Only then did he welcome the dark, knowing she would be waiting for him on the other side.

"Was she an agent, too?"

Ciaran rested his head against the pillow, staring up at the ceiling. His palm paused mid-stroke over Sloane's sweat-slickened back as her question seemed to boom and reverberate in the living room like a shout in a cave.

Sex on the bar had been soon followed by sex in his bedroom. She'd ridden them both to orgasm, and the bone-weary lethargy that was a consequence of amazing sex had just fallen over him when her soft question had plummeted into the room like a boulder in a still pool. Tension rippled outward in ever widening circles.

He closed his eyes, as if that could shut out the imminent conversation. But he couldn't reject her like that. Sloane wouldn't have broached the subject out of morbid curiosity—she had too big of a heart, was too sensitive to cause him pain just to pry. And the truth was, he owed her answers. He'd just been balls-deep inside her body but couldn't bring himself to rise yet because he knew—he *knew*—he wouldn't be able to stay here, lying down beside her.

With the other women, he'd had no desire to sleep with them. But her? He craved it. Which made the desire even more of a betrayal to the woman he'd loved and let down in the most devastating and final way possible.

Sloane shifted, as if about to slide off his chest and thighs, but he pressed his palm harder against her spine, halting the movement. After several seconds, she relaxed, her body curling into his once more, the warm puffs of her breath tickling the damp skin of his neck.

"No. She was a CI, a criminal informant," he murmured into the shadowed darkness. "I didn't know it when we first met at a local dive bar four years ago. I heard her laugh before I even saw her. The sound of it...the sheer joy of it filled a room. And when I turned around? Beautiful. Hair the color of dark fire, a smile that was contagious, and she was so sweet.

Samantha Genoa, although she only responded to Sam." He huffed a soft chuckled at her remembered stubbornness. "For the first time in my life, I'd fallen hard for a woman. And months later, when she confessed why she never brought me home to meet her family, it was too late. I'd already given my heart to her—the niece of a *capo* in the Lucchese crime family."

He could still feel the shock and sickness that had rolled through him when she'd confessed the truth. "At first I'd felt so betrayed, angry, disillusioned. I was in law enforcement, for God's sake, and she'd held back something so important from me, jeopardizing my career, my life. But then she admitted she was also a criminal informant for the FBI. That's when fear for her safety trumped my anger over her secrets. Somehow I convinced Sam to enter Witness Protection, to trust the system—and me—to protect her and offer her a fresh start where we could leave New York and be together."

But some dreams belonged only in the darkest hours of night with hushed lovers' talk and soft embraces. He swallowed the lump that rose in his throat, strangling him for a moment. He tightened his arm around Sloane, as if grounding himself in the present even as he slipped further into the past. The darkest, most painful, bloodiest moments of his past.

"A week after she entered the program, I received a call from the FBI agent on Sam's case. The location had been compromised. Unknown assailants had killed the US Marshals on duty, and the agent believed Sam had been taken since her body hadn't been located at the scene. As soon as I ended the call, I strapped on my weapon and headed to Queens, radioing for backup along the way. Sam had confided in me about a hangout in the Queens neighborhood of Ozone Park that she hadn't mentioned to the FBI. She'd warned me that if something happened to her, look there, because the backroom had a notorious—and bloody—reputation within the family."

He paused, his breathing harsh in the heavy silence. Only the gentle caress to his jaw and cheek allowed him to continue.

"I-I found her there. She died... murdered. Right in front of me with a gunshot to the head. And I couldn't do a damn thing to stop it."

Her fingers brushed the two scars on his chest where Sam's murderers had shot him, almost killing him, too.

"Yes," he rasped. "I was shot, too. Except back-up reached me in time. They did for me what I couldn't do for her. I failed her. I urged her to go into Witness Protection, to trust me. I promised her I wouldn't let anything happen to her. And I failed to save the life of the woman I loved."

A deep quiet suffused the room as his voice trailed off. At some point he'd slid his hand into her hair, tangled the strands around his fingers and held on as if she were his anchor.

"I think Samantha was a very lucky woman to have your love." A feather-light caress brushed his jaw. "Not many women have men willing to come to their rescue. To sacrifice their lives for theirs."

"I didn't rescue her. I didn't give my life for hers," he objected, voice hoarse with the pain and grief that never failed to swarm him when he thought on the darkest period of his life. *Thought on*, not spoke. Because aside from a drunken night about a year after he'd left the DEA, and Shane had scraped Ciaran off his bedroom floor, Ciaran hadn't talked about Sam, her death, or being shot. "She stared right at me, knowing she was going to die. Knowing I wouldn't save her."

A fist of emotion blocked his throat, and he swallowed convulsively.

"Ciaran." A soft palm cradled his face, tipped his head down from the back of the couch so he had no choice but to meet Sloane's tender, but unwavering contemplation. "Maybe she did know she was going to die. No, look at me," she said when he closed his eyes. She gently shook his head, and when he looked up at her again, she rubbed the pad of her thumb over his lip. "She might have known, but she also died knowing she was loved."

"I couldn't—"

"No, you couldn't save her." She brushed a fingertip over the bullet wounds hidden under his tattoos. "But sometimes it's enough for a woman to realize and acknowledge in the deepest part of her heart and soul that she was worth the effort. That come hell or high water, you'll go to bat for her... lay down your life for her. And that's what you did, Ciaran. Why you survived that night, only God knows, but it doesn't negate that she was so precious and necessary you went there to save her. And she died knowing that certainty. Love, not failure."

He stared into her eyes, glimpsed the conviction there. He wanted to feel the same surety, to accept it. Desperately.

"I can tell you don't believe me." She swept a kiss across his mouth. "But that's okay." Another kiss. "I'll believe for both of us until you get there." And another kiss, longer, deeper, wetter.

He opened wide, letting her take the lead. Letting her convince him to believe.

Letting her begin to heal him.

Ciaran jerked awake, blinking into the darkness, the echo of shouting, gunfire, and cries ringing in his ear. Sweat coated his face, neck, and bare chest. His chest that heaved with rough, deep gasps for breath.

Jesus Christ. He sat up on the couch cushion and scrubbed his palms down his face. It'd been a while since he'd had that dream. No, not dream—a nightmare. Of blood and death. Of the night he'd lost Sam. Only it hadn't been Sam with the gun to her head, fear darkening her eyes. It hadn't been Sam who'd slumped to the floor. It hadn't been Sam he'd failed to save.

It'd been Sloane. Her dark hair even darker, matted with blood and brain matter.

Ciaran moaned, a shiver racking his body like an earthquake. The terror and grief hadn't faded yet, and he tasted both on his tongue, acrid and slick.

Oh God. He couldn't do it again. He couldn't survive it again.

And she died knowing that certainty. Love, not failure.

Sloane's words from earlier rang in his head, growing louder and louder like the shrill whistle of an oncoming train.

She died…she died…

Maybe Sam had gone knowing he loved her. *But she'd died.* Because he hadn't been fast enough. Smart enough. Strong enough. Because he'd been blinded by emotion instead of relying on the training that had been ingrained in him.

And he was repeating the same mistake with Sloane. Again the image from his nightmare flashed across his mind's eye. Another blank stare. Another life snuffed out. Another stain of guilt on his soul.

"Ciaran?"

He lifted his head at the murmur coming from the direction of the living room entrance. For just a second the vision from his dream superimposed itself over Sloane's features, and he flinched, his chest seizing. But then he blinked and the gory image disappeared, leaving her face softened by sleep and clear of blood.

She moved further into the room, but he remained glued to the couch, unable to move. Shit, at this moment, unable to speak.

With a sigh, Sloane sank to the love seat across from the sofa he'd been dozing on. The sofa he'd sought after she'd fallen asleep in the bed they'd made love in. Remorse and shame packed into his already crowded chest.

"When Phillip left, and I had to take a good hard look at myself and all that I had allowed, I came to several realizations. One, you teach people how to treat you. Two, if that was love, I can do bad all by myself. And three, I would never allow myself to be controlled again. None of those resolutions were—are—easy, but you were my first real test. Because of the assaults and stalking, I've had to bend and submit when I wanted to tell you to go to hell. When I wanted to run and demand that you don't follow. I've also come to know your heart in these past days. Although you can be harder to read than the Sphinx, you're a man of honor, kindness, humor, and incredible passion."

"Sloane, I—"

But she held up her hand to halt the apology he would have uttered. Apology for what, he didn't exactly know. For the hurt smudging her unwavering gaze? For whatever had woken her and driven her out into the living room?

"Let me finish, please. I feel like I know your heart, Ciaran, but as of tonight, I also know your demons. I hate that you've suffered. Hate that you bear the burden of pain and guilt. Especially over something you had no control over. But I also know I woke up alone in that bed."

He surged to his feet as if propelled. Thrusting his fingers through his hair, he stalked across the room, away from her, away from the shame that had nothing to do with Sam and everything to do with the pain he'd unintentionally inflicted.

No, a voice whispered against his skull. *At least here be honest*. When he'd slid across that mattress and walked out of the bedroom door, a part of him realized what he was doing. Placing distance. Telling her without words that sex was all they had, nothing more. That his quiet confession and unloading of a past he never spoke of didn't mean anything.

He'd been firing his warning shot across her bow, putting her on notice.

And she'd just called him on it.

"Sloane." He turned to face her, his voice hoarse from the nightmare and the confusion cycling inside him. "I made it clear from the beginning what my first priority was. Protecting you, keeping you alive. God knows I wasn't expecting you. I shouldn't have touched you, but I did. I broke my rule about getting involved with a client; I fucked up. Even now I'm fucking up because I want you. But, I can't"—he shook his head, curled his fingers into tight fists—"I can't have a repeat of Sam. I *won't*. Not with you."

"And what about me? What I want? Do my choices factor in at all?"

He clenched his jaw, trapping the "No, not when it comes to this," inside. But he might as well as have said it for the sad comprehension that dawned on her face.

"I can concede to your experience with keeping me safe. But deciding my life for me as if I'm too naive? No. You don't have that right, that power."

"I'm not trying to control—"

"Yes, you are. Even if you think it's for my own good. Even if it's from a well-intentioned place. You're not doing it out of malice or contempt like Phillip. No, yours is from fear of pain, of guilt and shame." She rose, her long hair tumbling over her shoulders and his shirt that concealed her curves from him. "I get that you don't want any involvement with me to distract you from keeping me alive. But if you were honest with yourself, you'd admit it's not just redemption you're looking for. You're afraid. Afraid to feel, to risk loving and losing. To forgive yourself because it would mean living again. Afraid of pain."

"You don't know what you're talking about," he rasped, heart thudding against his sternum. *Stop talking now*, the wounded beast inside of him howled. *I don't want to hear any more.*

"I do. I've been there. Living with Phillip was horrible, but looking at myself after he left was one of the most terrifying things I've ever done. I've lived in fear. Fear of failure, of risking my heart again, of disappointing those I love, of never being enough. It's crippling, but there comes a time when you stop coping and start *being*. You're still coping. By walling yourself off from others. By not letting anyone in but so far… By not sleeping next to a woman."

Her shoulders straightened, and she notched her chin up. The gesture, while proud, couldn't deflect from the pain in her gaze. Pain he'd placed there.

"When I woke up alone, I laid there, staring at the ceiling, beating myself up because I so hoped you would be there when my eyes opened." She briefly closed her eyes. "But then I realized I choose not to let you treat me like the other women you've slept with. I choose to be worth more than a screw that you can easily walk away from. Not for you, but for myself. I'm so sorry for your loss, Ciaran," she whispered. "But you can't let go, and I can't give in."

She turned and on silent, bare feet retraced her steps across the room.

"Sloane," he murmured, and she paused without turning around to look at him. Sadness and regret throbbed inside of him. Sadness, regret, and a yawning, foreboding sense of precious sand slipping through his fingers. "I wish I could be who you need."

"You could," she said softly. "If you chose to be."

She left the room. Left him exactly as he claimed he desired.

Alone.

Chapter Seventeen

Mid-morning sunlight beamed through the windows of Sloane's Hamptons bedroom. At ten o'clock the streams only reached mid-way across the room, but in another couple of hours, the bright sunshine would bathe the west-facing room in its light.

Standing at the window and staring down at the English gardens and considering the direction of the sun prohibited her from thinking about the silent, brooding man in the room. And the pain that crawled through her like a virus.

After their "talk" last night, they'd both risen early—not that she'd gone back to sleep—and returned to the Hamptons. The ride had been quiet, the silence heavy, deafening. What she'd said to him the night before…it'd needed to be said, for herself as well as him. But God, did she regret the distance it'd placed between them. It'd only been a few days since they'd known each other, but the absence of the closeness they'd shared hollowed out a hole in her heart.

Had it only been a few days? So much had happened in that time. She'd faced her ex. She'd been attacked. Her former student had been arrested on stalking charges. And she and Ciaran had become lovers.

The biggest change, though, had been in her. A couple days ago, she'd entered this house with anxiety curdling her stomach. Nervous about seeing her family, enduring social events she hated, facing Phillip. Today, the same tests remained, but she possessed a confidence that had been missing for far too long. Ciaran hadn't instilled the strength and esteem…he'd reminded her they were already there.

And it had been that same confidence and esteem that had allowed her to walk away from him last night. No matter how much it hurt.

"We've been gone overnight, so I'm going to go downstairs and make a couple of quick phone calls. Will you be okay staying here for the next thirty minutes or so?"

"Yes, of course," she replied. So polite.

A hard sigh. "Sloane, I—"

A knock interrupted whatever he'd been about to say. Instead of finishing, he strode across the room and opened the door.

"Good morning, Ciaran," Chelsea greeted, her tone as bright as the morning. "Is my sister decent?"

"Yes, I am," Sloane called out, humor breaching the heaviness in her heart.

"Damn," she chirped, entering the room.

With a snort, Ciaran shook his head. "I'll be back in few," he reminded Sloane, then left, pulling the door shut behind him.

"Sloane," Chelsea drawled, sinking to the bed and crossing her long, pretty legs, bared by a stylish, white pair of shorts. "I have to tell you, if he were my man, neither of us would be decent. Ever."

Waving her hand, Sloane barked with laughter. "You're crazy. I think Mother's having a bit of a crisis trying to figure you out now."

Her sister snickered. "Speaking of Mother," she said, eyes narrowing. "Fair warning. She's in a tizzy wondering why you and Ciaran left so abruptly last night. You know you messed up the after-dinner cocktail count." She grinned, her blond ponytail swinging with her theatrical head toss.

"I know, but it couldn't be helped. Ciaran had an emergency call from his job, and I insisted on accompanying him for the long drive back to Boston. I didn't want him traveling by himself so late at night," she said, delivering the explanation she and Ciaran had come up with to explain their sudden exodus.

"Oh, well, she should understand that. Or just have Ciaran flash that pretty smile and she'll be a goner. We were all a little worried, but I'm glad everything's okay." Chelsea tipped her head to the side and studied Sloane. "Everything *is* okay, right?"

She parted her lips, prepared to give her pat answer of "Yes, of course," but what came out was, "No. I'm in love with Ciaran." Shock rippled through her, cold, paralyzing. "Oh my God, I love him."

Jesus, how stupid could she be? Falling for Ciaran Ross. And not because God had decided to borrow the DNA from some long distant Celtic warrior and create this virile, courageous, beautiful man. No, Ciaran had proven three times last night that he desired her.

She was stupid for falling in love with a man who was more unavailable than the president. Of course a stalker still hunted her. But even if that hurdle was jumped, he still loved his dead girlfriend. And how did Sloane fight a ghost?

She didn't. A shard of sadness sliced her chest.

"O-kay," Chelsea said, frowning. "And that's a bad thing, why? Even bitter as I am about Greg's cheating ass, I can still see what a catch Ciaran is. Especially after that jerk Phillip.

You deserve someone sweet."

Shaking her head, Sloane loosed a sharp crack of laughter. "Oh God, it's such a bad idea." And then she found herself unloading on her younger sister—a woman she would have never cast in the role of confidante. But there she was, telling Chelsea about Ciaran being in love with a dead woman, how he was afraid to risk loving again, the helplessness she was drowning in. She skipped the details, careful not to reveal how she and Ciaran met or the circumstances of him accompanying her to the anniversary party. But she admitted everything else to Chelsea, who sat quietly listening, not uttering a word. Just…listening.

"I didn't fool myself into believing that just because we had sex, a happily ever after loomed in our future. Girl meets guy, girl and guy face peril and survive, girl and guy fall in love and ride off together—that plot line belongs in million-dollar action thrillers directed by James Cameron, not real life. But somewhere along the line, I forgot that and fell for a man who can love but doesn't want to. Who makes me wonder if it's just me he won't love," she whispered, confessing her secret fear. The one she didn't reveal to him last night.

"That's bullshit," Chelsea growled, surprising Sloane. She jumped off the bed and stalked over to Sloane, grabbing her hand in a firm, implacable grip. "You are one of the most beautiful women I know. *He* is unworthy of *you* if he can't recognize the second chance standing right in front of him. When all the shit with Greg hit the fan, do you know who I thought of calling first after I kicked the rat bastard and his whore out? Not Mother. Not the tons of so-called friends I had who knew about his cheating all along and didn't tell me. You. I thought of calling you."

"Chelsea…" The question, "Why didn't you?" hovered on Sloane's tongue, but she knew why. It was the same reason that had almost prevented her from confiding in her sister only moments ago.

"I've always envied you," Chelsea said, knocking the air out of Sloane's lungs. "You were always the strong one, the smart one. The confident one. You knew what Daddy and Mother wanted for you, yet you forged your own path, lived your own life. I, on the other hand, took the easy way out and became a mini-me of Mother. And because I didn't have the balls to be my own person, I'm twenty-four, divorced, and a single mom with no prospects or idea how to support myself."

Strong. Smart. Confident. Was that really how Chelsea had seen her? All this time…

Sloane reached for her baby sister's other hand and squeezed. "Next time, call," she whispered.

Chelsea nodded, her eyes shining brighter with unshed tears. "Will do. But for now, you're going to fix your makeup, go find that man, and make him see the good thing he's passing up." She grinned. "And you can start in just an hour by putting on a sexy bathing suit and skimpy dress and showing off those curves. Everyone is headed out on the boat today. We're leaving shortly. Another reason I came to find you. Butter up Mother by not being late. And oh, Daddy wants to see you. I last saw him on the patio."

"Okay, thanks. I'll go find him. And, Chelsea?" She tugged her sister into a tight hug. Their first true embrace in, well, years. "Thank you."

"If you make my mascara run, I'll hurt you," Chelsea threatened, her voice suspiciously soggy. Her arms squeezed Sloane. "Any time, sis. Any time."

A t ten o'clock on a Saturday morning, the house didn't yet buzz with much activity. Guests would be awakening and preparing for the outing her mother had planned for the day. So locating her father on the patio, sipping from a cup was easy and unencumbered. As she moved down the hallway, she scanned the living room and family room for Ciaran but didn't see him. He definitely wouldn't be happy when he returned to the bedroom and found her gone. But going straight from her room to the patio, she would be fine.

"Hey, Dad." She eased next to John, her elbow brushing his on the rail he leaned against. Smiling, John slid his free arm over her shoulders, hugging her into his side. Long seconds of silence settled between them like a comforting blanket. Times like these with him were rare, with his workaholic schedule and her job. But these were the moments she cherished. "I'm sorry about skipping out last night. Ciaran had a bit of an emergency back in Boston that couldn't be helped."

John clucked his tongue, flicking his free hand. "I knew if you left in a hurry, it had to be important. And it didn't ruin the evening. Although, I am glad you made it back in time to see Matthew. He has to leave early, so he'll be happy to see you before then."

"Oh, that's too bad. Aunt Grace, too?"

John shook his head. "No, she's staying. Business came up." He sipped from his cup, and the dark, fragrant scent of coffee tickled her nose. "Phillip was also looking for you last night."

"Really?" She fought to keep the distaste and anger out of her voice. God, why didn't Phillip go away?

"Hmm." He tipped the cup to his mouth once more, and after a lengthy beat, mused, "I don't understand why your mother insisted on inviting him."

Sloane gaped at her father, unable to close her lips that had parted in shock. "Mother said you wanted him here."

He *tsked*. "We have business dealings, and I believe your mother didn't want to put me in a tough spot by uninviting him. When I would've preferred if she had done just that. I tolerate Phillip—I always have. He's okay. Adequate at his job. I suppose women consider him handsome." He shrugged a shoulder. "Still, he always struck me as...oily. And I never did grasp what you saw in him. You two were so different, and frankly, you were—are—too good for him. But since you seemed to love him, I accepted him. Besides, as your father, no one will ever probably be good enough for you."

She barely felt the squeeze to her shoulders. She stared at him, her mind trying to compute his stunning revelation. *He'd never...why hadn't he said...*

"But this Ciaran fellow. I must admit I like him so far. Although, your mother thinks he's too 'masculine.'" He loosed a bark of laughter. "Not sure if I should've been offended by that or not. Besides, I like that about him. He's his own man. And he seems taken with you. That might be his best selling point." He chuckled, but before she could disabuse him of becoming too attached to Ciaran, he sobered. The smile fell away, and the tired, almost pensive expression she'd observed her first night home returned. As did her worry. "Promise me you'll be happy, Sloane. No matter others' opinions and the pressure they might apply, be happy."

The moisture fled her mouth, and she swallowed. Inside her chest, her heart drummed away. *Don't let fear hold you back.* Ciaran's words from the previous day drifted through her mind like a cool, comforting breeze.

"Dad." She cleared her throat. "Dad, there's something I wanted to talk with you about. There's an opportunity I've been offered..." And she told him about the charter school, leaving none of the details out. As she talked, a peace and sense of certainty settled in her soul and heart. She would be taking the job. Even if her father disagreed or tried to argue her out of the decision, she would still accept the position. It was where she belonged. And more important, it was what she wanted. A weight evaporated from her shoulders.

Look at that. She'd grown up.

John stared out over the massive backyard, his mouth pursed as if in thought. Finally, with a sigh, he returned his regard to her. "Sloane, if this job is what you want, then I support you. I arranged that position at Kennedy-Lewis because I wanted to help you achieve your goals. Just because they aren't mine, doesn't mean they're not worth pursuing. Will I worry? Of course, that's my job as a parent. But your dreams and your happiness are important, not mine. They will be lucky to have you."

Joy and gratitude choked her, tears stinging her eyes at his unconditional support. Why hadn't they ever had this talk before? The wasted time. She smiled, though the gesture was more than a little wobbly. "Thank you," she rasped. Then hugged him. Tight. Pressing her cheek to his chest like she once did as a little girl. Chuckling, he embraced her, kissing the top of her head.

"All I ever wanted was for you and your sister to find joy and security. Your sister? Now, there's a work in progress, but I don't doubt she'll find her way. But you? You're the strongest of this lot. You always have been."

She lifted her head and studied the lines bracketing his mouth and fanning from the corners of his eyes that appeared deeper. Inspected the shadows that darkened his eyes. "Dad? Is everything okay? With you, I mean?"

"I'm fine, honey," he assured her, brushing another kiss to her forehead. He grasped her shoulders and held her. "And in case I haven't told you so lately. I love you."

"I love you, too," she whispered.

"I hope I'm not interrupting," a smooth, all-too-familiar voice interjected.

Phillip. Like a freaking bad penny, he'd turned up again. Once more Ciaran's voice—his warning—haunted her.

"...that wasn't a man with no hard feelings. There was

anger there...he followed you out on that patio for a purpose, and he was going to see it through..."

"Phillip," her father greeted. "You're down early. I don't think the boat leaves for another couple of hours."

"I'm an early riser, John," Phillip replied with an easy-going grin. Oily, her father had called him. How accurate. Too bad it'd taken her so damn long to recognize it. "If you don't mind, can I borrow Sloane for a moment?"

"Well, I would say that's Sloane's decision." He glanced down at her, an eyebrow arched. His voice sounded pleasant, but a steely glint in his eyes assured her he would tell Phillip to get lost.

"It's fine, Dad. I'll see you inside." As loath as she was to be anywhere in the same vicinity as her ex, she wanted to find out what he wanted from her. And then maybe he would go away for good.

John nodded, and with a last squeeze to her shoulders, exited the patio. As soon as he disappeared inside, the laid back smile vanished from Phillip's face, replaced by the smirk that had become more common place in the last few months of their relationship.

"You have been very hard to catch up with, Sloane," he drawled, striding closer until he infiltrated her personal space.

"You mentioned that earlier." As well as employed this little intimidation tactic. He really should see about acquiring a new script. "Dad told me you were looking for me last night. What do you want?"

"Look who grew a backbone?" he jeered, then with much exaggeration, scanned the patio. "I don't see your bodyguard around. Still feeling bold without him?"

Her bodyguard? A trickle of unease filtered through her annoyance. Why had Phillip used that particular term?

"What do you want, Phillip?" she repeated. "As far as I'm concerned we have nothing left to talk about."

"Oh but we do," he snapped. "It seems that once I got rid of you, your *daddy*," he sneered, "revoked all support from me. I've been losing clients just because I dumped his precious daughter."

What the hell was he talking about? True, her father had recommended several of his friends and business associates to Phillip's bank, but John wouldn't...would he? A slow rush of delight burst in her chest, emanating a glow that fairly pulsed "Daddy's girl." Was it right? Probably not. But damn if it didn't make her feel good. Feel loved.

"You think this is funny?" Phillip shoved his face into hers. "I earned those contacts, and now he's trying to ruin me. I put up with your lazy ass for two years, so you're going to talk to your father, and do whatever it takes to convince him to back off."

Lazy ass. Lazyasslazyasslazyass. How many times had she heard that phrase over the course of their relationship? And each time it'd sliced deep, wounding her and leaving scars. She sucked in a breath, fury flickering to life in her belly. Not anymore. Not. One. More. Time. He didn't have the right to demean her. No one did.

"If you lost clients maybe it's because they finally saw through the shiny veneer to the shitty-ass truth beneath," she snapped in return. Jesus, this had been a long time in coming. And now that she'd opened the gate, the words flooded out like a raging deluge. "Maybe they discovered what a petty, insecure, spiteful, small man you are and decided to take their business elsewhere. I don't know. And honestly, I don't give a damn. But one thing I do know"—she jabbed a finger at him before slapping both palms to his chest—"You will never speak to me again as you have in the past. As a matter of fact, you just won't speak to me. You put up with *me*? I put up with your anger, your vindictiveness, your abuse. But no more. And if the vandalism and assaults are your way of trying to bully me into doing what you want, it's not going to work."

He gaped at her, eyes wide, mouth gaping. But in seconds, rage burned away the astonishment, staining his face an unattractive crimson. His lips curled in a snarl, he spat, "Who the hell do you—"

"Phillip, I think it's time you go," John appeared in the patio entrance. And from the rigid lines of his face, she guessed her father hadn't gone that far away.

"J-John," Phillip sputtered. "I didn't—"

"I figured," John said, voice harsh and cutting as a December wind. "Leave. You can wait outside while I have someone pack your things and deliver them to you."

"John, you misunderstood," Phillip babbled, a pleading note straining his explanation.

"I seriously doubt I misunderstood anything about you verbally abusing my daughter. Now, if I need to have someone physically remove you, I will. While I might take a hell of a lot of pleasure in it, you will be embarrassed and so will my wife. So you have a choice. But not for long." John's fingers curled into fists at his sides. "Sloane," he murmured, not removing his gaze from her ex-fiancé. "Why don't you go upstairs? I'll make sure this is handled."

Wow. She'd never seen her father so angry before. Forget angry. Enraged. Maybe she should feel sorry for Phillip.

Yeah, nope. Sliding past her soon-to-be-vacated ex, she brushed a kiss over her father's cheek and left the patio without once looking back. Phillip was her past, and she was never going back there again.

Still, she grinned, climbing the staircase. The look on his face...she chuckled.

"Excuse me, Ms. Barrett?"

Sloane halted on the third step, turning around. A staff member she didn't recognize stood at the bottom of the stairs, a note extended toward her. Of course with the extra people her mother had hired for the weekend, there were more than a few unfamiliar faces around.

"Yes?" She descended the couple of steps, reaching for the slip of paper. "For me?"

"Yes, I was told to pass it along to you."

"Thank you," she said, flipping open the note. The young man nodded and headed toward the hall and back of the house. She immediately identified Matthew's spidery handwriting.

Sloane, I was hoping to catch you before I left today so I could say good-bye. Please come by my room if you return before noon.

Smiling, she pivoted and strode up the staircase once more to the second floor. Whenever Matt and Grace visited, they always stayed in the same guest room down the hall from Sloane's. In seconds, she stood in front of Matt's door. She rapped on the panel, and her uncle opened the door, already dressed in a suit. With a smile, he shifted to the side, and she sailed inside the room.

"Oh good," Sloane gushed. "I was afraid I might've missed you—"

A sharp pain radiated from the back of her head. Blinding, sickening. On reflex, she reached behind her, touching the source of the agony. A sticky, warm substance coated her fingertips, and before she glimpsed her hand, she knew she would find blood.

She jerked her attention to Matt, reached for him.

Concern and sympathy twisted his much loved features... even as he backed away from her.

"I'm sorry," he whispered.

Then nothing. Her world crashed into darkness.

Chapter Eighteen

Ciaran ended his call with a client who had left a message on his voicemail and entered the living room from the French doors leading to the gardens. Nothing that couldn't hold until he returned to Boston. Sloane was his priority now and for the foreseeable future until GDG or the cops caught the person behind the attacks.

And after? a sly voice whispered inside his head.

He stared down at the home screen of his phone. But the organized mess of apps jeered him from their colorful display. *Hell, I don't know.*

When he'd taken on this assignment, his goals had been clear, uncluttered. Keep Sloane safe and alive. And keep his dick away from her. So far he'd managed one, and totally fucked up the other.

All morning—actually from the moment she'd walked away from him in his condo—he'd been replaying her words in his head. Was he the coward she'd accused him of being? No, she hadn't used that word, but the implication was there. At least for him. Afraid. He, who had dedicated his life and career to placing his body and life on the line for others, was afraid. She'd said he was scared to feel, to risk loving and losing, to feel pain. All of them were true. But she'd missed one.

He was afraid of her.

Because some time between the scorching hot bout on the bar and his confession about Sam, they'd ceased fucking and had started making love. He couldn't place the consuming passion and soul-scattering connection and pleasure they'd shared on the base, meaningless level of what he'd had with other women.

So why couldn't you sleep beside her, then? Why did you cop out by staying on the couch all night?

Shit, was there a way to turn that aggravating, nagging voice in his mind off? Sighing, he thrust his fingers through his hair and stalked over to the tall living room windows. Fear. Cowardice. Neither tasted good or went down well.

Sloane understood what lying down beside a woman meant to him. And though he'd wanted—hungered—to curl up behind her on his big bed, he'd hesitated. This regal, intelligent, gorgeous woman had everything at her fingertips. The world. But would she want to share it with a physically and emotionally scarred ex-DEA agent trying to build up a new security firm?

He didn't know. And after how his last relationship had ended, he was too much of a chicken shit to ask. To take a risk. Loving meant losing. Holding something close meant eventually it would be ripped away from you.

But what about the risk?

Was the time he'd spent with her, the secrets and laughter they'd shared, the combustible sex they'd experienced worth it?

Fuck. Yes.

More so, *she* was worth it.

Because Sloane wasn't Sam. At some point between watching the sun rise and pulling up in front of her parents' home, he realized Sloane was not Sam. He'd loved Samantha, but she'd had her flaws. Not being truthful with him. Not allowing him the choice of becoming involved with her by being honest from the beginning and telling him about her family and her connection with the FBI. Sloane didn't live a life riding the edge between law-abiding and criminality, surrounded by underworld figures. She didn't place herself in harm's way, in spite of being the target of some asshole who got off on terrorizing women. Sloane was strong, honorable, a survivor. And that same character had seen her through an abusive relationship, rising from the ashes of it like a beautiful phoenix burning bright.

By not trusting that strength, he was not only underestimating her, but belittling the courage and indomitable spirit she'd maintained and still kept after emerging from years of denigration. In his need to avoid being hurt, he'd hurt her.

No wonder she'd call him a coward.

Suddenly impatient to lay eyes on her, he strode toward the room's entrance and the staircase leading to the room where he'd left Sloane with her sister.

His phone vibrated in his palm.

"Damn," he growled. But then a glance down revealed Maddox's number. His irritation vanished as he swiped his thumb over the screen. "Yeah. What's up?"

"Ciaran." The sound of his given name and not his friend's usual annoying "Key-Key" sent disquiet rattling in his chest. "I have some information."

"Go ahead," Ciaran said, the calm in his voice belying the beginning of dread clenching his gut.

"First, we looked into the angle about Sloane's father." Pause. "Did you know he's about to be bankrupt?"

"What?" Shock sucker-punched Ciaran. *The hell?* The revelation seemed incongruent and outright ridiculous when he was surrounded by the signs of the man's wealth. "What do you mean?"

"Jake did some digging into his financials, both personal and business. In the last year he's made several investments that went belly-up. He and several investors have pretty much lost their shirts. If he can't find a fast and significant infusion of cash, he's going to be broke before the year is out. Did Sloane not mention it?"

"I don't think she knows," Ciaran murmured. "I don't think any of his family knows. Shit."

He could only imagine the impact this news would have on Sloane. Pain for her father, not over losing the money and lifestyle. She'd been paying her way for a while and didn't live off her family's wealth or status. But Sloane's mother and sister—*damn*. They would be devastated.

"Yeah, like I said, we had to do some digging to discover the information, but if the financial bleeding continues the way it has been these past months, I can't see it remaining covered up for much longer. But there's more." If possible, Maddox's tone became even more serious. "We also ran a check on the list of party guests and crossed it with her father's business associates."

The dread deepened, thickened, crawled up Ciaran's chest to the back of his throat.

"Of course there are several, as to be expected. But one stood out," Maddox continued. "Matthew Daniels. He's a longtime friend of John Barrett's and has had some dealings with her father in the past."

"Yeah," Ciaran murmured. An image of an older man coalesced in his mind's eye. Tall, slender, salt-and-pepper hair, quiet. "Sloane introduced me to him. He's her godfather, I think."

"Well, about four months ago, Matthew Daniels's son committed suicide. But a month before his death, he'd lost everything in an investment…an investment John Barrett had spearheaded."

"Goddamn." That quickly the jagged pieces that had never seemed to fit gathered together and formed a very ugly, deadly picture. The personal attacks, the intimidation, the attempted kidnapping, not murder. Yet, the inability to locate enemies other than a punk student and a disgruntled boyfriend.

Because the enemy hadn't been Sloane's. It'd been her father's.

Murder wasn't the only motive here. Retribution was.

Jesus Christ. And Ciaran had brought her back to the man behind the entire thing. "Maddox, Matthew Daniels is here at the house. And it's going to take for-fucking-ever to search," Ciaran growled. "I need to get Sloane, secure her, and then go look for Daniels while he has no idea we're on to him."

"We're on our way, and I called the detective investigating the incidents at her house and the school. They're probably coordinating with the police out there, but I have no clue how long that will take. If they'll do anything at all since all we have is a theory."

"Doesn't matter. I'm not going to wait. I'll find Daniels and ask him myself," Ciaran said, grim pleasure coursing through him.

"Copy that. We'll see you soon."

Ending the call, he stalked from the room and headed for the foyer, damn near running for the steps. The room. That's where he'd left her. But minutes later, after tearing the bedroom apart, he had to concede she wasn't there. Panic clawed at his ribs, strangled his throat. No. Christ. He forced the terror down, iced it over with hard-won calm and logic. The same kind he'd forged by fire with the DEA. Sloane needed him to think and save the emotion for later.

He charged out of the room and bounded down the steps. As he cleared the bottom step, a man wearing the white shirt and black pants of the serving staff passed by him.

"Excuse me." Ciaran grabbed the other man's arm to ensure he had his attention. "Have you seen Sloane Barrett?"

"Um, no, sir," the staff member stuttered. "I mean, yes, sir. About ten minutes ago. Adam was talking to her."

"Adam. Where is he?" Ciaran demanded.

"I-I'm not sure. The kitchen, maybe?"

Ciaran wheeled the younger man around, and led him back down the corridor. "Let's go find him."

"Wake up, Sloane." The gentle croon was followed by a hard, stinging slap to her cheek. Pain chased away the fuzziness that had already begun to lift. A palm caressed her face as if soothing away the soreness. "Come on, Sloane. Open your eyes. I don't want to have to hit you again."

She forced her eyelids up. Blinked away the heaviness. Slowly, she lifted her head, but a sharp agony pierced her skull. She cried out, tried to ease the pain. But her hands refused to cooperate. Cautiously, she wriggled her hands. Bound. They were bound behind her back.

Oh God. Fear, acrid and thick, swelled inside her, packed her throat, almost smothering her. Helplessness. Terror. It converged on her like a tidal wave, almost dragging her under its obsidian, choking depths. *No, no.* She shook her head, and this time, expecting the blast of agony, she used it to fully awaken. Swallowing convulsively, she pushed back the bile and blinked away the swarm of black and gold dots.

Focusing, she took note of her surroundings. A large bed. Cherry wood dresser and vanity. Blue and green comforters and drapes. The deep aqua sparkle of the pool and lush greenery beyond the window.

The pool house. She sat on the bedroom floor of the pool house.

"There you go, honey." Matt's face hovered in front of her. "I was getting worried he might have hit you too hard."

"He?" she questioned. Even the soft whisper set off a pounding in her head, but she shoved it aside.

Crouched down before her, Matt *tsked* as if in disappointment. "Leo. He's a bit…overzealous. I talked to him about that incident at the pool. But he's more trustworthy than those two now in police custody." He frowned, drumming his fingers on his thigh. "Last time I ever hire through someone else for such a sensitive task."

A sensitive task? Hurting and abducting her was a sensitive task? Who was this man who wore the face of the godfather she'd loved all her life? Who would have never harmed a hair on her head, but had now sanctioned her kidnapping?

"Matt," she said. Damned if she would ever call him "uncle" again. And if the softening of his face with what appeared to be regret was any indication, he didn't miss the slight. "Why? I loved you."

"Loved," he repeated. With a sigh, he rose to his feet, walking over to the window. But careful to stay out of the line of view, she noticed. "I'm sorry to hear you say it in the past tense, although not unexpected. Still, it hurts. You are the daughter I never had, Sloane. And this pains me so much."

Crazy. Matt had to be crazy. Had he snapped? What else could explain his claim of loving her even as he held her shackled on the floor?

"But the fact is, you're not my child, Sloane. My son killed himself. Do you know the utter devastation to walk into a room and find your son hanging? Dead by his own hand? I couldn't save him. I was too late. All I could do was cut him down, hold his body. As a father, you couldn't possibly comprehend the grief, the powerlessness, the failure. The desire to die right there beside him." A sob escaped him, wracking his body with the force of it. "He wanted to make me proud, prove to me he could build a business of his own as I had. He didn't need to, though. The reason I worked so hard was so he didn't have to. But he didn't believe it. So he went behind my back and joined in one of John's ventures, invested everything he had. And lost every. Bit. Of. It. Because of John."

Steel bled into his voice. The same flinty hardness glinted in his eyes, straightened his shoulders. In seconds, the man capable of masterminding a plan involving criminals, kidnapping, and assault stood in the same room as her.

"He cost me my son. If not for him convincing Matt to gamble everything he owned on a hope and a prayer, my son would be here. He wouldn't have felt like so much of a failure he took his life and left me and his mother." Matthew's thin frame shook with his rage, his fingers balling into tight fists that trembled. He no longer stared at her, but his narrowed gaze was fixed on the far wall at something only he could see. Taking advantage of his inattention, she inched her legs under her. "A child for a child," Matthew ranted. "That's the price for John's betrayal. A child for a child. He took mine, I'm going to take his in the same way I lost mine. Hanging. Struggling for breath. Having to loose the rope from around your throat. Only then will he feel the pain I've suffered."

He reached behind him, withdrawing a black gun that seemed longer than usual. A silencer. Horror propelled her to her knees, but the hefting of the weapon froze her.

"Don't think about getting up. I'd hate to cause you any unnecessary pain, but I will if you leave me no choice."

Slowly, she lowered to the floor again, but as her butt hit the floor, the room swerved to the side. Or maybe that was her. Woozy. Like she drank too much. But she hadn't even sipped coffee this morning.

"Ah," Matthew hummed, moving forward. "That must be the sedative taking effect. I didn't want you to suffer. Contrary to what you probably think of me right now, I'm not a monster."

Sedative? Her increasingly whirling mind tried to grasp the implication of the word, but then her focus zeroed in on the rope he picked up from the top of the dresser. A rope with a noose fashioned at the end.

Adrenaline kicked in like a mule, racing through her veins and momentarily dispelling the influence of the drug in her system. She struggled to her knees, tried to make it to her feet, not caring about the gun. Primal, survival instinct demanded she get away, escape. *Live.* But the sedative overwhelmed her and the rush to her system. She toppled over, her shoulder slamming into the wall with a *thud*. Pain jettisoned through her joints and down her arm, momentarily numbing it.

Above her, Matthew shook his head, that terrible mixture of sympathy, love, and resolve filling his expression again. Tenderly, he looped the rope around her neck and fit the knot to the nape.

"Don't move, Sloane," he warned her, the barrel of the gun fixed on her.

With a grunt, he tied the other end around a light fixture in the wall, then tugged on the cord. Most likely to ensure her weight didn't tear the fixture free.

"As you fall forward, your body weight will strangle you, but the sedative should eliminate your struggle and pain. I'm just going to wait here with you while the drug takes effect," he said, settling on the edge of the mattress. "Unlike Matt, you won't be alone when you die."

Was that supposed to comfort her?

"Matt," she pleaded, her words slurring as her tongue

grew thicker in her mouth. "Please don't do...this."

"I don't have a choice. It will be easier if you don't fight it."

How the hell would you know? The deafening scream rebounded off the walls of her head. But she couldn't say it. A heaviness infiltrated her limbs as her body mass doubled, and she strained to remain upright. But even as she fought the lethargy, Matthew wavered in front of her... *God, no.* Not like this. Not without saying good-bye. With her family believing she would do this to them. Without Ciaran knowing...

Crash.

She jerked her head around—or tried to. Her head slowly swayed in time to see glass implode into the room like a bomb had been detonated. A tall figure leapt through the window, crouching low. *Ciaran.*

Joy, relief, fear. They jumbled inside of her like a snarled ball of yarn.

Matthew launched from the bed, gun in hand. The muted percussion of a bullet leaving the gun silencer permeated the room, and she lurched forward as Ciaran ducked, his leg shooting out and connecting with Matthew's arm.

She choked as the noose tightened around her neck. On reflex she attempted to jolt back, but her muscles wouldn't comply. Her voice wouldn't cooperate.

She could do nothing as the noose slowly strangled her...

Chapter Nineteen

Ammonia. Laundry detergent. Wood chips and fresh rain.
Sloane pried her eyelids open, battling the peaceful,
seductive darkness that called to her. For a moment, she
surrendered, sinking back into its welcoming arms. But the
wood and rain. They both called to her, dragged her to the
surface…

An IV stand and clear bag of fluid. A monitor with
steadily blinking lights. Heavy green drapes and the ugliest
couch in creation.

The hospital. She was in the hospital. Searching her foggy
mind for how she ended up there and why, she shifted. Or
at least she tried to move. She glanced down where a heavy,
muscled arm banded her waist, holding her in place. Suddenly,
the mist cleared from her brain as if a strong, nor'easter had
blown in and driven the haze away. And she became aware of
a big frame pressed against her back and thighs, spooning her.

Holy hell.

Gingerly, careful not to pull on the needle taped to the
back of her right hand, she turned. And came face to face with

Ciaran.

Long, thick lashes rested under his eyes, and in sleep he appeared younger, less intense with those piercing blue eyes closed—wait. In sleep…

Ciaran was asleep.

Beside her. *With* her.

A snail can have about 25,000 teeth.

Her heart thudded in her chest, and the rapid pounding had nothing to do with waking up in a hospital with a fuzzy brain. What…why…did he?

Ciaran's lashes lifted. And they stared at one another for several long, silent moments.

"You're sleeping with me." *Jesus Christ.* Had she been hit on the head?

"I was." A smile tugged at the corner of his sensual mouth, but the humor faded as he cupped her jaw and studied her with the penetrating inspection she'd grown accustomed to. "How're you feeling?"

"Fine—" As if his question had twisted a faucet, the memories flooded into her head. Matthew. Pain. The rope. The sedative. Ciaran. The gun.

Gasping, she shot up, reaching for him. But a vicious throbbing in her head halted her, stealing her breath. Good *God.* It was like tiny men were whistling while they worked with little pick axes against her skull.

"Shh. Easy, sweetheart," Ciaran soothed, and cradling her shoulders, gently lowered her to the bed. "The doctor said your head would hurt for a little while because of the drugs and the concussion."

Swinging his legs over the bed rail, he rose and grabbed a dark brown carafe as well as a plastic cup. The muscles underneath his gray T-shirt flexed as he poured water into it, and just the sight of the clear liquid had her desperate for a taste. Slipping a straw into the cup, he cupped the nape of her neck and helped her tilt forward to sip the cold, delicious drink. God, had anything ever tasted as good? In this moment, no.

"Thank you," she murmured. Closing her eyes, she inhaled a deep breath, held it, and waited for the pounding to subside. Finally, she returned her attention to Ciaran, who studied her from his perch on the bed. Part of her wanted to ask him to lie down beside her again. But that same need held her back. "How long have I been here?"

"Two days. They had to make sure the sedative was completely out of your system, and then make sure there wasn't any swelling of the brain from the head injury."

Jesus, that sounded so scary.

"Matthew?" she whispered.

"In jail," he replied, voice as soft. "Him and the guy he hired to help him subdue and kidnap you." Ciaran went on to relay about Maddox's phone call, her father's dark financial situation, and how they figured out Matthew blamed John for his son's suicide. "I found the staff member who gave you the note from Matthew. Thank God he was nosy and read it. When I went to Matthew's room, this Leo Gardner was just coming out. Apparently, Matthew had sent him back to the room to ensure no sign of you remained. First thing I noticed about Leo was the scratches on his wrists and hands. With some persuasion"—a grim smile curved his lips—"he told me where you were. I was almost too late." He tangled his fingers with hers while the other hand brushed a caress over her cheek.

"The gun went off." The terrible horror of seeing the gun fire and being unable to move, to even speak, surged within her, threatening to drag her back under. "I thought you were..."

"No, sweetheart. He's a horrible shot." Again that half smile that helped battle back the terror of those memories.

She snorted. "Not funny."

"It kind of was."

Before she could reply the hospital room door opened, and her mother, father, and sister swept in. The candid relief and love on all of their faces when they saw her brought the prickle of tears to her eyes.

"Sloane." Mallory sailed to the other side of Sloane's bed, across from Ciaran. Eyes bright with moisture, she pressed a cool palm to her cheek and kissed the other. "We were so worried. Oh my God, you almost died. I can't believe Matthew would do this to you. To us. I still don't understand why," she practically wailed.

"Grief over Matt. I think he just snapped, but none of us are to blame," she murmured, meeting her father's stricken gaze over her mother's shoulder. Guilt and sadness lined his face, making him appear so much older than he had the last time she'd seen him on the patio. She glimpsed the truth in his eyes, realized he understood the motives behind his former best friend's deadly actions. He gave her a subtle nod. But she sensed John would bear the burden for a long while to come.

"We spoke to the doctor on the way in," her father said, voice tired, weary. "They're going to run a few more tests today, but if they come back clear, you can leave tomorrow morning."

"And you're coming back to the house so I can watch over you until you're fully recovered," Mallory interjected, her tone fierce as if anticipating Sloane's objection. In her mother's narrowed glare, Sloane glimpsed not just determination, but fear. Fear of almost losing her child.

A warmth suffused Sloane's chest, and she smiled. Hell, she wasn't turning down a little pampering either. Although after a couple of days she might want to plan a prison break. "Okay, Mother."

Mallory blinked. "Well…okay, then."

Chelsea snickered. "I think you just did the impossible and rendered her speechless."

"Chelsea," their mother hissed.

Her sister chuckled and squeezed Sloane's leg. "I'm glad you're okay, sis," she rasped. Clearing her throat, she wrapped her arm around John's waist. "And don't worry. Dad and I will run interference when you leave here. Just like this one"—she dipped her head toward Ciaran—"has been doing since they admitted you. He hasn't left your side once."

Sloane glanced at Ciaran, who steadily contemplated her.

"We're going to leave, honey. Let you get some rest." Her father circled the end of the bed and pressed a kiss to her forehead. "We'll be back tomorrow to bring you home."

"We're going to be okay, Dad," she whispered, clasping his hand.

He nodded, eyes glistening with unshed tears. Moments later, the door shut behind her family, leaving her alone with Ciaran, who hadn't moved from beside her on the bed.

"I'm sorry," she murmured.

He cocked his head to the side. "For?"

"For you having to go through this again." She started to shake her head, but stopped in time. "I can't imagine how you felt having to face almost the same situation as four years ago." *Oh God.* Had she just implied that he'd once more ridden to the rescue of a woman he loved? She flinched. "I mean, not that you...you know what I mean..."

Swallowing a curse, she pinched the bridge of her nose. It must be the head injury that had turned her into a babbling, blushing idiot.

"Sloane. Look at me." A gentle, but firm hand lowered hers back to the mattress. But he didn't let go. Just waited until she complied and met his unwavering regard. "I do. And yes, I know what you mean."

She stared at him. "I'm sorry, what?"

His full, sensual lips curled into a smile. One reflected in his gleaming blue eyes. "I do love you. And yes, I do know what you mean. I did risk my life for you. And I'd do it again."

Shock robbed her of her voice, but hope—fragile hope—fluttered in her chest.

A person consumes one tenth of a calorie with every lick of a stamp.

Dolphins sleep with one eye open.

A giraffe can clean its ears with its twenty-one-inch tongue.

He snorted. "I can imagine how convenient that is when a Q-Tip isn't around. Sweetheart." He lifted her hand, pressed his lips to her palm. "I wasn't looking for you. But from the moment you walked into that restaurant, I haven't been able to look away from you. Your beauty, your strength, your courage—you're this light burning away the dark place I've existed in for so long. Existed, not lived. For four years I've been afraid to feel, to love. But almost losing you, almost having to wake every day without you in this world made me realize I want to live. With you. Sleeping next to you every night knowing I'm holding everything I need in my arms." He crawled up on the bed, stretching out next to her and cradling her face in both of his hands. "I started this job hoping you would be my redemption, my absolution. You ended up being my heart. Let me be yours, duchess."

Joy, hope, and love welled inside her so she breathed it. Wondered how she'd ever functioned without it. Because in this moment, staring into the beautiful face of the man who owned her heart, soul, and spirit, she'd never been truly alive.

"Okay."

A grin quirked a corner of his gorgeous mouth. "Okay." Then, "Give me the words, duchess. I've discovered that with you I need to hear them."

"I love you," she whispered.

"You are worth the risk, Sloane." He captured her mouth in a kiss as tender and delicate as this emotion between them. Brushing his thumb over lips, he murmured. "You always were."

Acknowledgments

First and always, thank you. Father, for your inspiration and never-ending faithfulness. None of this would be possible without you, and I thank you for letting me be Your writing partner.

To Gary. Thank you for your patience—especially during deadline time. :) Your love and support means almost as much to me as you do.

To Debra Glass. Thank you for always answering the "I know this is last minute" call. I don't feel right unless you've vetted a book. You've been an awesome friend, critique partner, and cheerleader. And I love you for it!

To Jessica Lee. Thank you for brainstorming this series with me, and for the ear you let me bend and the shoulder you give me to lean on. Love you!

To Tracy Montoya. Gracias. Merci. Grazie. Go raibh maith agat. That last one is in Gaelic. LOL! Yeah, all these languages, and none of 'em can capture how much I just thank you for all that you are and all that you do. I have grown so much as an author, and it's because of your guidance, patience, and wisdom. Because English—and apparently other languages, too—fail me, all I have is thank you.

To the Saints and Sinners and Sirens. I'm like in the cool kids' club. The Pink Ladies. The popular crowd on one of those Disney Shows. And it's because I get to hang out with you guys. You're the best! MUAH!

About the Author

Naima Simone's love of romance was first stirred by Johanna Lindsey, Sandra Brown, and Linda Howard many years ago. Well, not that many. She is only eighteen…ish. Though her first attempt at a romance novel starring Ralph Tresvant from New Edition never saw the light of day, her love of romance, reading, and writing has endured. Published since 2009, she spends her days—and nights—creating stories of unique men and women who experience the first bites of desire, the dizzying heights of passion, and the tender, healing heat of love.

She is wife to Superman, or his non-Kryptonian, less bulletproof equivalent, and mother to the most awesome kids ever. They all live in perfect, sometimes domestically challenged bliss in the southern United States.

Come visit Naima at www.naimasimone.com.